THE SAINT
IN THE SUN

FOREWORD BY
MICK DAVIES

by the l[...]
v.hants.go[...]
o31

___

shire
Council

THE ADVENTURES OF THE SAINT

THE SAINT
IN THE SUN

LESLIE CHARTERIS

SERIES EDITOR: IAN DICKERSON

Text copyright © 2014 Interfund (London) Ltd.
Foreword © 2014 Mick Davis
Publication History and Author Biography © 2014 Ian Dickerson
All rights reserved.

Published by Thomas & Mercer, Seattle

www.apub.com

ISBN-13: 9781477842959
ISBN-10:1477842950

Cover design by David Drummond, www.salamanderhill.com

Printed in the United States of America.

To John Paddy Carstairs,
with thanks for many nice things
done for the Saint, and especially
for suggesting this title

PUBLISHER'S NOTE

FOREWORD TO THE

NEW EDITION

Growing up in a working class family, in the city of Glasgow, was about as tough as it gets. Throw in a dose of asthma, four people in a one-bedroom apartment with no bath or shower, unemployment, and a daily diet of uncertainty (apart from the rain), what's left but to dream? And my dream was very simple: I was going to live in Hollywood and make movies and TV shows. Of course if I shared that dream with anyone around me it was grounds for insanity, so it remained my secret. A secret I shared only with my heroes, who I sat cross-legged before, watching them in black and white, walk across our 12-inch screen to save the day . . . my day. *My life*. But there was one hero who stood out more than any other for me—the guy who looked up at the halo above his head as if to say, "Really? C'mon, you know how naughty I am."

Simon Templar was a Saint, but it was that devilish side of his cavalier, charismatic, bad-boy persona that I felt drawn to. A good old-fashioned cad whose guard was his cheeky smile and quick retort, and yet, underneath it all, I felt he was really quite lonely. I identified with that and it helped me to understand what a great, multi-dimensional character he really was. That was the genius of Charteris for me.

Cut to a few decades later and here I am living my dream in Hollywood, but did I ever imagine I'd get to meet Simon Templar, even write for Simon Templar, put words in his mouth, and have the privilege of mining that delicious melancholy I always thought he kept hidden? No chance!

And yet, I did.

And I have to tell you, he is exactly as I thought he'd be, a true Saint, with a little bit of devil tucked away for a rainy day.

—Mick Davis

THE SAINT
IN THE SUN

CANNES: THE BETTER

MOUSETRAP

Until his unfortunate accident, Mr Daniel Tench, in spite of having been christened with such an unglamorous name (though he had used others) had managed to lead what some people would consider quite a glamorous life. Born in a caravan on an English fairground, he had grown up with a traveling circus, and spent several years as a merely second-rate acrobat, by Ringling standards, before he graduated to become one of the most successful jewel thieves who ever operated in Europe.

A few small but profitable experiments during his last season under canvas had shown him that the limited athletic gifts which would never get him billing at Madison Square Garden were more than adequate for making illegal entries by various improbable routes, and when a neat second-story job in Deauville produced a pearl choker that brought a million francs even in the market where he had to sell it, Mr Tench decided that he had found a better way to use his nerve and muscle than by swinging on a trapeze for the niggardly applause of a small crowd of yokels.

One day, someone with more patience and earnestness than this reporter may write an original monograph on the influence of architectural styles upon trends in crime. It is quite possible that the frustrations of the Victorian home were responsible for the popularity of wife-poisoning as an indoor sport during that era. It is certain that the art of Mr Tench could only have reached its apogee in Europe, where most of the flossiest hotels are still monuments to a period in which ornateness was a synonym for luxury, and no caravanserai was considered palatial that did not have an abundance of balconies, ledges, cornices, gables, buttresses, groovings, ornaments, and curlicues that were made to order for a man of his somewhat simian talents. On the stark facade of the latest Hilton construction he would have been as confused as a cat on roller skates.

In fact, the obvious vulnerability of such gilded barracks long ago created a specialist known in French as a *souris d'hôtel,* or hotel mouse, who would stealthily make off with any valuables that careless guests left unlocked in their rooms. Traditionally, this operator wore only a suit of black tights, to be able to move without rustling and to be as invisible as possible in the dark; and in the merrier myths the tights were always filled to capacity by a beauteous female who, if caught in the act, always had one last card to play against the penalty of being turned over to the police. Mr Tench, of course, did not have the benefit of what we might call this ace in the hole, in normal situations, but he made up for it with a physical agility that consistently kept the problem from arising. Until the night when his hand slipped.

Personally he was not at all the gay and charming type that would have been portrayed in any self-respecting movie, and even his widow did not waste a minute mourning for him, though she was most annoyed to be so abruptly deprived of the loot he provided, especially the assortment that was his objective on the expedition which he concluded by falling four floors down the front of the Carlton Hotel in Cannes.

None of this might ever have concerned the Saint very much, but for the fact that the place where Mr Tench made his spectacularly unsuccessful attempt to bounce off a slab of concrete was situated vertically underneath the window of a room in which Simon Templar happened to be registered at the time. As a result, Simon was subjected to a long and hostile interrogation by an inspector of the *Police Judiciaire,* who was convinced that all thieves of Tench's type had an accomplice, and could see no suspect more obvious than a person of such notoriously equivocal reputation.

"Not that I can altogether blame him," Simon said to Natalie Sheridan. "Danny-boy could have fallen right off my balcony, so to any cop's way of thinking my room could have been his headquarters. This should teach me to stay away from places where the guests have jewels."

He usually stayed at the less showy but just as comfortable Majestic, but he had backed his luck too hard by arriving without a reservation at the height of the season, and had had to take anything he was lucky enough to get. But for that, he might not even have met Natalie as he had only two days ago, when he felt too lazy to go any further than the bar downstairs for his first apéritif.

The terrace of the Carlton at cocktail time is about the busiest place in Cannes, and some of the business is not the kind that the best hotels are conventionally supposed to welcome. But in France, a country with a realistic approach to everything except politics, it is recognized that the very classiest ladies of accommodating virtue, or *poules de luxe*, will inevitably forgather in the very classiest places, where they can expect to meet friends of equal distinction in other fields, and nothing much can be done about it. This does not mean that they are conspicuous, except by being often better looking, better dressed, and better behaved than most of the more strait-laced customers, or that their importunities are a menace to respectable citizens; but a man who looks lonely there always has a chance of catching a not indifferent eye.

Simon Templar was not on the prowl in that way, but he never said No to anything without a second look, and his second look at Natalie was what stopped him. At the first, she was only one of the sea of faces that he automatically scanned with extraordinary selectivity while he seemed to be merely looking for a vacant table—this was the habit of a lifetime whose duration could sometimes depend on seeing everyone before anyone saw him—and her eyes were not the first in which he could sense a possibility of welcome, or her lips the only ones that seemed on the verge of a tentative smile. But these features were so exceptionally attractive that after the first comprehensive glance he had to look at them again individually. And that was when the mouth actually smiled, with a quite brazen forthrightness that was not according to protocol for that place at all, and the possibility of invitation in the eyes bared itself as almost shameless pleading.

The Saint smiled back as if he had just seen her. Dismissing with a casual gesture the intrusive attentions of a waiter who was trying to sell him a seat on the other side of the terrace, he steered as direct a course towards her as the intervening tables permitted, and watched the near-panic in her eyes relax into simple nervousness as he approached.

"Darling," he murmured. "Have you been waiting long?"

"Long enough," she said.

He sat down.

"What would you have done if I hadn't shown up?"

"I don't know," she said. "Or if you'd turned out to speak nothing but French . . . But why did you speak to me in English? How did you know I wasn't—"

"Us old roués have educated hunches that pay off sometimes."

Another waiter intruded himself, a disinterested mercenary concerned only with one aspect of the encounter. Simon glanced at the Martini in front of the girl, which she had scarcely touched, and ordered a St Raphael.

"But you don't know," she said almost feverishly, as the waiter went away. "I've got to explain. I'm not the kind of girl you think!"

"Really?" Simon offered a cigarette. "Well, I've got nothing but time. Tell me the story of your life."

It could hardly cover much more than a quarter of a century, he estimated, and any debauchery that she might have crowded into the later years had not yet left any telltale marks on her face. Even at close quarters, her flawless skin did not betray an indebtedness to artful cosmetics. A master coiffeur had done ethereal sculpture to her hair, but would have mortgaged his soul to be able to duplicate with bleach and dye and rinse its cheerfully inconsistent shades of honey-blonde. And if her figure relied on prosthetic support or increment for its extremely interesting contours, that was a remotely potential disillusionment which in these days only nudists never have to risk. From all angles that could be determined in a respectable public place, she was as promising a temptation as any buccaneer ever made no exaggerated effort to resist.

"Natalie Sheridan," she said. "Canadian. Divorced one year. No torch, but I did feel like a fling, and I'd read so much about Europe. The only thing I hadn't thought about, practically, was just how a gal would make out from day to day, traveling alone. It was all right in London and Paris, because I was with friends all the time—but then they were going to Scandinavia and I wanted to see the Riviera. It was even all right in Monte Carlo, though, because I met an English woman on the train coming down, and we sort of stuck together. But I've been here on my own now for three days, and tonight I got desperate."

"It can be a problem, I imagine."

"The first night, I had dinner here and went straight to bed. Lunch wasn't so difficult, somehow. But the second night, I was afraid to go to any fancy place: I went into another restaurant very early, it was almost empty, and then I went to a movie and went to bed. Tonight I decided it was just silly. I could waste a whole vacation like that, and why shouldn't I act like a healthy modern gal with her own traveler's checks? So I got all dressed up and swore I would have some fun. But—"

"Other people had other ideas about the kind of fun you ought to have?"

"Over here, they don't seem to understand that a gal can be alone because she wants to. If she isn't waiting for one man, she must be waiting for any man. I've never had so many strange men trying to be so charming. Of course, most of them were just devastatingly discreet, but all the same . . . after a while, it gets to be like a kind of nightmare.

And then when I felt the waiters beginning to worry about me, it was the end."

"So you decided that if everyone was thinking it, you might as well be it?" he asked, with lazy wickedness.

"Oh, no! But when you came in, I was about frantic, and you looked English or American or—or as if you might understand, anyway. And I did try to pick you up, and I shouldn't be wasting your time. But if you would just have your drink, so that I can sit here for a little while and enjoy staring at everyone else instead of them staring at me, and let me pay for it, and then escort me out so I can make a graceful exit—"

The Saint finally laughed, cutting off her spate of headlong clauses with a muted outburst of sheer delight. He threw back his head and shook with it irrepressibly, subduing only the sound of the guffaw, while the waiter delivered his St Raphael and went phlegmatically away.

"Natalie, I love you. I thought I'd been picked up in every way there was, in the course of a misspent life, but you've shown me that there can always be new things to live for." He sat up again, still smiling, and not unkindly. "I'll tell you what. We'll have this drink, and then another, on me, and enjoy the passing show together. And after that, if you can still stand the company, I'd like to introduce you to a little side-street restaurant, Chez Francis, where you can eat the best Provencal sea-foods in this town. Until you've tasted Francis's *coquillages farcis*, you've only been gastronomically slumming."

That had been the beginning of what looked at first like the most beautifully innocuous friendship in the Saint's life story. Her ignorance of everything European was abysmal, but her lively interest made kindergarten instruction surprisingly enjoyable. Experiencing for the first time places and foods and wines that were so familiar to him, she made them new to him again with the spice of her own excitement. He got almost a proprietary kick out of first emphasizing the murky waters and overcrowded sands of the Croisette beaches, until she was as saddened as a child with a broken toy, and then taking her on a mere fifteen-minute ferry ride to the Ile Ste Marguerite and over the eucalyptus-shaded walks to the clean rocky coves on the other side which only a few fortunate tourists ever find. And when he gave her one of the glass-and-rubber masks which are almost one of the minimum garments required of Mediterranean bathers today, and she made her personal discovery of the underwater fairyland that only encumbered divers had even glimpsed before this generation, she clung to him with real sexless tears flooding her big hazel eyes.

Except for that one spontaneous clutch, she was neither cold nor coquettish. It must be faced—or who are we kidding?—that few women could be with the Saint for long and want to leave him alone, and that passes had been made at him in more ways than a modest man would try to remember, and that he could scarcely help revealing even in subtle ways that he was prepared for the worst and poised for evasive action. But Natalie Sheridan gave him nothing to fight. She made no overt attempt to bring him closer to her bed, while at the same time leaving no doubt that he might be very welcome there, some other night, when certain other conjunctions were auspicious. This alone was a refreshing change from more hackneyed hazards.

Nor was she asking to be rescued from any dragons or dead-falls, except the almost adolescent insecurity which had made her beseech him in the first place.

He had told her soon enough, inevitably, but with all the misgivings that could be rooted in a hundred prologues like this: "My name is Sebastian Tombs, believe it or not."

She had said: "Of course I believe it. People always do, when the Saint tells them that, don't they?"

It was at this memorable moment that he finally decided that the time had come at last when the pseudonym which had given him so much childish amusement for so many years must be put away in honorable retirement. He would never feel confident of fooling anyone with it again, and indeed he realized that he had been more than lucky to get away with it on the last several occasions when a perverse sentimental attachment had made him risk it just once more.

But even so, Natalie had surprised him again. She hadn't followed up the identification with the usual babble of silly questions, or embarrassing flattery, or the equally routine recollection of some flagrant injustice, public or private, which he simply must do something about. She seemed perfectly satisfied to enjoy his company as an attractive man, without pestering him for reminiscences or otherwise reminding him that he was a kind of international celebrity, in the most refreshingly natural camaraderie.

It was almost too good to be true.

On the third evening, she handed him a sealed envelope.

"That's for last night," she said. "I saw exactly what you spent—I've got very sharp eyes. Tonight is on you, if you like. But about every other time it has to be on me, if we're going on doing this. Now don't get on a high horse. I'm not going to insult you by offering more than my share, and don't you insult me by trying to make me a parasite. You don't have to pick up all the checks until you're married to me or keeping me, and I haven't heard you offer to do either yet."

This was altogether too much.

"What on earth did your husband divorce you for?" he asked.

"He didn't. I divorced him."

"Then put it another way. Why did he let you?"

"Why should I tell you what's wrong with me? If I don't, there's always a chance you may never find out."

Nothing else had beclouded the idyllic relationship until Mrs Bertha Noversham had arrived. Mrs Noversham was the English woman whom Natalie had met on the Blue Train and whose company in Monte Carlo had postponed the problems of solitude. She had been to Corsica on the yacht of some titled plutocrats whom she had met at a roulette table and adopted as old friends on the basis of having seen them several times in the most fashionable London restaurants—Natalie had already told Simon about Mrs Noversham's steamroller methods of enlarging her circle of acquaintances.

"Yes, dear, it was utterly divine," Mrs Noversham said, sinking massively into a chair at their table without waiting for an invitation. "It's a shame you couldn't have gone along, but they did only have the one spare berth, and even I practically had to ask myself. They're such snobs, though—Sir Oswald wasn't knighted more than five years ago, and they couldn't get over me having the Duke of Camford for a great-uncle, and calling him a silly old fool, which he is."

She was a woman with a gross torso and short skinny legs, who masked whatever complexion she may have had with an impenetrable coating of powder and rouge, and dissimulated her possibly graying hair with a tint of magenta that never sprang from human follicle. In spite of this misguided effort, she failed to look a day under forty-five, which may have been all she was. Her dress looked as if it had been bought from a black-and-white illustration in a mail-order catalog. But like magic charms to obscure and nullify all such cheap crudities, she wore jewels.

It was a long time since the Saint had seen jewels in quite such ostentatious quantity, even in that traditional paradise of jewel thieves. Mrs Noversham wore them in every conceivable place and form, and a few that required a long stretch of the imagination as well. She wore them in an assortment of settings so garish that she must have designed them herself, because no jeweller with a vestige of sanity would have banked on a customer falling in love with them in his shop window. If the most casual observer was to be left in doubt as to how she was loaded, it was not going to be her fault.

"I'll have a champagne cocktail," she told the waiter. "This wasn't some itty bitty little yacht, Mr Templar. It's a small liner. Natalie can tell you—she came to dinner on board before we sailed. But do you know, with all that money, Lady Fisbee still insists on having all the wine iced, even the claret."

"You must have been glad it wasn't a longer trip," said the Saint earnestly.

"Well, you know what did cut it short?" Mrs Noversham said, with the unction of a born connoisseur of catastrophes. "We had a robbery!"

"What, not another?" Natalie exclaimed.

"Yes, dear. Right in the harbor at Ajaccio. Lady Fisbee had given most of the crew a day off to go ashore—it's quite ridiculous the way she pampers those people—and all of us had dinner at the Hotel so that they wouldn't have to work. She's obviously still frightened of servants and thinks that she has to make them happy instead of it being the other way 'round. So there were only two men on board, and they were playing cards and probably drinking, and somebody got on board and jimmied the safe in Lady Fisbee's cabin and cleaned out the two other guests who had anything worth stealing as well."

Natalie turned to Simon and explained, "There was a robbery at the Métropole in Monte Carlo, too, while we were there. We must attract them."

"One of us does, dear. Perhaps it's a good job they couldn't find room for you, after all—you might have lost that nice collar of sparklers."

Natalie fingered the exquisitely mounted string of white fire around her throat almost self-consciously and said, "I'm not really surprised. That wall safe that Lady Fisbee showed us looked terribly flimsy to me. The best thing about it was the way it was hidden. And that Italian actress said that she'd never needed anything safer than the bottom of a wardrobe under a pile of dirty laundry. As if professional thieves didn't already know all the hiding places that anyone could think of. Some people almost deserve to be robbed."

"Not me, dear," said Bertha Noversham smugly. "You know where I keep everything I'm not wearing, and nobody could get at that even in my sleep without me raising Cain, unless I was knocked out first, and that kind of thief never goes in for rough stuff. He wants to sneak in and sneak away without anyone having a chance to see him."

"But there are stick-up men, too," Simon mentioned.

"I hope I meet one some day—I'll have a surprise for him," said Mrs Noversham darkly. "Where are you having dinner?"

She continued to anticipate and accept unuttered invitations with an aplomb that was paralyzing, and never stopped dominating the conversation with the bland assumption that they had only been waiting for her to relieve their boredom.

Before the meal was over, she had blithely devastated a dozen other characters or reputations, some of them belonging to people whom Simon did not even know by name, always in a way that obliquely underlined the impeccability of her own status as a social arbiter. She had a trick of flattering her listeners by taking it for granted that they would sneer at the same things she sneered at, while at the same time implying ominously that they would be wise to make positive efforts to continue in her good graces.

She accompanied them from dinner to the Palm-Beach Casino, and only left them to themselves again when she spotted a famous Hollywood producer and his richly panoplied wife, to whom she was sure she had passed the sugar at tea in the Royal Enclosure at Ascot.

"I'm dreadfully sorry," Natalie said. "She's quite awful, isn't she? But I was so desperately glad to know anyone at all when I first got here, as I told you, that I didn't realize how overpowering she was."

"She has a fabulous technique," Simon admitted mildly. "I can see how anyone with the least insecurity would be a sitting duck for her. Before she's through, that popcorn potentate will be terrified of sticking the wrong fork in his caviar, in case Bertha changes her mind about introducing his wife to the Duchess of Camford, which he would never hear the last of."

"The point is, what are we going to do? If—well, if you're interested."

The Saint grinned.

"Tell her who I am. I don't think it really penetrated, when you introduced me. Rub it in. I think that'll scare her off. Of course, she'll try to scare you off too, but I'm counting on you to resist that."

"I don't think I'd be too shocked if you did steal her jewels. Somebody ought to stop her being so superior about everyone else."

"Where does she keep them, by the way?"

"She has a specially-made sort of apron with zipper pockets that she wears all the time; but with her figure, when she's dressed, it doesn't show because it hangs under the bulge, if you know what I mean."

"You couldn't be more discreetly graphic."

Natalie's lovely eyes dilated slightly with belated comprehension.

"I told you, didn't I? Just what you'd want to know if you were a jewel thief. She was right—some people almost deserve to be robbed."

"I thought you were the one who said that, darling."

"Well, it was right anyway. Don't start to get me confused and frightened, Simon. We've had such a lot of fun these few days. And I haven't bothered you with any silly questions, have I? Don't let me start now. But you were telling the truth, weren't you, when you told me you were strictly here on vacation?"

"Most strictly," he smiled. "As long as nobody makes the path too straight and narrow for my tottering tootsies. Talking of which, why don't we see if they can still keep time with this team of paranoiac Paraguayans, who are obviously subsidized by the local Society of Osteopaths?"

But that had been the very night during which, somewhat later, Mr Daniel Tench made his catastrophic verification of the laws of gravity.

The Saint had been detained all morning by the skeptical inspector of the *Police Judiciaire*, and when he got back he had found a brief note from Natalie saying that she had gone to Eden Roc with Mrs Noversham. By that time it was already late for lunch, and in any case he thought it might be more opportune to leave them on their own. He left an answering message for her to call him when she came in, and thus it was tea-time when she asked him to meet her at the Martinez, and it was there that he got off the wry reflection that could have been an epitaph on their brief friendship.

"This is another place where the guests often have jewels," she pointed out.

"There are so damn many of them," he complained, "Staying away from them is easier said than done."

"And you do like some of the people, don't you?"

"I never thought of you as one of the jewelled ones. Which is a compliment to someone's good taste in settings. Because now I come to think of it, the choice bits of ice I've seen you wearing could be worth twice as much as all Bertha Noversham's rocks, if they're real. You see how I must have reformed? Something like this has to happen before I even start thinking like a jewel thief."

"That isn't the way Bertha sees it."

Her voice was so cool that he stared at her.

"This is very interesting," he said. "I know it was my idea for you to give me a build-up, but could you have oversold yourself?"

"I don't know, but I couldn't cover up for you. When Bertha called me about seven o'clock this morning, she'd just woken up and discovered that someone had taken that precious apron-bag of hers, which she was so sure couldn't be done. I almost got the giggles when I remembered that the last thing she talked about on the way home last night was how she was going to break down and take something for her insomnia. But by the time I got to her room, she'd already called the manager, and of course they'd already found that man who fell off a balcony, so the police were there, and she'd told them that I knew about her apron and so you certainly knew too. She was much more hep than you thought—she knew who you were all the time. She didn't blame me for letting you get so much out of me, but I couldn't deny that you had."

"Naturally," said the Saint, without rancor. "I gathered most of that while I was being grilled, though the inspector did his best not to let on. But it seems to be bothering you more than it does me."

She twisted her fingers together—he had not seen her so tensely defensive since their first meeting.

"How do you explain that man being on your balcony?"

"Just what the inspector asked me. I asked him if there was a French version of the English or American parable that we all know, only don't ask me where it's from, which says that 'if a man only makes a better mousetrap than his neighbor, though he lives in the heart of a wilderness, the world will beat a path to his door.' I'd hate to calculate how many billions the advertising industry has spent to prove that this is the silliest old saw that ever lost its teeth, but it still works for me. At one time in the shocking days you've heard about, I managed to become the best-known alleged crook since Raffles. Since then, there has been the dreariest procession of otherwise bright lads who could think of no more dazzling climax to their careers than to leave their tracks on my doorstep. Brother Tench was only the latest, but he won't be the last."

"He had Bertha's apron, with all her jewels—she got them all back, I suppose you know. But what would he have done with them in your room?"

"He could've afforded to drop one piece, or even just one stone. And then with only an anonymous phone call, he could've had all the cops concentrating on me for days, while he wrapped up his getaway. As it is, the only thing that really saved me from being stuck was that he had all the boodle on him when they scraped him up."

"Would you mind," Natalie said, in a fainting voice, "if I went back and took a little nap? I guess I'm not used to coping with things like this."

She made him walk back on the other side of the Croisette, the beach side, so that it was easy to look up at the facade of the Carlton as they approached it. When they were almost opposite, she stopped and pointed.

"That's your balcony, isn't it, to the right of the middle, on the fourth floor?"

"Yes."

"Bertha's on the sixth floor, the corner room on the left."

"Is she?"

"And I'm on the floor below you, just a little more to the right."

"I could have figured that from your room number, although you never invited me to see."

"This man Tench had already been to Bertha's room," she said. "Suppose he was on his way to my room from there. That could just as well have taken him past your balcony, just because it was on the way, without him necessarily having the idea of planting something in your room."

The Saint frowned. He had tried hard not to be unduly sensitive, but she was making it a little more difficult with every sentence.

"I suppose so," he said. "I had a theory, but anyone else is entitled to another. I'm only the guy who was in the middle—as you've rather neatly pointed out."

"But that's the whole point, isn't it?" she said. "They don't seem to know where Tench started climbing around from. He didn't have a room of his own in the hotel, apparently. Bertha swears that her door was bolted on the inside, but once he'd got into her room he could still have gone out by the door—and why wouldn't he have done that, instead of risking his neck on the outside, if he was in cahoots with you and only wanted to bring you the jewels?"

"Thank you," murmured the Saint, with a trace of irony. "I should have had you with me when I was trying to convince that inspector."

"The only other reason that Tench would have to be on your balcony, except for your theory that he meant to try to frame you, would be if he was on his way somewhere else. To my room, perhaps."

Simon gazed at her for quite a long time.

"Did you figure all that out in your own little head?"

"You don't need to be sarcastic. Of course Bertha and I talked about—everything. And I feel rather ashamed of some of the things we said last night. She was just having a bad spell, but she isn't a bad person."

"Good. Then you don't want me to steal her jewels, after all?"

"Or mine either. I'll take all the blame, I've loved every minute of it, but Bertha reminded me of an old saying—'Lead us not into temptation'. One can ask too much even of a Saint, can't one?" She put out her hand suddenly. "Let's just say good-bye now, and nothing else."

"If that's how you want it, darling. It's your script."

He raised her fingers to his lips, in a gesture that added a uniquely cavalier insolence to a Latin flourish, and watched her force her own way through the endlessly crawling cross-streams of traffic.

If that was how she wanted it, so be it.

He couldn't remember when he had last felt so recklessly resentful. It had become almost a standing joke, for him, to protest that he was always being driven back towards the old bad ways by the people who refused to believe that he had ever forsaken them. But seldom had his admittedly equivocal past been raised to slap him in the face as unfairly as this.

Natalie Sheridan deserved to lose her bloody diamonds.

So did Mrs Noversham, for helping to put that bee in her bonnet. Simon would have bet anything that Natalie would never have reached the same conclusion by herself. But put two women together, and the ultimate outcome of their mutual catalysis can be predicted by no laws of chemistry or logic.

Simon scowled up again at the front of the hotel into which Natalie had already disappeared, imprinting a certain pattern on his mind.

Then he went up to his room and scowled vaguely out the other way, over the blue bay where speedboats towing aimless but tireless water-skiers cut random patterns between lazily graceful sailing skiffs and mechanically crawling pedalos, but in his mind he saw the same pattern, reversed, in which his window was still a kind of focal center.

Eventually it was the telephone which interrupted his brooding, with a strident abruptness that left him with what he recognized at once as a purely wishful flutter of hope. The uncompromisingly materialistic voice that greeted his response quickly reduced that pipedream to its basic fatuity.

"This is Bertha Noversham, Mr Templar. I'd like you to have a cocktail with me."

"Well, thank you, but I'm not sure that I—"

"Don't tell me that you've got another engagement, because I'm fairly sure you haven't. Anyhow, this needn't take long, and if you'll come to my room you can be sure you won't be embarrassed in public. Just tell me what you like to drink, and I'll order it while you're getting here."

"I remember that you liked champagne cocktails," said the Saint slowly. "Get in a bottle of Bollinger, and I'll help you with it."

The Bollinger was on ice when he arrived, but it was no frostier than the self-assurance of her welcome.

"I'm quite sure you didn't think for a moment that this was just a social invitation," she said, "so I'll come to the point as soon as you've done the pouring. Please use only half a lump of sugar, and scrape it well on the lemon peel—don't put the lemon in. That small glass is cognac, in case you have the common American idea that that improves the taste."

Simon performed the dispensing with imperturbable good humor.

"All right," he said. "Start shooting."

"Very well. I find you quite a likeable person, Mr Templar, in spite of some things that everyone knows about you. So I'd like to save you from making a serious mistake."

"What about?"

"I understand that until yesterday Natalie was amusing herself by letting you think you were showing her the Côte d'Azur. I don't know how often she's done it before, but she certainly told the same tale to the man who gave her some of her diamonds. That was last year, when I first met her. I knew him from one of the garden parties at Camford Castle—a nice old duffer, but quite senile of course."

The Saint's eyebrows did not go up through his hair-line like rockets through the ionosphere, but that was only because he had spent more time with poker hands than ballistic missiles.

"Now I know why you thought you had to offer me a drink, anyway," he remarked.

"Bernie Kovar was at Eden Roc today—you remember, I was talking to him at the Casino last night. We had lunch together. His wife left for Rome this morning, to do the shops and the museums for a week or two, while he's supposed to be reading scripts. Of course she knows perfectly well what the old goat will be up to most of the time—the gossip columns would tell her if nobody else did—but she only brings it up if he dares to say a word about the money she spends. He didn't waste a minute inviting Natalie to dinner and asking why no one had ever offered her a screen test. It may make you feel a bit better to know that that's the real reason why she has to shake you off in such a hurry—not because she seriously thinks you might rob her."

"That does sound considerate."

"I don't know what Natalie has told you about her background, but I've heard enough contradictory fragments to believe none of them. I think of her simply as an ambitious girl who is determined to get the most out of her undoubted attractions while they last. That is what every woman does who isn't a 'career woman,' God help her. That's what I was like at her age, and I'm sure you think I haven't outgrown it. The difference is that Natalie wants to get away with murder and still have everyone loving her. She's a dear girl, and I've done a lot for her, and I may go on doing it."

"Then why are you telling me all this?"

Mrs Noversham took a very healthy, unequivocal swig at her champagne cocktail, and indicated that Simon should replenish the glass.

"Because I'm just selfish enough to want to protect myself. It's all very well for Natalie to spare your vanity by pretending she just thinks it'd be safer not to see you again. But she doesn't even want to take the responsibility for that idea. She had to make you think I put the idea into her head. I didn't care at first, until it dawned on me how dangerous that could be, with a man like you. You'd be perfectly capable of stealing my jewels, if you could, just to pay me back for a thing like that—wouldn't you, Mr Templar?"

Simon brought the refill back to her, and lighted a cigarette.

"When you phoned, I was thinking along those lines," he said candidly.

"I was sure of it. I don't like being disloyal to Natalie, but there's a limit to how far I can go to cover up for her. My jewels mean a lot to me, and I don't want to worry about your intentions for the rest of the season."

"It's nice of you not to put it that I'd be the first person you'd remind the police about if anything happened to you again like last night."

"I'd prefer to keep this conversation entirely on a pleasant plane. And in any case, I can assure you that nobody, including Natalie, would have much chance of persuading me to take another sleeping pill unless my jewels were in a strong-room."

The Saint released smoke in a very careful ring. He had thought himself beyond being jolted by any magnitude of female duplicity, but he had never personally encountered anything as transcendent as this.

"This makes life rather difficult," he said. "Because now I'm liable to think about unkind things I might do to Natalie, rather than to you. Perhaps that hadn't occurred to you when you decided to save me from myself."

"I thought I'd made it clear that I was only trying to save myself. Or my possessions. To me, you, Natalie Sheridan, Bernie Kovar, and a lot of other people I meet, are all birds of a feather. I think you all deserve anything you do to each other. That's why I can still be amused by Natalie, in spite of what I know about her. But she shouldn't have thrown me to the wolves—or wolf, if I may call you that. If she suffers for it, she has only herself to blame."

"I'd like to put it more bluntly. Suppose she did get robbed— would you feel obliged to tell the police about this conversation?"

She looked him straight in the eye.

"Mr Templar, if I were sure that as of now you had no grudge against me, I should think it much wiser to mind my own business. It isn't as if Natalie's loss would be irreparable. Bernie will give her plenty more jewels, if she plays her cards right"

"I wish I met more people who were so broadminded."

"However, it won't be easy," Mrs Noversham said briskly. "Since what happened last night, she swears she'll put all her valuables in the hotel safe the minute she walks into the lobby, each and every time she comes home. There'd have to be a hold-up outside, or somewhere like Bernie's suite AA1 in the new wing of the Hôtel du Cap, where he's sure to have her reading scenes after dinner."

"It would be a rather dramatic interruption."

"I didn't hear you, Mr Templar. But since you were obviously going to dine alone, you can take me with you to this Chez Francis place, where I have heard the chef turns himself inside out for you. Afterwards we can come back here and play Bézique for as long or as short a time as you can stand it."

"I'll make myself a little more presentable," said the Saint, "and pick you up at eight."

When he returned he was very presentable indeed, by conventional standards, having changed into a double-breasted dinner jacket of impeccably inconspicuous style and blackness, and she looked him over with visible surprise.

"Don't think I'm overdoing it," he said. "This just happens to be the most anonymous costume I know, in a place like this, for stick-ups and such jobs. With an old nylon stocking over the head, it gives nobody anything worth a damn to describe."

"You needn't have told me that," she retorted. "You almost had me believing that there could be some basis for the legend of the gentleman crook."

Otherwise they spent quite a civilized and sometimes even amusing two and a half hours, and nothing so crude as crime was mentioned again even when the Saint returned her to her sitting-room, played one hand of Bézique with her, and then asked with deliberate expressionlessness if he might call it a night.

"I shall be up for a long time yet," she said flatly. "Probably playing Patience, since you won't finish this game."

Simon took shameless advantage of this when he returned to his own room some time after midnight and found the unfriendly inspector of the *Police Judiciaire* already ensconced proprietarily in the most comfortable armchair, and polluting the atmosphere with a cigar which some countries would have classified as a secret weapon.

"*Alors*, Monsieur Templar. Let us continue. There is a hold-up reported from Cap d'Antibes. The man is tall, slender but well-built, his features disguised with a stocking, but wearing a *smoking* like yourself—"

"And like a few thousand other dopes who've settled for the idea that women must change their styles every season, but men have now achieved the ultimate costume which they must expect to wear from here to eternity, or until civilization comes to its glorious radioactive end."

"I am not here to discuss the philosophy of clothing," said the inspector. "I would like to finish this business and go to bed."

He was a small dark man with beady eyes and an impatient manner, as if he was perpetually exasperated by people who gratuitously wasted his time by pretending to be innocent.

"I understand your eagerness," said the Saint mildly. "But isn't it stretching things a bit for you to be waiting here even before I get home from this alleged caper?"

"This is very easy to explain. Your victims would not have waited two seconds to report the robbery. The gendarmerie at Cap d'Antibes immediately notified me, as is their duty. And electricity travels on telephone wires much faster than you could drive here, especially at this time of the season. While I only had three blocks to walk."

"Okay," said the Saint. "I'll try to finish this even faster. If you'll permit me . . ."

He picked up the telephone and asked for Mrs Noversham's suite by number. She answered so promptly that she might have been waiting for the call.

"This is Simon Templar," he said. "Would you be amused to hear that I've already got a policeman in my room accusing me of a stick-up out at Cap d'Antibes?"

"Does he have any evidence?"

"None that I know of. But it's the same character who gave me such a bad time this morning. I think he's just decided to blame me for everything that happens around here, on general principles."

"How ridiculous," she said. "Have you told him that you only left me a few minutes ago, after playing Bézique with me all evening?"

"I was wondering if you'd mind telling him yourself."

She arrived in a few minutes, an overwhelming figure in her warpaint and jangling jewels, and gave Simon an alibi that was a classic of unblushing perjury, even adorning it with details of some of the hands they had played and waving a piece of paper which she said carried the complete scores for the session. In addition, her phraseology left no doubt of her majestic contempt for the intelligence of the police, and of one policeman in particular.

"*Alors, mon vieux,*" the Saint said to him finally. "You were anxious to get home, I believe. What else is keeping you?"

The inspector stood up, looking somewhat crushed.

"It is only my job," he mumbled. "*Je m'excuse—*"

"*Je vous en prie,*" said the Saint, with exaggerated courtesy, accompanying him to the small vestibule. "*Et dormez bien.*"

He closed the outer door and returned to the room where Bertha Noversham still stood looking somewhat Wagnerian.

"I don't know how I should thank you," he began, and she cut him off unceremoniously.

"Don't bother. Just hand over those jewels of Natalie's. I think I can get as good a price for them as you can, and you'll get your share eventually, but I'll do the divvying."

He stared at her frozenly.

"It was nice of you to help me out," he said, "but I didn't think you were planning to make a career of it."

"I can scarcely believe that you're so naïve, Mr Templar. I'm sure I don't look like a starry-eyed ingénue who'd do something like this for love. I didn't even do it for love for Danny Tench."

"You mean—the man who—"

"My husband. Legally, too, though I never used his name—it sounded too frightfully common."

"But he had your jewels on him when he fell," said the Saint slowly. "No, wait a second—I get it. After the yacht job at Ajaccio, and the Métropole at Monte Carlo before that, and God knows how many others before those two, it would have begun to look suspicious if you were always around but never got robbed yourself."

She nodded.

"It's pretty easy for a gabby middle-aged frump like me to make friends with a lot of stupid women, and in no time at all we're comparing jewels and telling each other where we hide them. Danny couldn't have done half as well without me, and he was the first to admit it. But when he slipped last night—and it would never have happened if he hadn't had that clever idea of planting something in your room—I made up my mind I still wasn't going to give up on Natalie's diamonds, and you were the man to swipe them for me."

"So you actually did talk her into distrusting me."

"And I had to be pretty clever about it, too. And it was even more of a job to set up that date with Bernie Kovar. But she really is quite a babe in the woods, if that does anything for your ego. I never set eyes on her before I found her on the Blue Train a few weeks ago, of course . . . And now," Mrs Noversham said coldly, "are you going to hand over those sparklers, or shall I have to tell that police inspector what you did to force me to back up your story?"

Simon turned rather sadly towards the little vestibule, at the inevitable identical instant when the inspector made his return entrance from it, on the inevitably unmistakable cue.

He was followed by two agents in uniform, one with a notebook and one carrying a small tape recorder, and both of them trying not to look as if they had strayed out of the *Tales of Hoffman*.

Without any need to speak, they all watched Mrs Noversham's face whiten and sag under the crust of make-up which suddenly did not seem to fit any more.

"Now don't jump to any conclusions," she said at last, with a desperate attempt to keep the old brassy dominance in her voice. "If you had anyone listening in when he phoned me, you know that I asked if you had any evidence, and he said no, it was only suspicion. So I thought that if I pretended to give him an alibi, and made him believe I was as big a crook as he is, I'd get a confession out of him that you could use. And he was just ready for it when you busted in and spoiled it all. But you can't guillotine me for trying to help you do the job the taxpayers pay you for. If you even had the gumption to search him right now, he's probably still got those jewels on him—"

"I'm sorry, Bertha," Simon said. "But there never was any hold-up. I only asked the Inspector to act as if there had been one, and I promised him that you would do the confessing. He took quite a lot of convincing, and I hate to think what he'd've done if you'd let me down."

Mrs Noversham had one succinct response to that, and she squeezed it through her teeth with all the venom of a professional.

"Stool pigeon!"

"It was rather against my principles," said the Saint, and he meant it. "In some ways I'd rather have stolen your jewels and called it quits. But you and Danny-boy started the routine by trying to get me in trouble, and then I wanted to get the record straight for Natalie."

The little inspector cleared his throat irritably.

"*Madame*, this is not a performance at the *Comédie Française*. You understand that you will have to accompany us?"

"Only too well, Alphonse," said Bertha Noversham insultingly.

She started regally towards the door, but as the two agents nervously made way for her she turned back.

"Mr Templar," she said almost humbly, "why?"

"To use a phrase of your own," said the Saint, "you shouldn't have thrown Natalie to the wolves—or wolf. You made her out to be such an outrageous all-time phony that after I got over the first shock I started to think that if any woman could be such a colossal barefaced liar, so could any other. But I'd never caught Natalie in the smallest dishonesty, myself, whereas I always knew that there's no such person as the Duke of Camford. And once the question of credibility had come up, there was no doubt about which of you had done the hottest job of selling me the idea of robbing the other . . . There are several morals in this, Bertha, but I'd say the best one is that before you start beating a path to the door of a man who makes better mousetraps, you should be sure that you're not a mouse."

"*Madame*," said the inspector impatiently, "one cannot wait for you all night."

However, he had the grace to pause, albeit restively, before following his cohorts and their evidence and his prize.

"I am indebted for your assistance, *Monsieur le Saint*, and if perhaps some day I can—"

"I knew you'd think of that, Alphonse," Simon took him up cheerily, and the little man winced. "Mrs Sheridan may be home already, or she should be at any moment, and I'm sure you won't mind waiting to vouch for the true story of the last twenty-four hours. There'll be so many other nights when you can go to bed early, and sleep like a cherub, once you know I've got something better to do than climb in and out of windows, at my age."

ST TROPEZ: THE UGLY

IMPRESARIO

"That," observed Simon Templar, "is quite a sight, even for these parts."

"And that," said Maureen Herald, "is what I've got to talk to."

They lay on the dazzling sands of Pampelonne, which are the beaches of St Tropez, gazing out at the sun-drenched Mediterranean where a few white-sailed skiffs criss-crossed on lazy tacks, an assortment of speedboats with water-skiers in tow traced evanescent arabesques among them, and, much closer in, the object of Simon's comment cruised southwards along the shore line where its occupants could comfortably observe and be observed by the heliophiles on the strand.

It was an open Chris-Craft runabout which would have photographed exactly like any other similarly expensive standard model, except in color. The color was a brilliant purple which no shipyard can ever have been asked to apply to a hull before. And to offset it, the upholstery of the cockpit and the lounging pad covering the engine hatch were an equally brilliant orange. As an aid to identifying the owner of this chromatic monstrosity, the sides of the craft were emblazoned with a large capital J nestling inside a still larger capital U, the monogram being surrounded by a circle of large golden metal stars.

The owner of the boat and the initials, Sir Jasper Undine himself, sat on the port gunwale controlling the course with one hand. Apparently to insure that he would not be eclipsed by his own setting, he wore fluorescent green shorts, a baggy fluorescent crimson windbreaker, and a long-peaked fluorescent yellow cap. Under its exaggerated eye-shade he wore a pair of huge white-plastic blue-lensed sunglasses which, with the help of a torpedo-sized cigar clamped in his mouth and the gray goatee below it, balked any analysis of his features even at that comparatively short range: one had mainly the impression of some goggle-eyed, balloon-torsoed, spindle-legged visitor from Outer Space which had arrayed itself in human garments selected to conform with the prismatic prejudices of Alpha Centauri. But no one who paid any attention to the sophisticated chatter of those times would have been so misled as to fail to identify Sir

Jasper Undine, whose ostentatious eccentricities (suitably embroidered and broadcast by a tireless press agent) had established him as the most garish current character in a coterie which has seldom been distinguished by coyness and self-effacement.

Sir Jasper Undine was, in fact, at that moment one of the indisputable kingpins of the entertainment world in Europe. The story of his rise from part-time usher in a run-down movie theater in South London, to his present control of a complex of motion picture and television producing and distributing companies with ramifications in five countries, in versions flattering or calumnious according to their source, has been told too often to need repeating here. It certainly vouched for an outstanding talent, although some stuffy critics might say that this leaned more towards a ruthless dexterity at brain-picking, idea-stealing, cheating, finagling, and double-dealing, than to any creative or artistic ability. But having achieved success, he had made a second career of indulging every appetite it would gratify, up to and including the knighthood which had cost him many expensive contributions to good causes with which he had no sympathy.

"Is he really as horrible as one would think?" Simon asked.

"Even worse, I believe. But he's got the final say-so on a job that I need very much."

"Don't you have an agent to handle things like that?"

"Of course. My agent's got everything on the contract except Undine's signature. And Undine won't make up his mind about that without meeting me himself."

Maureen Herald was an actress. She had entered Simon's life with a letter from David Lewin of *The Daily Express:*

Dear Saint,

Enclosed please find Maureen Herald. I don't need to tell

*you who she is, but I can tell you that I wish everyone I
know in show business was as nice a person. She has to go to
St Tropez to talk to someone who is not so nice. She doesn't
know anyone else there, and she can't go places alone, and
she may well want a change of company. I've told her that
you also are a good friend and comparatively nice and can
behave yourself if you have to. No wonder some people think
I'm crazy.*

She had gray eyes and what he could only have described as
hair-colored hair, something between brown and black with natural
variations of shading that had not been submerged by the artificial
uniformity of a rinse. It was a perfect complement to her rather thin
patrician features, which would only have been hardened by any
obvious embellishments. She had a gracefully lean-moulded figure to
match, interestingly feminine but without the exaggerated curvature in
the balcony which most of the reigning royalty of her profession found
it necessary to possess or simulate. His first guess would have been that
she had started out as a high fashion model, but he learned that in
fact she had been a nurse at the Hollywood Hospital when a famous
director was brought in for treatment of an acute ulcer and offered
her a screen test before he left. Her rise to stardom had been swift and
outwardly effortless.

"But my last two pictures were commercial flops," she told Simon
candidly. "I say they were stinkers, of course, but some other people
found it easier to blame it on me. A nice girl, they said, but death at the
box office. And just when my first contract had run out—it was no star
salary to start with—and I should have been able to ask for some real
money. They just aren't bidding for me in Hollywood at the moment,
and if I don't do something soon I could be washed up for good."

"That would be a pity," he said. "And nothing but a few annuities to live on."

"That isn't even half funny," she retorted. "After taxes and clothes and publicity and all the other expenses you have to go for, there's very little left out of what I took home. And I've got a mother in a sanatorium with TB and a kid brother just starting medical school. I can't afford not to get this part."

The purple speedboat veered closer to the shore, farther along. There was another man in the cockpit, but he had hardly been noticeable as he sat down, even though he had ginger hair and a complexion exactly the tint of a boiled langouste, they could not compete with the gaudy coloration surrounding him. Now he got up and began throwing out water skis and a tow-rope. He was short and scrawny, and his torso was fish-white up to where his narrow shoulders turned the same painful pink as his face.

Three girls had come down to the water's edge nearest the boat, shouting and giggling. They had almost identical slim but bubble-bosomed figures displayed by the uttermost minimum of bikini. One was raven-haired and the two others were platinum-bleached. One of the blondes began to put on the skis while the other two girls waded out to the boat and climbed in.

"Sir Jasper seems to be casting starlets too, if I recognize the types," Simon remarked. "And he doesn't seem to have much difficulty picking them up."

"When I phoned him this morning for an appointment he said he'd be busy all day until cocktail time."

"He probably figures it's good psychology to keep you cooling your heels for a while. And after all, he is busy."

"From what I've heard, next to making money that's his favorite business."

The Saint recalled photos that he had seen published of Sir Jasper Undine in various night clubs and casinos, where he was always accompanied by at least one conspicuously glamorous damsel and frequently two or three. It was also common gossip that he did not merely cultivate the impression that he lived like a sultan but aspired to substantiate it.

"I wonder if I could resist the temptation, if I were in his position."

"You've probably had plenty of practice resisting temptations," Miss Herald said. "But I'm not looking forward to this interview."

The two dolls who were riding deployed themselves artistically on the orange coverings, the red-haired factotum scrambled down again into insignificance, the Chris-Craft's sulky muttering rose to a hearty roar, the tow-rope tightened, and the skier came up out of the water a little wobbly at first and then steadying and straightening up and skimming out of the wake as the boat came to planing speed.

Undine drove at full throttle, curling across the bay on a course that seemed cold-bloodedly improvised to score as many near-misses as possible on all the pedalos, floaters, dinghies, and other slower vessels in the area.

"Do you water-ski?" Simon asked, as they watched.

"I've tried it. But I don't much like being whipped around like the tail of a kite, wherever the boat takes you. If someone would invent a way of steering the boat yourself while you're skiing, it might be fun."

"Water-skiers must be the worst kind of exhibitionists. Haven't you noticed that their whole fun is in showing off? If they just enjoyed water-skiing for its own sake, they could do it all over the ocean without bothering anyone. But no. They always have to work as close as they can to what they hope is an admiring audience, and half-swamp anyone who's only trying to have a quiet peaceful time on the water."

"But the girl who's skiing isn't doing that," Maureen pointed out. "It's Undine who's driving."

"Using her to get more attention." The skier fell off then, trying to jump the wake, and Simon sat up with a short laugh. "What a pity that wasn't him! But I'm sure he wouldn't ski himself and risk anything so undignified . . . Come on, let's forget him for a while and have a dunk."

She swam well and with surprising endurance for her slight build, not with the brief burst of speed fizzling out into breathlessness that he would have expected. He followed her for about five hundred yards, and when they turned around she seemed quite capable of making it five kilometers.

"I won all the athletic prizes in school," she said when he complimented her. "That's probably my trouble, being the good sister instead of the home-wrecker type."

"If I treat you like a brother," he said, "it's only because David stuck me with it."

After the sun had dried them again she said, "I don't want to spoil your day, but I'm not tanned like you are, and it might ruin everything if I meet Undine this evening looking like a raspberry sundae."

"It's lunch-time, anyway. I have an idea. Let's drive up to Ramatuelle. There's a little restaurant there, Chez Cauvière, where they make the best *paella* this side of the Pyrenees and perhaps the other side too. Then I'll take you back to the hotel for a siesta, and by seven o'clock you'll feel fit to cope with a carload of Undines—if you can stand the thought."

The ambrosial hodge-podge of lobster, chicken, octopus, vegetables, and saffron-tinted rice was as good as he boasted; the unlabelled *rosé* of the house was cool insidious nectar; and by the end of the meal they were almost old friends. He felt an almost genuinely brotherly concern when he left her and had to remember that all this had been only an interlude.

"Is there anything else I can do?" he asked.

"Yes," she said. "I've been thinking about it. Do you suppose you could come by the café about eight o'clock, and say hullo to me? Then if it seems like a good idea by that time, I can make like we had a date. It might get me out of something. Even just as a card up my sleeve, it'd do a lot for my morale. That is, if you aren't already tied up—"

"I can't think of anything better," he smiled. "You can count on me."

She had already told him which café was referred to. The quais which face the harbor of St Tropez are lined almost solidly with restaurants and cafes, where everyone who knows the routine turns out in the evening to be seen and to see who else is being seen, but ever since "Saint-Trop" became known as the rendezvous of a certain artistic-bohemian set for whom the Riviera westward from Cannes was either too princely or too bourgeois, "the" café has always been the Sénéquier, and the others have to be content with its overflow—which is usually enough to swamp them anyway. Although many of the original celebrities have since migrated to less publicized havens, the invading sightseers who put them to flight continue to swarm there and stare hopefully around, most of the time at each other. But even in this era a permanently reserved table at Sénéquier was still a status symbol which Sir Jasper Undine would inevitably have had to display, whatever the price.

Simon strolled slowly along the Quai Jean-Jaurès a little before eight, allowing himself a leisured study of the scene as he approached.

It was impossible not to spot Undine at any distance: he stood out even amidst the rainbow patchwork of holiday garb on the terrace with the help of a blazer with broad black and yellow horizontal stripes, which with the help of his oversized sunglasses made him look something like a large bumblebee in a field of butterflies—if you could imagine a bumblebee wearing a red-and-white-checkered tam-o'-shanter.

Besides the ginger-haired young man who had served as mate on the speedboat in the morning, and two of the shapely playthings they had picked up (or two almost indistinguishable chippies off the same block), Sir Jasper's entourage had been augmented not only by Maureen Herald, who had been privileged to sit on one side of him, but also by a reddish-blonde young woman with a voluptuous authority that made the starlet types look adolescent.

As he came closer, Simon recognized the sulky sensual face as that of Dominique Rousse, a French actress whose eminence, some competitors asserted, was based mainly on certain prominences, which contrived to get uncovered in all her pictures on one pretext or another. On her other side was a black-browed heavy-set individual who seemed to be watching and absorbing everything with brooding intensity but to be deliberately withholding any contribution of his own.

As Simon came within earshot, Undine was saying, " . . . and rub his nose in it. The banks don't make any loans on artistic integrity, and a producer who isn't as tough as a bank better learn to print his own money. I know what I can do for anyone and I figure what they've got to do for me to pull their weight in the package, or I'm not interested—"

He broke off, cigar and goatee cocked challengingly, as the Saint stopped at the table.

Maureen Herald's face lighted up momentarily, and then masked itself with a kind of cordial restraint.

"Oh, hullo, Simon," she said, and turned smoothly to the others. "This is Mr—Thomas." The hesitation was barely perceptible. "Sir Jasper Undine. Mr and Mrs Carozza—that is, Dominique Rousse." The dark withdrawn man, then, was the lush actress's husband. "I'm afraid I didn't get all the other names—"

Undine did not bother to supply them. He stared at the Saint steadily. The impenetrable sunglasses hid his eyes, but at this range it could be seen that his nose was fleshy and his mouth large-lipped and moist.

He asked brusquely, "Any relation of the Thomas brothers—Ralph and Gerald—the directors?"

"No," said the Saint, pleasantly.

"Not an actor?"

"No."

"You can sit down, then. Get him a chair, Wilbert."

The carroty young man gave up his own seat and went looking for another. He was the only customer in the place who was a wearing a tie, and even a shiny serge jacket as well. They were like symbols of servitude amid the surrounding riot of casual garb, and obviously defined his part in Undine's retinue.

"There's nothing wrong with actors except when they're trying to get a job, and then there's a limit to how many you can 'ave around at the same time," said Sir Jasper. His origins revealed themselves in his speech more consistently through its intonation and subject matter than by the dropping of h's, which he did only occasionally. "One day somebody'll make a robot that you just wind up and it says what you put on a tape, and then they can all butter themselves. Get him a drink, Wilbert."

"And who would make the tape recording?" Simon inquired, mildly.

"The writers would be glad to do that themselves. They always know 'ow their precious lines ought to be spoken better than anybody else—don't they, Lee?"

The taciturn Carozza, whose profession was thus revealed, gave a tight-lipped smile without answering. Now the Saint remembered having seen his name in print as one of Europe's avant-garde new dramatists, but was vague about his actual achievements. It was not a sphere in which Simon Templar had more than a superficial interest.

"These brainy chaps can do anything," Undine pursued. "Look at him. There's Dominique, who gets made love to by all the matinée idols—on the set, of course—and papers her bathroom with mash notes from millionaires, and I could go for her myself, but she falls for his intellectual act. He's hired to work on my script, and she wants to play the lead in it, but he goes and marries her. That's what you do with brains."

"You promised me the part before that," said Dominique Rousse sullenly.

"I said you were the best bet I'd seen. But what am I betting on now? All you'll be thinking about is what Lee wants, not what I want. I'm kidding, of course."

If he was, it was with a touch that tickled like a club.

"Does that mean you were kidding when you asked me to come here for an interview?" Maureen Herald asked.

"Get me another cigar, Wilbert." Undine brought his opaque gaze back to her. "Listen, you remember in 'Olly-wood about six years ago, right after the premeer of your first picture, which I saw—I was giving a party, and I sent you an invitation, but you didn't come then."

"I'd never met you, and I happened to have another date."

"I knew it couldn't've been because you felt too grand for the likes of me. After all, you came all the way here this time, didn't you?"

"So all this was just your way of getting even?" she asked steadily.

"Now why would I go to all that trouble? I'm reminding you, that's all. I didn't let it make any difference when I told my lawyers to go ahead and draw up a contract with everything your agent was able to get out of me. I rang 'em up this afternoon and they said they'd already sent it off. It should be here in the first post tomorrow. Then all I got to do is make up my mind to be big-'earted and sign it."

"But if—"

"Who said you and Dominique couldn't both be starred? There's two female parts in the script that could be built up equal, if we can stop Lee trying to give all the best of it to his wife."

"I'm sorry," Carozza said, speaking at last. "But I don't see that." He had only a trace of accent, which was as much Oxford as Latin. "Unless Messalina dominates everything—"

Sir Jasper clutched his temples.

"There 'e goes. Just like I told you." He turned to Maureen again, and dropped a heavy hand on her knee. "But don't worry—he'll come 'round when he thinks about all that lolly I could stop paying him every week. So let's you and me go to dinner and talk about this part." He stood up, royally. "Wilbert, order one more round and pay the bill. So long, everybody."

Simon met Maureen's eyes as they looked at him, letting her take the cue, and they said as plainly as if she had spoken, "Forgive me, but I guess I am stuck with it. What else can I do?"

The Saint smiled his understanding, and said, "I'll call you tomorrow."

He accepted another Peter Dawson without compunction, and made it a double just to reciprocate the courtesy with which it had been offered. The Carozzas also shrug-nodded acceptance, but the two starlet types, after ogling the Saint speculatively and receiving little encouragement, twittered obliquely to each other and took their leave.

While Wilbert (whether that was his first or his last name, it fitted his function and personality like a glove) was twisting one way and another trying to flag down a waiter, Dominique Rousse exploded in a furious aside to her husband which was pitched too low for any other ear, but Carozza silenced her with a warning down-drift of his brows. He was studying the Saint now with the undeviating concentration which he seemed to aim at its objects like a gun.

"Did I hear Miss Herald say you were Mr Simon Thomas?" he inquired.

"You did," Simon replied easily.

"I was wondering if it should have been Simon Templar."

"Why?"

"You have a great resemblance to a picture I saw once—of a person who is called the Saint."

"Have I?"

"I think you are being modest."

The Saint grinned at him blandly and indulgently, and drawled: "I hope that's a compliment."

The ginger-haired Wilbert had finally accomplished his assignment, which had kept him out of this exchange, and now as if he had not heard any of it he pulled a notebook and a ball-point pen from his pocket and leaned towards the Saint like a college-magazine reporter.

"What hotel are you staying at, Mr Thomas?"

"I'm staying in a friend's apartment. He lent it to me while he's away."

"Would you give me the address? And the telephone number, if there is one?"

The Saint was mildly surprised.

"Whatever for?"

"Sir Jasper will expect me to know," Wilbert said. "If he wanted to get in touch with you again for any reason, and I didn't know where to find you, he'd skin me alive."

With, his jug-handle ears and slightly protruding eyes and teeth, and the complexion that looked as if it had been sandpapered, he was so pathetically earnest, like a boy scout trying for a badge, that Simon didn't have the heart to be evasive with that information. But in return he asked where Undine was staying.

"He has a villa for the season—*Les Cigales*," Wilbert told him . . . "You take the Avenue Foch out of the town, and it's three or four kilometers out, on your left, right on the water. Sir Jasper has had signs posted along the road with his initials, so you won't have any trouble finding it if he invites you there."

"Thanks," murmured, the Saint. "But I hardly think we've struck up that kind of friendship."

Carozza was still scrutinizing him with unalleviated curiosity, and to head off any further interrogation, Simon deliberately took the lead in another direction.

"What is this epic you're working on?" he asked.

"*Messalina*," Carozza said curtly. He was plainly irritated at being forced off at a tangent from the subject that intrigued him.

"Based on the dear old Roman mama of the same name?"

"Yes."

"I can see why it would be difficult to build up another female part and make it as important as hers."

"With any historical truth or dramatic integrity, yes. But those are never Sir Jasper's first considerations."

"His first being the box office?"

"Usually. And after that, his personal reasons."

"This Maureen Herald," Dominique Rousse said. "She is a good friend of yours?"

In French, the words "good friend" applied to one of the opposite sex have a possible delicate ambiguity which Simon did not overlook.

"I only met her yesterday," he answered. "But I think she's very nice."

"Do you want her to have this part?"

"I wish her luck, but I don't wish anyone else any bad luck," said the Saint diplomatically. "I hope it all works out so that everybody's happy."

He mentally excluded Sir Jasper Undine from that general benevolence, but decided not to bring up that issue. He could see that Lee Carozza was getting set to resume his inquisition, and he was instinctively disinclined to remain available for it. He finished his drink and stood up briskly.

"Well, it was nice meeting all of you, but I must be going. Maybe I'll see you around."

Because Undine had turned to the right when he left, Simon turned the other way, to obviate any risk of running into them again and seeming to have followed. In the direction thus imposed on him, opening off a narrow and unpromising alley, was the surprisingly atmospheric and attractive patio of the Auberge des Maures, which it was no hardship to settle for. He found a table in a quiet corner; and presently over a splendid *bouillabaisse* and a bottle of cool *rosé* he found himself inevitably considering the phenomenon of Sir Jasper Undine.

It was a frustrating kind of review, because in spite of Undine's resplendent qualifications as a person on whom something unpleasant ought to be inflicted, the appropriate form of visitation was not at all easy to determine.

A simple extermination was naturally the most complete and tempting prescription, but might have seemed a bit drastic to a jury of tender hearts.

At the other end of the scale, a financial penalty, levied by such straightforward means as burglary, was not likely to be practically productive. Sir Jasper, for all his ostentation, would not be packing a load of jewels like his female equivalent would have, and in a rented villa he would not have any other personal treasures. Nor was there much chance of finding a lot of cash on the premises or on Sir Jasper's person. Wilbert had paid for the drinks from a modest wallet and entered the amount in his notebook: it was evident that among his various duties was that of personal paymaster, and he was the prim and prudent type who would be certain to keep most of the funds in the form of traveler's checks.

The only possibility in between would be one of those elaborately plotted and engineered swindles which delighted the Saint's artistic soul, but for which none of the elements of the situation seemed to offer a readymade springboard.

It was quite a problem for a buccaneer with a proper sense of responsibility to his life's mission, and Simon Templar was not much closer to a solution when he walked back to his temporary home at what for St Tropez was a comparatively rectangular hour of the night, having decided that some new factor might have to be added before an inspiration would get off the ground.

He was at the entrance when the door of one of the parked cars in the driveway opened, and quick footsteps sounded behind him, and a woman said, "*Pardon*, Monsieur Templar—"

The voice was halfway familiar, enough to make him turn unguardedly before he fully recognized it, and then he also recognized Dominique Rousse and it was too late.

She smiled.

"So my husband was right," she said. "You are *le Saint*."

"He wins the bet," Simon said resignedly. "Is he here?"

"No. He is at the Casino. He will be there until dawn. For him, gambling is a passion. I told him I had a headache and could not stand any more. Do you have an aspirin?"

The Saint contemplated her amiably for a profound moment.

"I'll see if I can find one."

He took her up in the self-service elevator, sat her down in the living room, and went foraging. He came back with Old Curio, ice cubes, water, and two tablets which he punctiliously placed beside the glass he mixed for her.

She laughed with a sudden abandon which shattered the unreal sultriness of her face.

"You are wonderful."

"I only try to oblige."

"You make this much easier for me. You know that I want something more—"

"More difficult?"

"Much more. I want to be Messalina in this film of Undine's. It is the most important thing in the world."

His eyebrows slanted banteringly.

"That's a considerable statement."

"It is important for me. I am a star in Europe, yes. In England and America they have heard of me—they have seen pictures in special theaters, with subtitles or with another voice speaking for me—but I am not a star. To become a star internationally, to be paid the biggest money, I must be seen in a great picture made in English. All of us have to do this, like Lollobrigida and Loren and Bardot. Undine will make that kind of picture."

Simon swirled the amber liquid in his glass gently around the floes.

"You know I just met him for the first time. What makes you think I can influence him?"

"Perhaps you can influence Maureen Herald to look for another job."

"I'm quite sure she wouldn't listen to me. And why should she?"

"I must tell you something," she said with restrained vehemence. "I already have a contract to play Messalina. It was not spoken of this evening because it is still a secret between Undine and me. But I made him sign it before I would pay the price that he wanted." She stated it with such brutal directness that the Saint blinked. "He cannot get out of that. But if he is thinking of cheating by having another part made just as big, or bigger, I would like to see him killed."

"And have no picture at all?"

"There would still be a picture. The contract is with his company. They already have much money invested. The company would go on, but the producer would not have Undine telling him how he must change the script." She stood up, and came close. "If you can do nothing else, kill Undine for me."

He stared at her. Her arms went up, and her hands linked behind his neck, her eyes half closed and her mouth half open.

"I would be very grateful," she said.

"I'm sure you would," he said as lightly as possible. "And if the *flics* didn't pin it on me, your husband would only shoot me and get acquitted."

"Who would tell him? It is for his good, too, and what he does not know will not hurt him, any more than what I had to do before with Undine."

Simon realized, almost against credibility, that she was perfectly sober and completely serious. It was one of the most stunning revelations of total amorality that even he had ever encountered—and ethical revulsion made it no easier to forget that it came with the bait of a face and body that might have bothered even St Anthony.

He let his head be drawn down until their lips met and clung, and then as he responded more experimentally she drew back.

"You will do it?"

The Saint had reached an age when it seemed only common sense to avoid gratuitously tangling with the kind of woman which hell hath no fury like, but he never lied if he could avoid it.

"I'll think about it," he said, truthfully.

"Do not think too long," she said. "You would do it cleverly, but another person could also do it, not so cleverly, but to be acquitted. Only then I would not owe you anything."

"You aren't offering a down payment?" he said with a shade of mockery.

"No. But I am not like Undine. I would not cheat in that way."

She looked searchingly into his eyes for some seconds longer, but the pouting mask of her beauty gave no hint of whatever she thought she found. Then abruptly she turned and walked to the door. Before he could be quite sure of her intention, she had opened it without a pause and gone out; it closed behind her, and the click of her heels went away uninterruptedly down the stone hall and ended in the metallic rattle of the elevator gate.

The Saint took a long slow breath and passed the back of a hand across his forehead.

Then he picked up his glass again and emptied it.

He knew then that his strange destiny was running true to form, and that all the apparently random and pointless incidents of the past thirty-six hours, which have been recorded here as casually as they happened, could only be building towards the kind of eruptive climax in which he was always getting involved. But now he could go to sleep peacefully, secure in the certainty that something else would have to happen and that this would quite possibly show him what he had to do.

But he never dreamed how bizarre the dénouement was to be.

He made his own breakfast of eggs and instant coffee the next morning, and after that it seemed not too early to call Maureen Herald. He was prepared to have been told that there was a Do Not Disturb on her telephone, but instead the hotel operator reported eventually: *"Elle ne répond pas."* He was surprised enough to have it repeated, making sure there was no mistake.

He had his call transferred to the concierge, and pressed the question of when she had gone out. He was told about nine o'clock, and was happy to be ashamed of his trend of thought.

He would have to be patient a while longer, then, for the next development.

He drove to the section of the Pampelonne beach which they call "Tahiti," and walked along the sand far enough to get away from the densest crowd, which naturally clustered near the end of the road. Peeled down to his trunks, he stretched himself out to enjoy the sun and the scene with the timeless tranquillity of a lizard.

It seemed only a matter of minutes before the purple and orange Chris-Craft came around the point on his left and cruised slowly across the bay, just as it had done the day before. The same grotesque monster with blue-lensed eyes and giant cigar, clad in the same horrible combination of fluorescent green and crimson and yellow, sat up on the side and steered it in the same negligent manner, scanning the shore, only this time it was alone. The servile Wilbert had apparently been left to some other chore.

From time to time Undine's cigar waved back in response to a wave from some would-be playmate on the beach, but the speedboat purred on without swerving. It looked as if Sir Jasper was not in the mood for company today, or as if his regular wolf-promenade would be satisfied with only one specific quarry which he had not yet flushed.

The speedboat voyaged all the way down to the "Epi Plage" at the southern end of the strand, where the more fanatical sun-worshippers regularly scandalize the conventional with their uninhibited exposures among the dunes, but even that did not seem to offer its colorific commodore what he was seeking. It turned, and retraced its course until it was almost opposite the Saint, and then suddenly poured on the power and veered out and away with a foaming arrogance that almost swamped two or three small craft which had the temerity to be near the path it had chosen, and disappeared to the northeast around the rocky salient of Cap du Pinet.

Simon glanced at his wrist watch, a habit of reference which was almost a reflex with him, and it showed a quarter to eleven.

He wondered what connection, if any, Undine's disinterest might have had with the outcome of the previous night, but he knew that this speculation was only an idle pastime.

When the heat began to become oppressive he went for a swim, and then he enjoyed the sun all over again. And it was twenty minutes to one before he felt restive—and recognized that the feeling was as much due to a plain gastric announcement of lunch-time as to any psychic impatience for new events.

Then he rolled over and saw Maureen Herald coming towards him.

In sunglasses and a chiffon scarf cowled over her head and knotted under her chin in the style of that season, she was like a hundred other girls on the beach except for the distinctively long-lined greyhound figure which her wet bikini clung to like paint—until she was close enough to reveal the classical delicacy of her face.

"Hi," she said.

Simon unwound himself vertically with a delight which surprised himself.

"Hi," he said. "I was wondering where we'd catch up. I called you about half-past nine, but you'd already gone out."

"I had to see Undine. I called you as soon as I could, but your phone didn't answer. I hoped I'd find you here."

"How did it go?"

She met his eyes squarely.

"He signed the contract."

She sat down, and he gave her a cigarette.

"Was it difficult?"

"It nearly was," she said. "You were wonderful to say nothing, the way you did, when I stood you up at the Sénéquier. But later on I was wishing you hadn't been such a good sport. He wasn't so bad at the restaurant, except that it was like being out with a brass band, but after dinner we had to go to his villa."

"Not to see etchings?"

"Not quite. To see if the contract had arrived. It might have come, he said, if it was sent special delivery. But of course it hadn't." She inhaled deeply. "Then he laid it on the line anyhow—what I'd have to do if he was going to sign. It was as corny as any old melodrama, but he was flying high by that time and he meant it. I was scared stiff."

"But Heaven will protect the working girl . . . the song says."

She gazed out towards the horizon unseeingly, as though she were watching a movie that was being projected on a screen inside her sunglasses, and her voice was a toneless commentary on what she saw replayed.

"The only thing I could think of was just as hysterically corny. I told him about my mother and my brother, and I said, 'That's the only reason I can't say no, but I can't make myself pretend to enjoy it. If you can enjoy it like that, go ahead.' And I lay down limp like a rag doll." She turned to Simon again, and gripped his arm in a sudden gesture that was more like a convulsive release of suppressed tension than anything personal. "And it worked!"

"It licked him?"

"He told me to get out and come back in the morning for the contract. He even let me take his car to go home and come back in."

"So that's where you were when I called."

She nodded.

"Of course I was afraid he'd have changed his mind. But he hadn't. He said if he'd had a sister who would have been ready to do as much for him, he might have felt a lot differently about women. It was a real tear-jerker. But he signed the contract, and that was that. I mailed it to my agent and came looking for you."

"Did he say you could play Messalina?"

"No. But it has to be a big part, for what they're paying. And however it turns out, I'll get the money, and that's the most important thing to me."

The Saint stood up, grinning, and put out a hand to help her to her feet.

"Then we've got something to celebrate. Let's go to the *Voile d'Or* at St Raphael and introduce you to Monsieur Saquet's *bourride*. It's only the best on the whole Coast."

"Yes. I'm starving. You always have the most wonderful ideas."

As they trudged towards the road, he asked, "Do you still have Undine's car?"

"No. I was glad to return it. Do you know, it's a Rolls Royce painted exactly like his speedboat, including the big monogram on the side. I took a taxi."

"In that outfit?"

She laughed.

"I'm afraid I'm not quite emancipated enough for that." She opened the plastic zipper bag she carried and took out a roll of cloth not much bigger than his fist, which shook out into a one-piece play-suit of some wrinkle-proof synthetic. In five seconds she was what daytime St Tropez would have considered almost overdressed. "See?"

"What won't they make next," said the Saint admiringly. "So we can head straight for the fish kettle without any footling about."

Thus it was that they made no stop in St Tropez until mid-afternoon, and had no preliminary intimation of the mystery which was going to climax Sir Jasper Undine's career with its last headlines.

Maureen Herald said she would have to find a travel agency in the town to check on her return flight to London, so the Saint stopped in the parking lot near the Casino and walked with her to the Quai de Suffren. And there they ran into, or more literally were run into by a hustling and vaguely frantic Wilbert.

"Oh, it's you," he said brilliantly, when the fact had registered. "Do you know anything about Sir Jasper?"

"Several things," said the Saint. "And nearly all of them are uncomplimentary. What aspect would you like to hear about?"

"I mean, have you seen him, or anything?"

"I saw him making his usual prowl in the speedboat this morning. But he went off without any passengers. That was about a quarter to eleven. Why, what's the excitement?"

"Hadn't you heard?" spluttered the tycoon's stooge. "Sir Jasper has disappeared!"

Simon raised his eyebrows.

"Theoretically, I'd say that was impossible," he murmured. "He must be easily the most visible man in this hemisphere. He's probably even luminous in the dark."

"But he has! The Chris-Craft was found forty miles out at sea, with nobody in it. I just got a message that a French Navy patrol boat had brought it in."

"You're headed the wrong way," Simon said. "The Navy jetty is on the north side of the port, that-a-way. Let's go and view the salvage."

As they went, Wilbert managed to calm down sufficiently to supply some details.

"He had an engagement for lunch with the manager of one of his Italian subsidiaries who was coming specially from Rome, but he never got back for it. I know it was an important meeting and nothing but an accident would have kept him away. Of course, I was a bit surprised that he'd already taken the boat out alone when I arrived at ten-thirty. He's never done that before—"

"You don't sleep at the villa?"

"No, I'm staying at a hotel in town."

"Did he say anything to the servants?"

55

"They don't sleep in, either. They come in at two o'clock, Sir Jasper doesn't like anyone in the house at night, except people he might invite. You know . . ."

The Saint thought he knew, but he avoided catching Maureen's eye.

A Naval rating and a police sergeant were jointly standing guard over Sir Jasper's effulgent sampan when they arrived and Wilbert identified himself. Both representatives of the State promptly produced notebooks and began jabbering at him at once, and Simon had to step in as interpreter. It appeared that the Navy was putting a lien on the boat for the cost of bringing it in, and at the same time considering the possibility of prosecuting the owner for endangering navigation by abandoning it on the high seas, while the Police were convinced that someone should be arrested but were trying to decide who and for what. Simon cheerfully assured them that Wilbert would take full responsibility for everything, and they were finally allowed on board.

In an open runabout of that kind there was not much to examine that could not have been seen from the wharf, but Simon switched on the ignition and pressed the starter buttons one after the other. Each engine turned over vigorously but did not fire, and he saw that the needle of the fuel gauge remained at zero.

"Ran out of gas," he remarked. "Do you suppose he tried to swim back for some?"

"He could only swim a few strokes," Wilbert said, "and the boat was forty miles out!"

"He could have been picked up by another boat," Maureen said.

"Then they'd have brought him home before this," said the Saint. "Or if it was a liner that couldn't just turn around, they'd have a radio, and he'd've got through to Wilbert right away."

"Suppose he was kidnapped?" Wilbert suggested.

Simon rubbed his chin.

"I guess you can suppose it. But who on earth would pay anything to get him back?"

Any fingerprints that might be found on the boat would be hopelessly confused by all the sailors who must have handled it, but there were no immediately visible traces of the salvage operation, or of any unusual behavior on board. In fact, everything was commendably neat and clean, as Simon pointed out.

"I hosed her down and tidied up myself when we came in yesterday," Wilbert said. "It's one of my jobs."

The Saint frowned thoughtfully.

"I suppose he made a lot of mess with those cigars?"

"Yes—ashes everywhere—" The carroty young man caught his breath, and his Adam's apple bobbed. He looked around the boat in a startled way. "Good heavens! You mean—"

"I don't see any ashes," said the Saint.

Maureen bit her lip.

"This is fascinating," she said. "Just like playing detectives . . . Listen. Sir Jasper was really quite plastered last night. He must have had an awful hangover this morning. That would account for him not being in the mood to pick any girls up. And if his tummy was upset he probably couldn't stand to light a cigar. Was his cigar alight, Simon?"

"I'm damned if I know," said the Saint. "He didn't come in close enough. And who would've noticed, anyhow?"

Then there was a new commotion on the dock, and they looked up and saw Lee Carozza and Dominique chattering with the guard detail. There was nothing more worth staying on the Chris-Craft for, and Simon and Maureen climbed back up and joined them, with Wilbert following.

"They told us at the Pinède," Carozza explained. "We were having the siesta, and they woke us up. But it's hard to believe he's been murdered."

"Who said he was?" Simon asked.

"That was the rumor. It is not true?"

Wilbert repeated the facts, very precisely, with the addition of what they had observed and discussed in the boat, like a new member of an undergraduate committee making his first report.

"I am not a criminal expert," Carozza said at the end, looking very significantly at the Saint, "but how can it be anything but murder? I knew him, and he was not a man who would take a boat forty miles towards Africa by himself, with no one to admire him. He was taken out by someone who killed him and threw him overboard, and escaped in another boat."

"Why in another boat?" Simon inquired.

"To make a mystery. Like the famous *Marie Celeste,* the ship from which all the passengers and crew disappeared and left everything in perfect order. This was the work of an artist!"

His wife studied him fixedly.

"You are not often so quick to talk," she said. "Be careful that someone does not think you are describing yourself."

She had not given the Saint more than the most perfunctory recognition at the beginning, and she continued to ignore him as calmly as if they had never had anything but the casual introduction of the previous evening. It was hard even for him to believe in the reality of the tempting pressure of her body and the tantalization of her mouth that he had known in between, or the monstrous bargain that she had offered. Indubitably she was an actress with more intelligence than her detractors gave her credit for, and if only as a tribute to that talent he had to nudge her off a hazardous tack.

"If there's going to be any murder investigation," he said, "we might all have to look to our alibis."

"Lee and I could have nothing to do with it," she said scornfully. "All this morning we were in Nice, at the studio, where I do an interview for the television. And afterward we have lunch with a reporter from *France-Soir*. And we come back to our hotel, the Pinède, for the siesta. We have no time for anything else."

"Simon and I were together," Maureen said, "from—when was it?—about a quarter to one until we met Mr Wilbert just now."

"I was at the villa," Wilbert said weakly. "Doing the petty cash accounts, going through letters, making a few phone calls—"

He was suddenly very helpless and bewildered.

"*Alors*," said the police sergeant, who had been trying to regain command for a long while, "there must now be a proper statement from everyone."

"By all means," said the Saint. "And let me start with a simple debunking of the whole razzmatazz. Undine was drunk last night, as witnessed by Miss Herald and doubtless many restaurateurs and waiters. This morning he had the *gueule de bois*. He also had an important business meeting to cope with. He went out for a spin in the speedboat to clear his head. And everyone knows he was a crazy boat driver. He made a turn too fast, and in his condition he lost his balance and fell overboard, and the boat went on without him. And let us all think kindly of him when we eat lobsters."

There was a sequel to this rambling anecdote almost a year later, when a production entitled *Messalina*, in Colossoscope and Kaleidocolor, was world-premiered with all the standard fanfares at the Caracalla auditorium in Rome, Italy, with simultaneous openings in six other towns called Rome in the United States.

Simon Templar, who was by nature attracted to such functions as irresistibly as he would have been drawn to a cholera epidemic, was a notable guest, and one of the first personages that he encountered was a ginger-haired bat-eared apparition upon whom a white tie and tails conferred an appallingly pasteboard dignity.

"I gather that you were able to satisfy the flics about the loose joints in your alibi," Simon greeted him genially.

"Of course, they had to accept it eventually." Wilbert inevitably reddened. "They could hardly get around the various people I'd talked to on the phone, which wouldn't have given me time to get far away from the villa. But it was rather awkward when it came out that Sir Jasper had made me the trustee of his will, and it was so loosely worded that I could do almost anything I liked."

"What did he leave his money to?"

"Most of it to found a motion picture museum, with the provision that one whole section has to be devoted to relics of himself and his productions."

"Modest to the last," murmured the Saint. "Well, you certainly gave him service while he was alive. But what I liked best was the way you cleaned up his boat the last time. If you hadn't been so conscientious, we wouldn't have had the cigar-ash clue."

"That didn't make a lot of difference, did it?"

"It helped, Wilbert. It helped."

Dominique Rousse was posing for photographers while her husband stood a little apart, watching with his usual introspective detachment.

"Good evening, Mr Thomas," he said ironically, as Simon came towards him. "I suppose you couldn't wait to see how the picture turned out."

"I do feel a sort of personal interest," Simon confessed.

"I think you'll like what I did with Maureen Herald's part. It is big enough to justify her co-starring, without upsetting the balance of the play."

"Or upsetting Dominique, no doubt," said the Saint. "You don't need me to tell you you're a good writer. But you ought to be more careful of your own dialog."

"In what way?"

"You must know that one of the stock routines for a character to trip himself up in a detective story is to talk about a murder before he's been told that there's been one. If that police sergeant had understood English and been on the ball when you dropped that clanger, you might have had to finish your script in the pokey."

One of the photographers recognized the Saint, grabbed him unceremoniously, and dragged him over to Dominique.

With her sullen beauty, and a rope of diamonds twined in her red-blonde hair, and her stupendous figure revealed by a skin-tight green silk sheath cut low enough to prove to everyone that her world-famous bosom owed nothing to artificial enrichment, it took no effort at all to visualize her as a queen who could have had a pagan mob at her feet, even though she had demonstrated the moral instincts of a cat.

"Pretend to be pointing a gun at her," urged the photographer. "No, that's no good. Put a judo hold on her."

Simon took her by the wrist and twisted her arm gently behind her in such a way that she was pressed against him face to face.

"You could have done this long ago," she said in a whisper that scarcely moved her lips. "I told you I do not break my promise. Why have you not come to claim it?"

He smiled into her eyes.

"Some day I may," he said. "When I can make myself unscrupulous enough."

Finally he was able to rejoin Maureen Herald as another group of photographers tired of her.

"It was nice of you to come all this way to put up with this sort of thing," she said, taking his arm. "But I felt you ought to be here. After all, if you hadn't come up with the explanation of the Undine business, any of us might have been in an awkward spot."

"Somebody certainly owes me something," he admitted, "for helping to hide a murder."

They were moving into the theater, but she stopped to stare at him.

"You mean you've changed your mind since?"

"I always did think it was murder." He got her moving again. "It wasn't just the cigar-ash business, though that started me thinking. When Wilbert let out that Undine never took the boat out alone, I tried to fit that in. Then I remembered the clothes Undine was wearing, and that was the clincher. Undine's taste in color schemes was ghastly, but it wasn't monotonous. Undine wouldn't have just one hideous outfit, he'd've had dozens, and he'd've loved to knock your eye out with a different one every day. *Therefore the man I saw in the boat on the second day wasn't Undine.*"

"Then who was it?"

"Somebody wearing his clothes and flourishing his cigar, padded out to his size with a cushion under the windbreaker. Between those huge sunglasses and the goatee, which could even have been his own hair glued on, at the distance the boat stayed out, it was easy to get away with. Hundreds of people would swear it was Undine they'd seen. But Jasper himself was probably in the bottom of the cockpit with the anchor tied to him, waiting to be dumped overboard out of sight off the cape. Then all the murderer had to do was head the boat out to sea, jump out at a safe distance, and swim back."

"But why did you—"

"I wouldn't want anyone to get in trouble for killing Undine. I can't feel he was any loss to the world."

They found their seats at last and settled down.

"Anyway," he said, "I wouldn't have missed your performance for anything."

"It's not much of a part," she said, "but it'll help me. And the money was just like Christmas."

"I'm not talking about the picture," Simon said. "I'm talking about your performance at St Tropez. Only your material wasn't quite good enough. I was having a hard time believing that a bastard like Undine had really been put off by your sob story. And then you were in just a little too much of a hurry to explain why there were no cigar ashes in the boat, when that came up. And then I realized that nobody else had a better motive for making it seem that Undine was still alive that morning. Several people had heard him say that your contract wouldn't arrive until then, and you had to wait to get it and forge his signature. Of course it took plenty of nerve, but I remembered that you'd started out as a nurse, so you wouldn't panic at the idea of handling a dead body, and I knew how well you could swim."

She turned her face to him with a kind of quiet pride.

"I didn't kill him," she said. "But when it came to the point I couldn't go through with what he wanted, I was struggling for my life, and he was like a madman—it meant that much to him, to get even for the time he thought I'd snubbed him in Hollywood. And then he suddenly collapsed. A heart attack. But all the rest is true."

"That makes it all the better," said the Saint.

He held her hand as the lights dimmed and the credit titles began.

ENGLAND: THE PRODIGAL MISER

Contrary to the belief of many inhabitants of less rugged climes, the sun really does sometimes shine in England, though it is admittedly a fickle phenomenon which imparts a strong element of gambling to the planning of any outdoor activity. But when it shines, perhaps because familiarity never has a chance to breed satiety, it seems to have a special beauty and excitement which is lacking in the places where sunny days are commonplace.

It was on one of those golden days in early autumn that Simon Templar drove out to Marlow, that pleasantly placid village on the Thames made famous by Izaak Walton, the first of all fishing pundits, in *The Compleat Angler*, to take Mrs Penelope Lynch out to lunch. He had met her only a few days before, in London, at a small and highly informal party to celebrate the seventh anniversary of a couple who have no other part in this story, and when he found out where she lived there had been the inevitable comparing of notes on places of interest in the neighborhood.

"Do you know my old pal Giulio Trapani at Skindle's?" he asked.

"Of course. We often used to go there. But for a smaller place, with more of a country-pub atmosphere, do you know the King's Arms at Cookham?"

"No, but I've been to the Crown, where they have wonderful home-made pasties."

"Yes, I've had them. But one day you must try the steak-and-kidney pie at the King's Arms. Mrs Baker makes it herself, and it's the best I know anywhere—if you like steak-and-kidney pie."

"I love it." This was a natural opening that could hardly be passed by. "Would you like to show it to me sometime?"

"Don't make that too definite, or you might find yourself stuck with it."

"How about next Sunday?"

"That would be perfect. In fact, since I'm a working girl, it's about the only day."

He guessed her age at about twenty six, and had learned that she was a widow—her husband had been the export manager of a manufacturing firm in Slough, who had taken an overdose of sleeping pills when he learned that he had lung cancer about six months ago. That was all he knew about her, aside from what his eyes told him, which was that she had short chestnut hair and a short nose, a wide brow, and a wide mouth that smiled very easily, the ingredients combining into a gay gamin look which formed an intriguing counterpoint to her sensuously modelled figure. To a true connoisseur of feminine attractions, which the Saint candidly confessed himself to be, she had an allure that was far more captivating than most conventional forms of pulchritude, and that was rare enough to demand at least a better acquaintance.

She was ready when he arrived, in a tweed skirt and a cardigan over a simple blouse, and sensible suede shoes, and she said, "I'm glad you're early, because it'll give us time to walk over instead of driving. That is, if you won't think that's too frighteningly hearty. It's only about four miles."

"I'm glad to know you're so healthy," he grinned. "Most girls these days would think a fellow was an unchivalrous cad if he suggested walking around the block. But it's such a beautiful day, it'd be a shame not to take advantage of it."

Her house was near the southern end of the village, a tiled and half-timbered doll's-house with a walled garden that needed tidying but was still a carnival of color. They walked down a lane to the main road and across the bridge, then took a secondary fork to the end of the flat land, hair-pinned up through Quarry Wood, and then branched off the pavement altogether to follow a well-worn footpath that rambled along the side of the slope around Winter Hill. The leaves which had fallen into a carpet underfoot had left myriad lacy openings in the canopy overhead through which the light came with fragmented brilliance, and the air was delicately perfumed with the damp scents of bark and foliage.

"Thank you for doing this," she said, after a while during which their flimsy acquaintance had been warming and easing through the exchange of trivialities not worth recording and the sense of companionship in sharing an uncomplicated pleasure. "I can see from your tan that you must be out of doors so much that you don't have to think about it, but it means a lot to me after being cooped up in an office all week."

"What sort of work do you do?"

"You'd never guess."

"Then I won't try."

"I'm secretary to a sort of horse-racing tipster. Or a kind of horse-playing service."

"That's certainly a bit out of the ordinary. How does it operate?"

"People give this man money to bet with, like an investment, and he sends them dividends from his profits."

"He really does?"

"Oh, yes. Every month."

And suddenly, in a flash, the pleasure of the walk was no longer uncomplicated. The air was the same, the loveliness of the leaf-tones and the dappled light were the same, but something else had intruded that was as out of place there as a neon bulb.

"It sounds interesting," said the Saint cautiously. "Where do you do this?"

"In Maidenhead, which is quite convenient. Much better than having to go into London. And it came along just in time. When my husband died"—he liked the way she didn't hesitate before the word, or after it, "I was left practically broke, except for the cottage with the usual mortgage. He made a good salary, but we'd had a good time with it and hardly saved anything. And no insurance. It was when he went to take out a policy that they found out he had cancer. I thought I was going to have to sell the cottage and move into a little flat in town and look for a job there, which I'd've hated, so this was almost like a miracle."

"People always will believe in miracles, I suppose."

"Well, perhaps I'm exaggerating. It wasn't quite the same as hearing that I'd inherited a couple of million from some distant relative that I'd never heard of."

"Or winning the Irish Sweep, or one of those fabulous football pools, I guess those are the simplest fantasies that most people who aren't millionaires have played with at one time or another. What would rank after that? Messing about with an old bureau and finding a secret compartment full of jewels? Stumbling over a suitcase full of cash that some bank robbers had dropped during their getaway? But that wouldn't be so easy to be dishonest about as you might think, unless you were fairly well-heeled already: somebody might get curious about how you became so rich overnight. No, I suppose some fast scheme to beat the stock market, the casinos, or the bookies, would be the next most popular get-rich-quick gimmick."

They walked on for a while in silence.

"What you're trying to say," she accused him at last, rather stiffly, "is that you think I'm in something crooked."

"I don't say that you're an accomplice," he replied calmly. "But I'd want a lot of convincing that some day the police aren't going to be looking for your boss."

"That's what I've been afraid of," she said. "That's why I made Anne and Hilton promise to introduce us as soon as you came to England, when they happened to mention that they knew you."

He looked at her admiringly.

"A conniving female!" he said. "And I liked you so much because you never asked any of the usual silly questions about my life as the Saint and so forth."

"I was afraid if I did you'd be too leery of letting me get you alone."

"So you had this date all planned before you let me think I thought of it."

"Worse than that. I might have tried to drag you out on this walk even if it'd been pouring with rain."

The path had come down again from under the trees to curve inside the bend of the river. Ahead and to one side there were three green mounds that must have been ancient tumuli, and farther off yet the ridge of a railway embankment cut across a marshy stretch of lowland. From the place where Penelope Lynch stopped, pointing through a chance gap in an intervening coppice, could be seen close up against the embankment a wooden shack with a tar-paper roof, a rectangular box perhaps ten feet long which might once have been built to shelter a maintenance crew or their tools, with a door at one end and a single small window in one side. It was occupied Simon realized from a thin wisp of smoke that curled up from a stovepipe projecting through the roof, and as he gazed at it puzzledly, wondering why Penelope was showing it to him, a man came out with a bucket.

He wore a brown pullover and dark trousers loosely tucked into rubber knee-boots. He was broad-shouldered and a little paunchy, and he moved with the plodding deliberation of a farm laborer rather than a construction worker. At that distance, even the Saint's keen eyes could not make out much more than that he had plentiful gray hair and a ruddy complexion. He carried the pail a few yards from the hut, emptied it on the ground, and plodded back inside.

"My boss," Penelope said.

Simon had to hold back the stereotyped "You're kidding!" because it was perfectly obvious from her expression that she wasn't. Instead, he said with determined nonchalance, "It's nice to see a man who hasn't been spoiled by success, still living the simple life."

"He used to be our gardener," Penelope said.

The Saint clung doggedly to his composure.

"Democracy is a wonderful thing," he remarked, as they resumed their walk. "And you may get a medal from some bleeding-heart committee for being so cheerful about changing places. But not for your story-telling technique. I've heard of quite nice girls getting their pretty heads bashed in with blunt instruments because they tantalized someone a lot less than you've already done to me."

"All right," she said. "If you'll forgive me for trapping you like this. But I couldn't think of any other way to do it. It's such a fantastic story . . ."

It was.

It began when she told the gardener, whose name was Tom Gull, that she couldn't afford to keep him on any longer, and that in any case she was going to have to put the house on the market and move away.

This was nothing like casting a faithful old retainer out to starve, for he only came one day a week, and served five other houses within a few miles' radius on the same basis. She had known nothing else about him except that he had knocked on the door one morning and announced that the garden looked as if it needed attention and he had a day to spare. He was unkempt and unshaven and smelled strongly of beer, but in those days gardeners were as hard to find as any other household help, and after a trial she had let him become a weekly fixture. He was not exactly an artist at his craft, nor did he ever risk injuring himself from over-exertion, but he was better than nothing, and both she and her husband were glad to be relieved of some chores for which neither of them happened to have any inclination.

He took his dismissal phlegmatically, but at the end of the day he came back with a proposition.

"I've got something 'ere, ma'm," he said, extracting a grubby and much-folded piece of paper from his pocket. "It needs correcting my spelling an' putting in good English, an' typing out neat an' proper. I know you've got a typewriter, 'cos I've 'eard you using it. Do you think you could 'elp me out?"

"Of course, I'll be glad to," she said, feeling some kind of obligation because of the employment she had just taken away from him.

"I wouldn't ask you to do it for nothink," he said. "You fix it up for me, an' I'll give you a bit more work in the garden."

She had protested that that wasn't necessary, but after she had done the job she was not so sure.

As deciphered and edited by her, the document finally ran:

YOU CAN BEAT THE BOOKIES!

But not by studying the form book! The professionals who set the handicaps are much better at that than you, and in theory they should make every race end in a dead heat, but how often do they do it?

And not by following "information!" who knows what secret plans have been made for every horse in a race?

The only method which can show a steady profit in the long run is a coldly mechanical mathematical method which will scientifically eliminate the element of chance. In other words, a System.

Now, I know there are dozens of systems on the market, but it should be obvious that none of them can really be any good. If it were, the news would finally get around, and everybody would be using it, and all the bookies would be broke.

But after a lifetime of study I have developed and tested and proved a system which is infallible—which points out winner after winner, week after week, year after year!

Obviously, this system is not for sale. Even if I charged £100 for it, somebody would buy it and turn around and sell copies to 200 other people for £5 each, and I should be left out in the cold.

I dare not even disclose the names of the horses indicated by the System, because after studying them for a while someone else might be clever enough to deduce the method by which they were found. And in any case, if people all over the country were backing these horses and telling their friends, the prices would come down until they all started at odds on, and there would be nothing in it for anybody.

What I will do is operate the System myself for a limited number of clients who will invest in units of £100 with me, to be staked entirely at my discretion, from which I Guarantee to pay monthly dividends of £5 per unit.

Where else can you buy such an income at such a price? Don't delay! Send me your Cash today!

TOM GULL
116 WATKINS STREET, MAIDENHEAD, BERKS

The Saint read it as it appeared in print, on a page torn from *The Sportsman's Guide* which she gave him, and was profoundly awed.

"I've seen some fancy boob-bait in my time," he said, "but this is about the most preposterous pitch I think I've ever come across. Don't tell me that anyone actually falls for it."

"They've been doing it ever since the first advertisement came out."

It was she who had found the one-room office and furnished it, on Gull's insistence that the service was worth a good week's pay and that he would have to get someone to do it in any case.

"Ain't no use me going to see the agents," he said. "The way I look an' the way I talk, they wouldn't want to rent me anythink. An' I don't know wot you oughter 'ave in an office to run this job proper. But I can pay for it." He dug into his trousers and brought out a fistful of crumpled currency.

"'Ere—take this, an' let me know if you need any more. I got a bit put away, wot I bin saving up till I was ready to start this business."

"If your system is so perfect, why don't you just work it for your own benefit?" she argued.

"Because it needs plenty o' capital, more 'n I could save up," he said seriously. "You got to 'ave reserves to see you through the losing runs, but if you keep going you can't 'elp winning in the end. So I got to 'ave share'olders, just like Woolworth's."

When the office was ready and the first advertisements had been placed, he had worked up to his culminating offer.

"I got to 'ave someone in the office answering letters an' all that. I wouldn't be much good at that meself, an' besides I better 'ang on to me gardening jobs till I see 'ow many share'olders I get. An' after that I'll 'ave to be going to the races or the betting shops every day, making the bets."

"But suppose you didn't get any answers?"

"Then we pack up an' go 'ome. That's my little gamble. But we'll worry about that when it 'appens. I know you got to find a job, an' if you ain't too proud to take my money I'd be much obliged if you'd give it a try."

She had finally consented, not without a guilty feeling that she was helping him to throw away the last of his life's savings, but justifying herself with the thought that since he was stubbornly determined to go through with it she might as well take the job as let anyone else have it. She never dreamed that there would be such a response as she found herself coping with.

In the first week, five of the coupons which concluded the advertisement were returned, each accompanied by £100 in cash. In the second week there were ten, and Tom Gull went with her to a bank and opened an account. In the third week she banked £1600, and Mr Gull showed up with a shave and a clean shirt and announced that he was going to begin working his System. The following Friday, after she had banked another £ 1400 for that week, he came in smelling more strongly of liquor and pulling packages of five-pound notes from every pocket.

"Not a bad start," he said. "Now we got to do somethink about paying them dividends."

He turned down her suggestion of writing checks, on the grounds that since their investments had been made in cash they were entitled to dividends in the same form, and that some people in such circumstances as he had been in himself not long ago might have difficulty in cashing a check. He had her address envelopes to all the subscribers, in which he would put the fivers they were entitled to, and which he would take to the post office himself.

"Not that I don't trust you," he said. "But if I post 'em meself, if there's ever any question, I can swear that everyone's bin paid."

So it had gone on ever since, with new investors enrolling at a rate of between twelve and twenty a week, besides additional £100 units sent in by presumably satisfied earlier subscribers. And each week Mr Gull (as she was now used to calling him) displayed thick wads of winnings he also allowed her to bank, except for what had to be set aside once a month for the payment of dividends, and the thousand pounds which he carried for "operating capital."

When she suggested that it would be safer for him to open credit accounts with bookmakers, he shook his head.

"Them chaps are all in league," he said darkly. "They'd soon catch on to wot I was doing, an' then they'd all close my accounts. They might even put me in 'ospital to get even. I make my bets on the courses, picking different bookies every time, or sometimes on the tote, or goin' around the betting shops in London—there's 'undreds of 'em to choose from, so nobody 'as a chance to get to know me."

The names and addresses of the subscribers were kept in a card index in the office, and also in a loose-leaf pocket address book which he bought himself and brought in twice a week for her to enter the latest additions. Against each of the names in this private list he made cryptic marks of his own. Altogether, there were now more than 200 members of this extraordinary syndicate, and a total of almost £30,000 had been invested. At which point Mr Gull told her to stop the advertisements, and the flow of funds abruptly dried up. "He told me it was as much as he could handle," Penelope said, "and if he had to make his bets any bigger he wouldn't be able to spread them around inconspicuously."

"And he still is betting?" Simon asked.

"Oh, yes. And he brought in some more winnings last week."

"Then why is he still living in that broken-down shanty?"

"He says it wouldn't be right for him to use the money that's been invested for anything else than it was given him for. And he wants to have all his own winnings till he can pay everyone back and have his own capital to work with."

"Penelope," said the Saint, "in spite of your unscrupulous methods, you've got me fascinated. But this has angles that need a bit of thinking about."

She refrained from pressing him until they were at the table and the steak-and-kidney pie had been served. The first taste told him that it amply fulfilled her promise, and gratitude alone would have obliged him to give attention to her problem even if it had been less provocative than it was.

"Do you know what I call the Ponzi Routine?" he said. "It's one of the classical sucker-traps. You offer investors a fantastic return on their money, and for a while you actually pay it—long enough for them to spread the good word and get more and more suckers enrolled. Of course, the 'dividends' are coming out of their own capital, but you can afford to pay out as long as enough new money is pouring in. It's been worked in all sorts of variations, but I call it the Ponzi in honor of the guy who may have been its most successful operator, who racked up several million dollars with it in America before I was around."

"But Mr Gull is winning more than enough money to pay the dividends."

"That's one of the angles I was talking about that doesn't fit. And wanting to stop the investments rolling in is another. And so is this business of not living it up himself, with all that dough in the bank. And even talking about paying it back."

"So you don't think I'm a complete idiot not to have gone to the police?"

"I can see why it might be a bit difficult. Your gardener hasn't done anything criminal yet. It isn't a crime to ask people to invest in any wildcat scheme, unless they can prove false pretenses. But under English law a man is innocent until he's proved guilty, and until Gull stops banking winnings or stops paying dividends, you'd have a job to prove false pretenses. Maybe you're doing the poor bastard a horrible injustice. Maybe he really has discovered an infallible system. But that's an awful lot to swallow."

"Is it impossible?"

Simon shrugged.

"I never heard of one yet. But lots of things are impossible until somebody does them. Like television, or rocket ships to Mars. I believe that some great scientists once proved that it was mathematically impossible for a helicopter to get off the ground. You can't convict a man of fraud because he claims to have discovered a trick that nobody could do before. Everything about Gull is still legitimate—until he falls on his face. And if and when that happens, he might be in South America—and you could have a tough time proving that you weren't an active confederate."

"That's why I thought it might be such a help if I could talk to you," she said.

The Saint scowled over his food, which was most unfair to it.

"One of Ponzi's best ploys," he said, "was when the first rumor got around that his golden-egg factory was goosey, and a few hundred stockholders panicked and came yelling for their money back. Ponzi produced sacks of bullion and cheerfully paid them off. The scare fizzled out, and in a few days more mugs than ever were begging him to accept their deposits."

"But nobody's asked Mr Gull for their money back, yet."

"Exactly. And so far he's only talking about this voluntary pay-off. If it goes beyond talking, it'll be something else to get quietly hysterical about. Meanwhile, I promise to lose some sleep over the contradictions you've given me already. I wish I could give you the answers right now, all gift-wrapped and tied up with ribbons, but the reports of my supernatural powers are slightly exaggerated. I'm only a human genius."

For the rest of the day he was nothing but human, but he repeated his promise before he left. And it was not for lack of mental effort that a solution to the mystery of Mr Gull continued to elude him. Some factor seemed to be missing which left all the equations open-ended, but he could not put his finger on it.

Then, on the following Thursday, Penelope Lynch phoned him.

"Well," she said, "it's happened."

His heart sank momentarily.

"What has? He's skipped?"

"No. He's going to start giving the money back. He came in this morning and told me to write letters to the first five people who invested, saying that he's decided to close down his business, thanking them for their help and confidence, and enclosed please find their original hundred pounds. He says he's planning to pay off at least that many people every week from now on."

"This I have got to see more of," said the Saint. "I'll be down this afternoon."

He thoughtfully packed a bag and put it in his car, and drove to Maidenhead immediately after lunch.

The office was above a tobacconist and newsagent on a turning off the High Street. It was minimally furnished with a filing cabinet, a bookcase which contained only boxes of stationery, and two desks, on one of which was a typewriter, behind which sat Penelope.

She showed him one of the letters which she had finished, but he was less interested in it than in the five envelopes she had prepared. He copied the addresses on a sheet of paper, and then asked to see the card index, but he could find nothing significant in the bare data on when their investments had been received and what dividends had been paid.

"Mr Gull left his own book here this morning," she mentioned, and Simon recalled what she had said about the cryptic marks that Mr Gull made on his own records.

He went carefully through the lists under each initial. Opposite some of the typewritten names had been pencilled an "O," and opposite some others appeared an "X." There were very few Xs—in fact, when he checked back, the total was only seven. He wrote those down also, but neither the names nor the addresses thus distinguished seemed to have any characteristic in common, at least on the surface. Only one of them happened to be among the five to whom the first refunds were going.

"You're not making out checks for these, either?" he asked.

"No. But they're to be registered, as you see."

"That's about all I can see," he said wryly. "If something doesn't click pretty soon, you're going to wonder how I ever got my reputation. And so am I . . . Now I'm going to beat it before he comes back, but I'll expect you for dinner at Skindle's. Will seven o'clock give you time to run home and change?"

When she arrived, and they had ordered cocktails in the bar, she told him that Gull had come in at five, laden with more money, and had approved and signed the refund letters.

"Then he said I could go home, and he'd make up the refund packages and mail them himself, like he always did the dividends. He had time to do it and get to the post office before it closed."

"You didn't happen to hang around outside and see whether he made it?"

"I thought of it, but I got cold feet. I was afraid he might see me, and it might spoil something for you."

"Well, assuming that he did catch the mail, the letters should be delivered tomorrow morning. And I just think I'll check on that."

She was beginning to seem a little troubled.

"Perhaps there is nothing wrong after all, and I'm wasting your time like an old maid who thinks every man on the street at night is Jack the Ripper. If that's how it turns out, I'll want to shoot myself."

"Somehow, I'm sure you'll never turn out to be an old maid," he said, cheerfully.

"But if Mr Gull really has a system—you said it was always possible—"

"It could still be just as dangerous. Perhaps I haven't been careful enough how I phrased some of the things I've said. There are theoretically infallible systems—but in practice they eventually blow up. For instance, it's a fact that about two out of five favorites win.

So in theory, you only have to double your stake after each loser, and fairly soon you must hit a winner and show a net profit. According to you, Uncle Tom is a rather simple soul, and he may have figured this out in his little head and thought he'd discovered something like atomic energy. But the snag is that the average two-out-of-five is the end result of a lot of very erratic winning and losing runs. There are plenty of days when no favorites win at all. Now, suppose you started with a bet of ten pounds; doubling up, you bet twenty, forty, eighty, a hundred and sixty, then three hundred and twenty on the sixth race. The next day, you have to start off betting six hundred and forty, twelve hundred and eighty, twenty-five hundred and sixty, five thousand one hundred and twenty—and if that one wins at even money, you net exactly ten pounds. If it goes down, your next bet would be more than ten thousand—and where would you find the bookies to take it?"

"And I suppose there have been two days in a row without a winning favorite?"

There have. Perhaps not often, but now and again they happen. I don't say that that's Uncle Tom's system, but it could be something along those lines. If so, he may have been lucky so far, but one day it's going to blow up with an almighty bang, as sure as there'll be a frost before summer."

"Then I only hope it lasts long enough for him to give everyone their money back."

"That'll take about ten months, on the present schedule," he said. "I don't think I can hold my breath that long."

It was hard enough for him to wait until after breakfast the next day and an hour at which the morning mail could be safely assumed to have been delivered and opened.

The one subscriber of the five earmarked for the first refunds who was also marked with an "X" on Mr Gull's private list had an address in North London and a telephone number in the directory.

"This is *The Sportsman's Guide*," said the Saint, to the cantankerous elderly voice that answered. "We understand that you were a client of one of our advertisers, Mr Tom Gull."

"That is correct."

"Mr Gull tells us that he is going out of business and is refunding all investments. Has he notified you of that?"

"I received a letter to that effect this morning, enclosing my money."

Simon took a deep breath.

"Until then, did you receive your dividends regularly?"

"I did. It was a most satisfactory service. In fact, I think it's most inconsiderate of him to discontinue it so arbitrarily. But there you are. Nothing seems to have any stability these days."

"That's what comes of keeping horses in them," said the Saint sympathetically, and hung up.

Another of the five was also in the London directory, but the number did not answer.

The other three addresses were in Beaconsfield, Windsor, and Staines. It took some time to find out and connect with the next number through the hotel switchboard—he had taken a room at Skindle's to remain closer to the subject of his investigation—but when he introduced himself with the same formula, the response was startlingly different.

"I never heard of him."

"You are Mr Eric Botolphome?"

"In a manner of speaking, yes."

"But you haven't had any dealings with Mr Gull."

"I have not. And I never heard of your publication, either."

"I'm sorry, Mr Botolphome," said the Saint slowly. "We must have been misinformed."

"The name," said his respondent plaintively, "is pronounced 'Boffam'."

"Congratulations," Simon said, and carefully cradled the hand-set again.

Scanning his lists, he realized that the process of having telephone numbers in a wide range of different towns researched and requested through the hotel switchboard and assorted exchanges would put a strain on the hotel operator and the lines at her disposal which would test her patience as much as his own. On the other hand, Windsor and Staines could both be reached in a single twelve-mile drive which might not take any more time and which would give a physical vent to his impatience—besides satisfying a foaming curiosity about the types who might or might not make up Mr Gull's strange inventory of contributors.

He threw on a coat and ran downstairs and began driving.

The address in Windsor turned out to be a weathered brick villa on Vansittart Road built on stark Edwardian lines that harmonized excellently with the complexion and corseted contours of the beldam who finally opened the door.

"Tom Gull?" she croaked. "What does he do?"

"He runs a kind of betting service."

She cupped a hand to her ear.

"Eh?"

"A kind of betting service."

"I don't need a vet. Haven't had any animals around since my last cat died."

"No, betting," Simon said, with increased projection. "You invest money with him, and he backs horses with it and sends you the profits."

"Young man," said the matriarch crustily, "if I had my way, I'd see all the bookmakers hanged, like they used to hang people for sheep-stealing. All this betting and bingo, it's no wonder we can't stop the

Russians occupying the moon. And people like you, trying to get customers for them, you're no better than they are."

She slammed the door in his face.

The nominee in Staines, a few miles further on, proved to be the proprietor of a small grocery store on the road out towards Laleham. In a more genial way, he was no less definite.

"Who, me? Not bloody likely. *The Guide*'s all right, but some o' those advertisements make me laugh. I like to have a little bet sometimes, but I want to know what I'm puttin' my half-crown on. Anyone who'd send someone a hundred quid to play with, like that, must be a proper Charley, if you don't mind my sayin' so."

Simon went back to his car and studied his second list—the names which had been singled out with an "X" in Mr Gull's personal register. Of the remaining six, one lived in Croydon, but the others were in Bournemouth, Worthing, Sevenoaks, Torquay, and Scarborough—a variety of respectable distances in too many different directions for it to be practicable to continue the investigation by personal visits.

He drove back to Skindle's, stopping on the way to buy a large and expensive box of chocolates, and hoping that the telephone operator had a sweet tooth and a sympathetic disposition.

Already he had an inkling of a pattern, but it was not until that evening that he had finally succeeded in contacting all the names and proving it beyond peradventure.

"The ones with the crosses are all satisfied customers," he told Penelope. "The others are real live people too—or at least the four I'd jotted down—but every one of them denies having had anything to do with Brother Gull."

Her eyes were big and wide.

"Why would they do that?"

"It could be because they're all ashamed to admit that they're secret gamblers. But I doubt it. I want to have another look at the original card index."

They went to the office after dinner, and he went through the cards one by one, confirming an impression which he had suddenly recalled that afternoon, during one of the waits between calls.

"Had you noticed that apart from the London addresses, which come up regularly, the earliest replies all came from the south and west, and not too far away? Later on they get more varied—here's St Albans, Cambridge, Clacton, Folkestone . . . But there isn't one of the "O" names with an address as far away as Torquay or Scarborough."

"No, I hadn't," she said, "Would it be because people living a long way from London aren't so interested in racing?"

"Not that I ever heard. Who do you think goes to all those tracks in the North—and even in Scotland?"

"Yes, that was silly. But then, what is the answer?"

"I think we may have stumbled on a Communist conspiracy to ruin the capitalist countries by debasing their currency. Tom Gull is a mad scientist who has invented a molecular multiplier which makes three or four fivers out of one. The advertisement is a code which tells all the cell captains to send in as much cash as they can; after a while they get it back, but the Central Committee has built up a store of perfect duplicates ready to flood the international exchanges. The "O" names, of course, are the egg-heads who are secretly cooperating in the scheme. The "X" is a shorthand form of the hammer and sickle, and indicates the élite of the organization. Tom Gull's cabin is actually a camouflaged rocket pad—"

"And he's got the fuel buried in all the flower-beds he digs up. I know. There's somebody who writes books like that."

The Saint's smile was a silent laugh.

"Is Gull going racing again tomorrow?" he asked.

"He said he was going to Ascot again. He was there today."

"Good. Then it should be safe to have a closer look at that shack of his in the afternoon."

"Do you have a theory, really?"

"It's such a wild one that I wouldn't dare tell you until I've proved it," he said. "Then if I'm wrong, you won't classify me with that writer. But invite me for cocktails tomorrow, and I may dazzle you with my brilliance."

He had one more call to make in the morning, to David Lewin of *The Mail,* and before lunch he had the answer to a question which gave him considerably more confidence when he set out for Cookham.

He enjoyed a couple of pasties and a pint of bitter at the Crown, and left his car parked there when he left soon after two o'clock to retrace the riverside footpath to the railroad track.

He stood hidden at the edge of the thicket for a while, studying the hut. This time there was no smoke coming from the chimney and no other sign of occupancy, but the only way to make finally sure of that was to go close enough to expose himself. He took a diagonal course that would lead him past it by at least fifteen yards, and studiously avoided any appearance of interest in it. Then when he was near enough he flashed a sidelong glance at the door without turning his head, and saw that there was a padlock in place which could not possibly have been fixed from inside.

He turned and went directly to it. The lock was a good one, but like many such installations it was betrayed by the hasp which it secured, which was fastened to the woodwork merely with four screws which offered no resistance to the screwdriver blade of the Saint's Swiss army pocket-knife. He put the screws in his pocket for future replacement, opened the door, and went in.

The interior, dimly lighted by the one grimy window, was stuffy with the mingled stalenesses of beer, smoke, and sweat. Gardening tools stood in three corners, and some soiled articles of clothing hung on hooks. A battered kettle and a dirty saucepan sat on the small black stove. There was a dresser with a stained and scarred top on which stood an enamel basin, a chipped cup and saucer, a couple of plates, some cheap flatware, and a can of beans. The only other furniture was an ancient armchair with the stuffing leaking through rents in the upholstery, and an iron bedstead with drab blankets carelessly heaped on a bare gray mattress.

If what he was looking for was there at all, there were not many places where it could be hidden. The dresser drawers yielded only a disorderly hodge-podge of clothing, canned food, old magazines, patent medicines, pieces of string and wire, and an empty gin bottle. Through the larger splits in the chair his probing fingers touched only springs and cotton batting. The mattress seams showed no signs of having been recently re-sewn. That left only the floor, which he checked board by board, until under the bed, when he moved it away from the wall, he found one that was loose and which came up easily.

From the hollow underneath he pulled out a stout canvas bag tied with a cord threaded through a row of grommets around the neck. Stencilled on one side were the words:

PETRIPLAST LTD SLOUGH

The bag bulged with a load that was half-hard but springy. He loosened the cord, plunged a hand in, and brought it out with a mass of paper money, most of it fives.

A change in the intensity of light, rather than anything positively seen, made him turn and look up sharply.

Tom Gull stood in the doorway. It could have been no one else, in a suit that looked as if it had been slept in but with a garish necktie knotted under a clean but threadbare collar. Tom Gull, dressed to go to the races, or to tell Penelope he was going, but already returned home instead. The untidy gray hair and ruddy face matched the impression that Simon had had from a distance, but at closer quarters it could be observed that the tint of cheeks and nose had not been produced by wind and sun without the assistance of internally administered colorants. The bear-like posture was the same, too, but not the speed with which he snatched up a pitchfork that leaned against the nearest wall.

"Hold it!" the Saint's voice crackled. "We mustn't get blood on it!"

For an instant the man was thrown off his mental stride, and that was sufficient to check him physically. But the fork was still levelled at the Saint's chest, the tines gleaming wickedly sharp, poised on the whim of the gardener's powerful arm like an arrow on the string of a drawn bow.

"Wot you think you're doing 'ere?"

"I know all about this," Simon said urgently, trying to keep his precarious hold on the other's attention. He threw the bag down on the bed so that the lettering on it was uppermost. "About a year ago this was stolen from the train to High Wycombe—the payroll for the Petriplast branch factory there. I was checking this morning on what robberies there'd been in the neighborhood where a lot of cash disappeared that'd never been found. There was about thirty-two thousand pounds in this. The guard put up a fight, and the men on the train were caught, but not before they'd thrown the bag out of a window. It was believed that they had accomplices waiting beside the line who got away with it and left them to take the rap, though they swore they didn't. I know what really happened. You were moseying around on your way to the local, and you stumbled over the bag and picked it up."

"Put down the rest of it," Gull growled.

Simon obeyed, slowly, and went on talking.

"Why don't you offer me a deal? Maybe a partnership in your horse-playing business? It's your only out, unless you want to kill me and bury me in the—"

Suddenly he realized that his improvisation, playing for time, had led him into a trap of its own. He had said the wrong thing to a man of Gull's limited but literal mentality. He saw it in the reddish glitter in the gardener's eyes, a tightening of the mouth, and a tensing of muscles, and knew that in the flick of another thought he would feel the steel in his flesh.

From behind Gull came a short shrill scream.

It distracted him just enough, at the very moment when he was starting his lunge, for the Saint to leap in under the pitchfork, deflecting the shaft with his left arm, while his right fist drove like a piston into the man's solar plexus, doubling him forward to meet the standard left uppercut that followed.

"Jolly good," said Penelope. "I'm not the screaming type, honestly, but it was the only way I could think of to help."

"It was the one great brainstorm of his life," Simon said later, at her cottage. "Having picked up all that loot and hidden it, he was faced with the problem of getting to use it. You can't walk into a bank and open an account with thirty-two thousand in cash without questions being asked. And you can't even start spending money like a Greek ship-owner, if you've been known for years as a slob who only worked hard enough to earn the wherewithal to keep slightly sozzled, without people talking, and pretty soon the cops hear about it. And if you tried to disappear and start somewhere else under another name, they'd soon be looking for you, remembering that you'd been in the vicinity when all that legal tender got lost. He had to find a way to legitimize it, or build a complete set-up to account for how he got it."

"So he just sent himself the money and filled out his own coupons," Penelope said. "I suppose he picked names and addresses from the phone books in different towns, because it was easier than inventing them."

"And then he began producing the rest of the money as winnings. And when he had you address envelopes for the dividends, he just took them home and burned them. The same with those refund letters. The money that should have gone in them would just be produced as more winnings, and gradually he could claim they were all his."

"But what about the man who said he really had had his dividends and his money back?"

"Frightening as it seems, there actually were seven suckers who sent in a hundred pounds of their own money. They were the ones marked with crosses in his private book. He had to keep track of them, and let them be paid, so that there wouldn't be any complaints that would get him investigated."

"How can people be so gullible?"

"You've invented a word. But don't forget that you went along with the gag for some time before you began to wonder if anything was wrong."

"And don't forget that if I hadn't decided to do some detecting on my own, since you were being so superior and mysterious, and followed him this afternoon, you'd've been stuck on his fork like a hot dog."

The Saint shuddered.

"Let's say you earned at least half the reward." He poured two more Peter Dawsons. "Do you think we should go out and celebrate, or just stay here by the fire?"

NASSAU: THE
FAST WOMEN

"You're the Saint," said Cynthia Quillen challengingly. "You kill nasty people, don't you?"

"Sometimes," said Simon Templar tolerantly.

Over the years, he had learned to speak tolerantly, on occasion, especially such occasions as being challenged at cocktail parties by beautiful women who had absorbed a little too much festive spirit.

Of course, not all men would have rated Cynthia Quillen as beautiful. She was a blonde who conspicuously refused to conform to the pneumatic cotton-candy type beloved of Hollywood press agents, which looks as if it would melt in your mouth or any other comfortably upholstered place. She had the kind of "good" features that with enough hard wear can become bony, and the other extensions of her nicely proportioned skeleton were also sufficiently short of adipose padding to entitle a fast assessor to call her skinny. Which is one of those misleading fronts that separate the men from the boys. But Simon Templar had survived long enough to have learned that plenty of slender women were kept that way by a nervous hunger that would have scared Don Juan out of his jockstrap.

"All right," she said. "How much would you charge to wash out that nasty sample over in the corner?"

Simon peered as best he could through an intervening hedge of standing guests, towards the indicated corner, where a rather short well-knit man with a chiseled curly head almost absurdly reminiscent of an ancient Greek statue was absorbed in animated chatter with an even more statuesque brunette.

The Saint did not have to be an automobile-racing fan to recognize him, for Godfrey Quillen was one of the most highly publicized drivers of that or the preceding season, a newcomer who was reportedly crowding the pros in their ratings.

"That's no way to talk about your husband," he reproved her patiently.

"I can talk about him any way I like—that phony, conceited, two-timing, chiseling, short-changing, free-boozing—"

"Hush, darling. You are speaking about God."

" 'God' Quillen! You should see the pit crew smirking when they call him that, when he isn't around! . . . But I don't have to waste a good bullet on him. A good subpoena would hurt him just as much. Only I'd never divorce him either, for somebody else to have. The one I'd like you to kill is the Continental indoor sports model with the slippery clutch, who's warming him up for another qualifying lap. Her name is Teresa Montesino, if you insist on a label on every tombstone."

Simon allowed his somewhat obstructed gaze to transfer itself to the exotic pulse-perturber on whom Godfrey Quillen was exerting his highest-octane charm. This was not an unbearably painful shift. The brunette had all the more obvious attractions that Mrs Quillen superficially lacked. She had the intense dark eyes and sensual lips that automatically inspire exploratory ideas, and the corporeal structure which it is always fun to explore. A hopeless cynic might have prognosticated that at some middle-aged future she could be just plain fat, but this was an unhappy conclusion that a less cautious soul did not have to envisage prematurely. At a similar age to Cynthia's, still safely under thirty, she offered the overwhelming sort of competition that any wife might reasonably have qualms about.

"You can't shoot him for having good eyesight," said the Saint soothingly.

"I told you, I'd rather keep him. I've been doing it for so long that I guess I've got to like the habit. How do you think he got to be a big racing driver?"

"Not by being good at it?"

"Oh, he's fairly good—for an amateur jockey who hardly knows how to change a spark plug. But General Motors doesn't build racing cars and sponsor teams like the European manufacturers. And if they did, they'd hire professionals who came up the hard way—not glamor boys with a rich wife."

"Are you a rich wife?"

"Loaded." She looked into her glass, and made a grimace. "In more ways than one. But he was what I wanted, and I could afford it, so I let him have fun spending my money. And brother, are those expensive toys! You have no idea what it costs to keep replacing those buggies, besides the care and feeding while they last. Nothing but the best of everything. Oil that Cleopatra should have a facial with, and a new set of tires every—"

"I know something about it. But most of us throw good money away on one silly plaything or another."

"And Godfrey is my bauble-boy. Thanks. I like your subtle touch, Saint. So you'll understand that if I feel like protecting my investment from that high-compression step-mother of Romulus and Remus—"

"Foster mother," Simon corrected her gently. "That is, if you're talking about the famous she-wolf. Well, it seems to me that all you'd have to do is yank the checkbook out from under him."

Cynthia Quillen exchanged her empty glass for a full one from the well-stocked tray of a hospitably roving waiter, with the dexterity of a veteran at such functions.

"You're not being very bright," she said peevishly. "If I did that, he'd sulk for weeks, and so what would that give me? You don't know what a brilliant sulker he is. Why make complications, when the obvious and effective answer is staring you in the face? Just exterminate the menace with the un-sealed-beam headlights. I'd pay quite a lot for it."

The Saint permitted himself one of his sometimes well-concealed sighs. This was a hell of a way to start a visit to Nassau, where he had gone only to take in that sub-tropical island's annual Speed Week—perhaps pleasantly leavened by the social festivities that considerately coincided therewith. He had enough friends in the Bahamas to be assured of all the incidental entertainment he wanted, and although the days when he himself had burned up a few tires under a certain cream-and-red Hirondel were now approaching the realms of reminiscence if not legend, he could still feel some of the old vibrations in the blood stream awakened by the smell of Castrol and the roar of beautifully tuned engines and the sight of sleek-wheeled monsters crowding each other through dizzying chicanes. But invitations to murder were even farther than those old road-racing days from anything he expected to be actively involved in on that trip.

"You're kidding, of course—I hope," he said, and had an uncomfortable presentiment of her answer before he heard it.

"Try me with a blank check and a good ball-point pen."

He shook his head.

"You can't take it with you, but don't throw it away. If Teresa is what you think, you could buy her off for much less than you could hire me."

Mrs Quillen scowled with increasing alcoholic frustration at the fresh drink which she had already half finished.

"You won't take me seriously," she complained. "If I have to do it myself, and I swing for it, I hope you'll be sorry. You could've got me out of that predicament. If you even only made love to her yourself, and took her away from him, which I'm sure you could do easily—"

"Now you're making sense," said the Saint, grasping the straw gratefully. "Why don't you introduce me?"

Before she could say anything else, he had taken her enthusiastically by the arm and was steering her through the throng with a firmness that was within an ounce of the closest that good manners could come to violence.

"Well," Cynthia said, almost breathlessly. "If it isn't my ever-loving husband. And the lovable Miss Montesino. Meet my new friend, Mr Templar."

"I was hoping I'd meet you, Mr Templar," Godfrey Quillen said, with an almost professionally fervent handshake and a wide smile of white teeth. "Sometimes I've almost wondered if you were real—my very favorite character!"

"Mine, too," said Teresa Montesino, with a softer and even warmer touch.

"That's wonderful, darling," Cynthia said, looking directly at her. "Because you just won him. Godfrey and I are late already for a dull old dinner party of respectably married couples."

Her spouse consulted his wrist watch with rather elaborate nonchalance.

"Why, so we are, sweetheart. How terribly tedious. Will you excuse us, Teresa? And Mr Templar—" He insisted on another, even heartier handshake. "Come and see us messing about in the pits tomorrow. You might give us some new ideas. I'd like to talk to you . . ."

His wife practically dragged him away, amiably protesting. She could do this convincingly, for they were almost the same height, though he had a well-knit breadth that made you think of him as a bigger man when you remembered him alone.

"Well, it was nice knowing him," Simon remarked, following the rest of the exit with his eyes. "Now the next time I meet some other road-racing buffs, I'll really be able to impress them with reminiscences of my great pal, Godfrey Quillen."

"Are you so unhappy to be stuck with me?" asked Teresa.

She had enough Mediterranean accent to give her voice a fascinatingly different intonation, but not enough to attract too much attention or to become quickly tiresome.

"By no means," said the Saint, and gave her another thorough inspection at this more convenient range. "I mean, am I stuck? If so, I have a sensational idea. Let's throw a dinner party of our own—for disreputably unmarried couples. And just to be sure we don't insult anybody, let's not invite anyone else."

"I must try not to wonder if you are insulting me, Simon. And if only I did not already have a date—"

"I'm sorry. I should have known that anyone as fabulous as you—"

"I should not have the embarrassment of breaking it," she concluded serenely, as if he had not interrupted. "Will you excuse me for a minute, to telephone?"

That was the beginning of an evening which he would remember for a long time. Not that he was likely to forget the important details of any adventure, but an evening with Teresa Montesino was quite an experience in its own right.

For all the tourist traffic that flows through it, Nassau is a very small town on a very, very small island, so that it has no secret dispensaries of ambrosial food and/or Dionysian entertainment known only to a fortunate élite. It takes a very large community to sustain a hideaway so famous that it is a privilege to be permitted to discover it. Simon could offer her nothing that she could not have found for herself by reading a few advertisements, and out of that selection she had already covered plenty of ground in other company. But nothing about the places they went to was new to him either, except what her presence contributed.

They began almost conventionally at a white table under an artistically lighted tree in the patio of Cumberland House, over the ritual turtle pie which is the best-known gastronomic specialty of the islands, and with the equally predictable conversational probings that have to be undergone at such first encounters. He learned that aside from any personal interest in a racing driver, she was one herself.

"But not a very good one yet," she said. "I need a lot more experience, and that is hard for a woman to get. It is a stupid prejudice. You don't need to be a gorilla with great muscles to drive a modern car. All it takes is strong nerves, and a skilful touch, and good judgment.

It is one of the few non-intellectual contests where a woman can start equal with a man. Perhaps that is why they make it so hard for us to prove ourselves. My own father discourages me."

"I thought the name sounded familiar." Simon was frowning. "But I couldn't place—"

"A woman. No, you were thinking of him. Enrico Montesino. He could have been one of the greatest. But he rolled over a mountain corner in the Mexico City race, trying to pass someone he thought had sneered at him. And he says I am too reckless and too emotional!"

"Is he here now?"

"Oh, yes. But not for me. Because he is a great mechanic, too, Ferrari still gave him a job when he could not drive again. And from that job, Godfrey hired him away to be his personal chief mechanic. For this his wife insults me, and perhaps I shall kill her."

Simon only blinked once, for by now the line had begun to sound faintly like a refrain.

"All by yourself?" he inquired hopefully.

"Who else would do it for me?"

He studiously evaded a direct entanglement with her witch's eyes, but after a moment she went on as she had done before, as if she would scarcely have heard anything he said anyway, "Besides, it would be most easy for me to do, in the Ladies' Trophy race. If there is an accident, you will be quite right to suspect me—but that is the most you will be able to do."

The Saint devoted himself to maintaining a sangfroid which would have been rated commendable by the sternest British standards.

"I didn't know she was a driver too," he said.

"She isn't. At least, not for any kind of professional racing. But she wants to prove something, and she has learned enough to get through a few qualifying laps. Godfrey is letting her drive his Ace Bristol. He can hardly refuse, since she bought it. She would drive his Ferrari if she could, but it is too big for the class. Another discrimination against women—we can only be trusted with smaller cars. But in my Maserati I shall show her some tricks. Do you know what a real driver can do to an amateur?"

Simon raptly allowed her to embroider some examples, while he made the most of his dinner. He was wise enough at that age not to take the initiative in convulsing his digestion.

Thus the rest of the meal meandered through pleasant trivialities, until over coffee and Benedictine and some background music at the Drake there came the inevitable lull in which he said, "Why do you care enough about Cynthia Quillen to want to knock her off? I gather from some things that have been said that you've got the inside track—if such a horsy metaphor isn't indecent in strictly horse-power circles—"

"To use your language, that is a position I would have to keep jockeying for, which is not dignified. I would rather have him all to myself. So I am only thinking of the kindest way to take him from her."

"Of course, how stupid of me. Not many girls I know would be so sensitive."

"If I merely steal him because I am more attractive," she went on calmly, without any hint of whether she was unconscious of his irony or ignoring it, "Cynthia would never get over the injury to her pride. She would rather die. So, it would be generous of me to let her."

Simon was glad now that he had waited for this until he had nothing in his mouth to choke on.

"And what does Godfrey think about this?"

"I have not asked. As you have seen, he is the charming type who likes a woman to tell him. The right woman, naturally."

"Yes, little mother."

"You should dance with me to this music," she said.

So for a while he danced with her, as casually as it could be done with anyone of her build and cooperative zeal. Another unfriendly woman might have commented that she was not very subtle about the way she made it difficult for her partner to be unaware for a moment of her architectural assets, but to a victim with hormones it was not a completely unendurable ordeal.

And then there was some other music at the Prince George, not for dancing, where he persuaded her to moderate the Benedictine to B-and-B and tapered himself into Old Curio on the rocks. She seemed to hold her fuel much more phlegmatically than Cynthia, but he wanted to be able to cope with any extra acceleration she might develop.

Thus, after many other bandyings of "relevancies which this chronicler has no space to quote," Simon only found himself verging back on the fatal subject when he said, "You must get tired of answering this, but why didn't those Roman talent scouts think they could get more dividends from you in a movie than a motor-car?"

"I have had those offers. And perhaps I would be as good as some others who have taken them." She was just brash enough to pull back her shoulders a trifle and take a slightly deeper breath, which on her was a seismic combination. Yet the Saint was far more devastated by the absolute certainty that he detected a downright twinkle in her gaze. "But the competition is much tougher, and I am very lazy. There are a thousand pretty girls who want to be movie stars, but so few who want to drive the Mille Miglia. So, while they scramble for the photographers' attention, the photographers scramble for mine. And while they must submit to many horrible people with influence, I can choose my important people."

"Thank you," said the Saint gravely. "But if Godfrey heard all that I have this evening, do you think his respiration would be running at the same r-p-m?"

"It might be accelerated a lot. But being a gentleman, you will not tell him. And if you did, being the kind of man he is, he would not believe you, and only punch your nose."

"Now I'm feeling miserable too. Where would you like to go next?"

She was in the mood then for some of the more boisterous native entertainment, so he walked her a couple of blocks up Bay Street to the Junkanoo, where it was noisy enough to make any but the most succinct and rudimentary forms of conversation impossible. It was a respite of sorts, if not exactly a soporific, and when she suggested another move after the deafening climax on the floor show that they had walked in on, he would have hated to be called for an appraisal of just how grateful he was.

"This is all wonderful for me," he said, with ingenious congeniality. "But I don't have to be needle-eyed and full of reflexes tomorrow."

"I know, you think I should go home. Very well, take me."

It would have been only another fairly short walk, and pleasant in the mild freshness of the night, but the little car he had rented was even closer, and he put her in and drove her up to the Royal Victoria, where she was quartered. "I think that is the word," she said. "The invited drivers are all guests of the meeting, and they deal us to the hotels like a pack of cards."

"A lot of people like it here," he said. "Personally, when I come to Nassau, I'm not looking for a sterling-area Miami Beach."

"Yes, it is a different atmosphere. But if one could choose whom to be near—"

"One might ask for trouble. Would you be really happy if the Quillens were here too?"

"They are at the Country Club."

"Are they? So am I. Now when I see you there, I'll have to wonder what brought you."

She looked up, through the car window on her side, at the four tiers of deep Colonial verandahs overlooking the driveway where he had stopped.

"My room is that corner one, on the second balcony."

"I'll wave to you, Juliet."

She turned closer to him, one arm partly on the back of the seat and partly on his shoulder, her eyes big and darkly luminous in the distant light from the entrance.

"Could you not be even a little interested in getting rid of Cynthia for me?" she asked. "You must be so clever at such things, you would not make the mistakes I might make."

"Such as talking so much about it," he said amusedly.

"You think I am drunk? A little, perhaps. But sober enough to know I can deny anything you say I said. But you too can deny anything you like. So, why not be honest?"

Simon reminded himself to remember next time that in alcoholic reaction some steady starters could ride a wild finish. But for that moment he could only fall back on the faintly flippant equanimity developed from some past experience of such challenges.

"All right, darling, what's in it for me? After I've freed Godfrey from his encumbrance, but he's inherited her money, and you've married him—"

"We could console ourselves," she said, "until he had an accident."

There must be extravagances for which plain silence is ineffectual and a guffaw is inadequate. Simon decided that they were close enough to that pinnacle. He said lightly: "This, I must think over."

"Come upstairs and think."

"The management wouldn't like that. And in the morning, you might be sorry too."

She leaned on him even more overwhelmingly, bringing her full relaxed lips within an inch of his mouth. He waited, well aware of the softness that pressed against him. Then she drew back sharply, and slapped his face.

"Thank you, dear," said the Saint, reaching across her to open the other door. "And happy dreams."

She got out of the car. And as she did so, there was one inevitably perfect moment in which she offered a transient target that the most careful posing could never have improved. With the palm of his hand, he gave it an accolade that added an unpremeditated zip to her disembarcation and left her in stinging stupefaction for long enough for him to shut the car door again and get it moving out of range of retribution.

Almost as soon as he turned the next corner he had cooled off. He had a violent aversion to being slapped, and the smack with which he had reciprocated had been uninhibitedly meant to hurt, but he realized that she had some material for self-justification. Any woman who candidly offers all her physical potential to a man, and has as much to offer as Teresa Montesino, and is rejected with even good-natured urbanity, can be expected to respond rather primitively.

Simon Templar had no virtuous feelings about the rejection. He was quite animal enough to be keenly aware of what she had in stock for the male animal, and he no longer had any lower-case saintly scruples about taking advantage of a grown woman whose natural impulses came more readily to the surface in the glow of certain liquid refreshments. He hadn't for one moment seriously contemplated making love to Teresa for any reward that Cynthia Quillen might have offered, but neither did that mean that he was resolved to fight to the death against letting her drag him into bed. He hadn't expected her to make any such effort, but when it happened he had found himself chilled by an unprecedented caution.

Recalling every one of the pertinent exchanges of their brief acquaintance, the slant of every second word that had been spoken, the Saint admitted to himself that he had been just plain scared. Discretion he could admire, and go along with; but a partnership in deception is another basis. He knew better than most people how many graveyards contain the headstones of men who listened too accommodatingly to the siren song which begins "If only something would happen to . . ." And Teresa had revealed herself much too acutely conscious of the rules of evidence for a free-wheeling freebooter's peace of mind. Getting into her bedroom might have been delightfully easy, but getting out again, unhooked by any whimsical barbs of her alcoholically precarious mood, might have been another deal altogether, and much more complicated than anything he had envisaged for that excursion.

"I must be getting old," he told himself wryly. And then he wondered how old you had to get before two totally differently attractive women each asked your advice about murdering the other, during the same evening. He thought that life might get really dull when there was no proposition you could afford to turn down and be satisfied with your own estimate of what you had passed up. He could see Teresa's last stunned expression as starkly frozen as a flash photo in his mind's eye, and was still laughing when he fell asleep. He did not see the Quillens at breakfast in the dining room the next morning, or while he swam and sunned himself on the beach. But they could as well have breakfasted in their room, and immediately afterwards have had mechanical details to concern themselves with at the track before the general public came to watch the vehicles vehicling. Simon did not concern himself unduly with the thought that there might be a fairly fresh cadaver on the premises somewhere, and he was right. Charlie and Brenda Bethell, who had offered him a seat in their box for that afternoon, lunched with him at the Club and drove him out to the track, and among the first people he saw as they came down off the bridge. At the end of the grandstand were Cynthia and Godfrey Quillen, both very much alive, even to a degree of visible vigor. In fact, from their gestures and attitudes, one might have thought at a distance that they were having a heated argument, and as Simon excused himself and strolled along the front of the pits towards them, they greeted him with a simultaneous cordiality which suggested that he might have been a welcome interruption.

"I suppose this is a tactical conference," said the Saint, with smiling tactlessness. "I'm sure that racing pilots don't commit back-seat driving, even by remote control."

"Hah!" Cynthia said tersely. "I was just asking the wizard, here, to stop nagging our boss mechanic about something that went wrong yesterday, as long as he's got to service the car I'm driving today."

"That's why I want to keep him up to the mark, sweetheart," Quillen said. "If he's going to take thirty-two seconds over a routine wheel change—"

"Besides fixing something in the ignition that might have left you waiting to be towed home from the next lap."

"So he says. I don't know. I'm a driver, not an engineer. Anyhow, that was when Moss passed me, and I never had a hope of catching him again."

"That wasn't Enrico's fault. You were the driver, my dear. But now he's sulking again, and he might easily feel mean enough to do something to the Bristol that'd make it crack up this afternoon, with me in it. Everybody knows about these Italian vendettas and the stiletto in your back."

Godfrey Quillen appealed to Simon with a deprecating grin that was a model of husbandly tolerance, effortless savoir faire, and older-boyish charm.

"Please tell her that all Italians aren't members of the Mafia or Sicilian bandits and all that nonsense."

"I've personally known at least five who weren't," Simon said solemnly. "And even if Enrico is a bad one, I'm sure his native chivalry wouldn't let him work off a grudge on you. When Godfrey loses a wheel in the chicane, you might start worrying."

Quillen clapped him heartily and happily on the back.

"Keep it up, pal," he said enthusiastically. "I'm late now for an interview I promised some dame who hooked me the last time I tried to sneak past the press box, but I'll look for you at the bar shortly."

He gave his wife's brow a quick brush of a kiss which she had no chance to freeze off or respond to, and was in full but delightfully definitive retreat before he could be caught in any more dispute.

Cynthia looked at the Saint defensively.

"I said a lot of silly things last night," she stated. "I wish you'd forget them."

"Consider them forgotten."

"Did you have fun?"

"I don't remember," he said, with his blandest smile.

Her eyes flashed with the involuntary exasperation of any woman caught in a trap of logic, but she was game enough to bite off any bid to wriggle out of it.

"All right," she said. "But at least you know what I mean when I tell you I really am scared of Enrico but I can't admit the true reason to Godfrey. You've got to admit it's an impossible situation, with him being the father of—you know who. Suppose they were ganging up to get rid of me?"

"It might be rather uncomfortable," Simon conceded soothingly. "Especially if you were bothered by wondering who thought of it first. Let's see what they're doing to your car now."

The "pits," which in petroleum-racing parlance are the stables in which mechanical steeds are groomed and babied for their decisive appearance on the track, were literally a figure of speech at this convocation, being completely unexcavated to any unprofessional eye. In effect, they were merely a long row of spaces divided by the pillars that supported the upper level of the "grandstand" where the reserved boxes flanked the press box and control tower and bar; the competitors who wanted and could afford more amenities than could be stacked on rough shelves between the pillars had station wagons and trucks and trailers of all sizes parked behind their berths. The start-and-finish straight was directly in front, where a procession of small noisy bugs was even then buzzing and blattering past in the last laps of an opening amateur event. She led him just a little way along the line, to a smoothly squat white car that looked momentarily like some sort of carnivorous robot preparing to swallow a human tidbit, which it had already engulfed except for the helplessly dangling legs.

"This is Enrico," Cynthia said.

After a second or two the snack squirmed back out of the gaping jaws of the monster, revealing itself to be a very short slight man with thinning hair and extraordinarily bright black eyes that were a perfect complement to his small bird-like beak of a nose.

"She is all-a ready, signora," he said, with a completely factual detachment. "All-a you got to do is-a drive her."

He shut down the hood and carefully wiped his oily finger-marks off the spotless paint. To pull out the rag to do it, he first had to put down the wrench he had been working with, for his left arm hung with an oddly twisted slackness at his side.

"Anyhow," Simon observed, "she must be one of the shiniest cars on the course."

Enrico Montesino's glance flickered over him with the same inscrutable impersonality.

"To me, signore, a car is as beautiful as a woman. More beautiful, sometimes."

"You're too modest," said the Saint easily. "I've met your wife's daughter."

The black hawk's eyes settled for a moment only.

"You too?" Montesino said enigmatically. "Yes, she is-a more beautiful than a car. But-a more crazy too, sometimes. So, I must see she is all-a right for da race."

"Now just a minute," Cynthia protested. "This is going too far. She's racing against me, let me remind you—and I'm paying you!"

"She is-a my daughter, signora. I only want to be sure her car is all right so she will not get 'urt. I can-a do no more for your car. If you drive good enough, you win—scusi!"

He turned brusquely and walked away, limping a little with the steady rhythm of a man to whom limping has become an integral part of walking, and Cynthia stared after him with her mouth open before she turned to the Saint again. "You see what I mean?"

"You've got other mechanics, haven't you?"

"Yes, those two working on Godfrey's Ferrari in the next stall."

"You could have them check everything over again."

"And make myself look like a jittery neurotic who shouldn't drive anything faster than a golf cart."

"Well, you are seeing a few bogeys, aren't you?" Simon said reasonably. "So far, my criminological museum hasn't collected any case of a father plotting a homicide to clear a track for his daughter, but I suppose there's a first time for everything."

"I need a drink," Cynthia said.

"That's a great idea. Then when you spin out, I won't have to wonder if it was sabotage."

She glared at him, but before she could formulate a retort the loud speakers above them were rasping an appeal for entrants in the Ladies' Trophy to get ready to move out to the starting line. Simon grinned and said, "I could be wrong, but I don't think you've any more to worry about than the next driver."

He beat his own retreat before she could argue any more against the reassurance.

It was not that he was determined to duck responsibility at any price. Almost any human being can legitimately claim to be a potential murder victim, if you go by the statistical count of seemingly inoffensive people who somehow get murdered every year. The Saint simply didn't think that Cynthia Quillen had more grounds for apprehension than anyone else, merely because she seemed to think more about it.

He could be wrong, as he admitted, but he had no idea how wrong when he apologetically rejoined the Bethells in their box.

"Did you find out who's going to win this 'Powder-puff Derby' as they call it?" Brenda asked.

"It'd be an awful event to have to give tips on," Simon said. "I'd be terrified of someone misunderstanding me if I told them I got it straight from the horse's mouth."

The cars below were already being manoeuvred on to their marks, while a waggish track steward from the secure anonymity of the public-address system begged the contestants to hurry it up and remember that they were getting lined up for a race and not getting dolled up for a dance. Simon quickly located Teresa Montesino as the focal point of a jostling circle of photographers, who found her custom-tailored skin-tight jade silk coveralls the perfect counterpoint to an otherwise sexless portrait of a somber green Maserati, and he had to grant that they knew their business almost as well as she did. When Cynthia Quillen's Bristol was manhandled into place with herself in it, they had almost run out of film.

And while Cynthia was getting herself snapped in the final scramble, Teresa was making herself comfortable in her seat and had time to sweep a long slow glance along the upper tier of spectators. Although she could only accidentally have recognized anyone from there, Simon was human enough to wonder how she would react if she saw him. But he figured it was more likely to be Godfrey Quillen that she was looking for, and he glanced casually around himself on the same quest. Almost at once he sighted the driver in a corner of the verandah near the bar at the back of the press box, where he could not have been seen from the track, in his usual kind of animated conversation with a striking auburn-haired woman whose flawless veneer of cosmetics made one think of a New York City model posing in resort clothes— but only for the smartest magazines.

"They certainly are raising a snazzy type of news-hen these days," Simon remarked. "I'll have to find out if that one who's interviewing Quillen would be interested in a few quotes from me."

"She might be," Charlie said mildly, when he had located the subject. "But she isn't what I think you mean by a news-hen. That's Mrs Santander, one of the richest women on the island."

"Oh. Pardon my ignorance."

"She's an ex-wife of José Santander, the Venezuelan oil man."

"Now that's more like type-casting," said the Saint, with an air of flippant relief, but a couple of knife-thin wrinkles remained between his brows as a throbbing crescendo of revving-up engines drew their attention back to the course.

The starter's flag dropped, and with a deafening roar the twelve tidily deployed automobiles surged forward, comfortably spread out three abreast for a bare instant before they broke ranks and crowded into one suicidal bid for position at the first bend. To the naive spectator who has never seen a shop open its doors to the first arrivals at a genuine bargain sale, or been caught on a suburban artery at the rush hour when a light turns green, these first few seconds are the most thrilling in any race of this kind. Even to Simon Templar it was still one of the peak excitements of every event.

Cynthia's white Bristol was off in front. Teresa's dark green Maserati, starting from one of the rear positions, shoved viciously through the pack like a bulldozing footballer, shouldering less ruthless drivers aside to left and right with an unswerving callousness which is the only ultimate factor in these jams. She was still only a close fourth at the turn, but the Saint thought she came out of it perceptibly faster than the two cars ahead of her as they flashed into the next short stretch and temporarily disappeared from view.

The track at that time was not laid out with much regard for the audience. Superimposed on the existing runways of Oakes Field, the former airport of Nassau, and making the most possible use of the already paved surfaces, it meandered off into backwaters previously known only to aviators, with little regard for the perspective of the cash customers. The most obvious thrills which the public comes to see in this kind of racing, of course, are on the corners, but practically none of these were clearly visible from the expensive boxes or the general admission stands, or accessible to either class of client. For most of the winding five-mile course, between their dashes through the short spectator stretches, the cars could be followed only in occasional tantalizing glimpses as they whizzed through the two or three fairly distant sections of which the terrain gave an unobstructed vista. This made it pleasantly painless to chat about other things or patronize the bar, without fear of missing too much of the race. On previous days, Simon had found this a fairly agreeable consolation for the inferior visibility, but this time he felt himself nagged by a faint far-down uneasiness, something like a tiny splinter might set up as it worked down into a calloused palm. He strained his eyes for the first cars to come out of the "chicane," two consecutive sharp turns that were at a bad head-on viewing angle from the club stand, and saw the white Bristol still leading, then another car, then another dark green one which had to be Teresa's, the only one of that color in the competition. She had already picked up one notch, through what he knew was some tricky territory.

"Pete won his heat in the Island Race," Brenda mentioned. "They finished just after we got here, while you were talking to the Quillens. They must have changed the starting time—we were supposed to be here for it. Don't tell him you didn't see that 'Saint' stick figure of yours on his bonnet—he only put it on for your benefit."

"Oh, hell," said the Saint contritely. "That's the last thing I would have missed. Where is he?"

"He just came up from the pits. He's in that box down there with Betty."

Peter Bethell was one of Charlie's brothers, and Betty was his wife. In another moment he was with them, still trying to wipe off the mask of track grime outside the stencil of his goggles.

"You shouldn't have done it," said the Saint. "That extra load of paint on my insignia might have cost you a track record."

"It was lighter than paint," Peter said boisterously. "We just had some masking tape left over when we got through putting on the numbers, and didn't know what else to do with it. Thought it might give you a laugh. And perhaps it was lucky for me. It may have been what scared off the ruddy saboteur who was going around messing up all the cars last night."

"The which?" Simon asked sharply.

"Some silly bugger who must've decided the races weren't exciting enough, so he was trying to arrange a few accidents. The night watchman was just taking a little nap, of course, but he finally woke up and heard this ghoul clanking about in the pits, and yelled at him. You know, 'Who dat?'—as if the fellow was going to be fool enough to give his name and address. So the chap ran off, very fast, and the watchman couldn't catch him. Anyhow, that's what he says. I expect he was so frightened himself he was running sideways."

"I hadn't heard about that," Charlie said.

"The watchman thought it was just somebody out stealing, and he knew from the way he ran off that he couldn't be carrying much weight. But when some of the crews came out this morning they started finding wheel hubs loose, and oil drain plugs unscrewed, and nails in the tires—a lot of that nonsense. After a while it dawned on them that it wasn't a lot of accidental coincidences, and they started making inquiries."

The Saint had been so fascinated that he realized he had missed the one other possible glimpse of the lady drivers before they would be passing the stands again. A thunder of exhausts was even then heralding the end of the first lap, and he turned to see the Bristol come first under the Esso bridge, a Jaguar after it, and then the smoky green Maserati gaining ground like a thunderbolt, overhauling the Jag by the end of the straight and coming out of the Prince George Corner with a measurable length's lead before they vanished again in pursuit of Cynthia's white steed behind the next topographical obstruction.

"It's between Quillen's wife and the Roman figure—if they don't kill each other," Peter said, with professional-sounding off-handedness.

"Couldn't the watchman give any description of this saboteur?" Simon persisted.

"Nothing that's any use. 'A medium small man,' he thinks, but he doesn't know if he was white or black. I know he must've been pretty stupid, because most of the things he did were bound to be spotted before anybody started driving. But even you couldn't catch anyone with as few clues as that."

There was a leaden feeling in the Saint's stomach, a sort of dull premonition of a premonition that was too essentially shocking to take complete form suddenly.

"Don't bet me, or I might have to go to work," he said mechanically.

"You've done your job, old boy. My buggy wasn't touched. This clot obviously saw your mark on it and got panicked. He knew that if he fooled around with that one, the vengeance of the Saint would land on him."

"What time was this?"

"About four o'clock in the morning . . . Ouf! I wonder if I'll ever get all this dust out of my mouth."

Simon's eyes shifted towards the back balcony again. The expensively glamorous Mrs Santander had disappeared, but Godfrey Quillen was still there, finishing a coke from the bottle and paying no immediate attention to anything else.

"Let's see what we can find to rinse it out," Simon suggested.

But he started moving towards the dispensing counter without waiting to see who would go with him. But Quillen saw him at once, and awaited his approach with expansive cordiality.

"Hi-yah, pal! This is the pause that refreshes, isn't it?—letting the back-seat drivers fight it out."

"Well, it's no strain on me," Simon assented amiably. "But I don't have a wife or a girlfriend driving right after some creep has been out in the small hours doing funny things to the hardware."

He knew by the switch of Quillen's eyes, without turning, that at least one of the Bethells had come with him, and went on, "I suppose you didn't tell Cynthia about that."

"Of course not. The poor girl was having the jitters badly enough already. Besides, this mysterious character can only have been a bit nutty. As Peter must have told you, the things he did weren't clever enough to be likely to cause any real damage."

"Or else he was being very cunning indeed," said the Saint. "Suppose there was only one particular car he wanted to wreck. No matter how clever he was about gaffing it, there was always a remote chance that an investigation would show that the accident mightn't've been quite accidental. It's those remote chances that give amateur plotters nightmares. Because the next phase of an inquiry, naturally, would be to ask who could have a motive for wanting that particular car to crash. So that's where our conspirator becomes a small-time genius. He figures that if it's established that some screwball was out

117

monkeying with a whole lot of cars, in various ways, the question of motive will be knocked out before it comes up. It'll just be accepted that this crackpot managed to sabotage one car in a way that unfortunately wasn't discovered in time."

"That's an interesting theory," said Charlie, who had come up on Simon's other side. "But what if the night watchman hadn't been asleep?"

"That wasn't much of a risk," Peter scoffed. "It's ten to one any night watchman would be taking a nap by that time, if he had any sense. Although this one didn't wake up until the prowler knocked over a couple of empty oil drums, or something like that."

"Which," Simon pointed out, "makes the prowler either extremely clumsy, extraordinarily unlucky—or a pretty cool operator. How do you sleep, Godfrey?"

"Me?" Quillen seemed slightly confused. "Like the proverbial top, pal. And spinning a bit, sometimes, especially after a night like last night. Man, those parties were rugged!"

He held his head graphically, and then all the sunny outgoing personality revived again as he said, "And me still waiting for the big race, so I can't even have a hair of the dog. You've done your stuff, haven't you, Peter? And nobody else has to abstain. Step up, gents, and name it. Take advantage of me."

Simon eased up to the bar with the others, and took part in the ordering. But it was one of the toughest exercises in restraint that he had ever undertaken. In his mind an hourglass was running out, and the last grains were pure explosive.

He swirled a shot of Peter Dawson around its crystal rocks, and said, "How about Cynthia?"

"Who?" Quillen said puzzledly. "Why?"

"How does she sleep?"

"Like a log, pal. Worse than me. Every morning I wonder if she's dead, and I have to try all sorts of things to find out."

"I don't know where your room is, but when I came in last night I tripped over some loose matting on the upstairs verandah, and nearly fell flat on my face. I was sure I'd woken up the whole joint."

"Not us, pal," Quillen said heartily. "It'd take an atomic bomb to do that."

Charlie Bethell said, in his diffident way, "I don't know how serious you meant to be about this prowler, Simon, but if you're right, it mightn't be so funny. Do you have any other ideas?"

" 'A medium-small man,' " Peter quoted. "Can't you tell us his name?"

Simon ignored them to look Quillen slowly up and down, and the driver had a sudden inspiration.

"Wait a minute! Could it have been a medium-big woman?"

"It ran away, didn't it, Peter?" Simon said. "Don't tell me that even this local Rip Van Winkle couldn't tell the difference between a man and a woman running."

"I don't know how many women he's chased," Peter said, "but I expect he'd've noticed."

"So if it was a man—"

"Oh, come now," Quillen protested. "You sound almost ready to buy that bee in Cynthia's bonnet. I know that Italians are hot-blooded, and all that, but I'll stand up for Enrico. Whatever the evidence is against him—"

"I don't know of any," Simon said gently. "I can imagine someone hoping he'd be a suspect, and trying to build that up on the side. An expert mechanic would be a wonderful fall guy for a job like this. But the evidence says that this prowler ran away, and the watchman couldn't catch him. I've seen Enrico walk, and I don't think he can run."

Quillen's teeth gleamed good-humoredly.

"Well, then, what's the answer, Sherlock?"

The Saint's gaze searched the baffling back stretches of the course with aching intensity. He had never felt that so much lost time had to be caught up so fast, but so smoothly. He had taken so long to be convinced that there was anything to be seriously perturbed about, and now he knew that any squandered second might be ticked off in blood. But only the most leisured nonchalance would convince a shrewd adversary that all his last cards were trumps.

"Don't ask me to be too brilliant," he said. "I was out rather late myself—as you may imagine."

"I don't imagine any more than I have to," Quillen said cheerfully. "But Teresa does tend to keep one up a bit."

"However, I did not trip on the matting when I came in."

"Good for you, pal. But don't feel guilty. Cynthia and I wouldn't've known the difference if you'd knocked over a row of ash-cans."

Simon lighted a cigarette.

"But when I did come home, I felt so good, and the moonlight was so fabulous, that I just couldn't go in at once. I had to stay out in the balmy air and soak it up. That's the thing I specially like about the Country Club, as against the other hotels: you've got all those rooms overlooking the beach from which you can, get straight out into the gardens, or on to a communal balcony with stairs at each end, and you can come and go as you please without having to pass through a formal lobby or be clocked in and out by any hired busy-bodies. So I was making the most of this, at about four-thirty this morning, when I saw you sneaking in . . . pal."

It was one of the most outrageous lies he had ever told in his life, but to his immoral credit he achieved it without a waver of expression. It was Godfrey Quillen whose face flushed and fluctuated through a fatal pause.

"I got restless," Quillen said. "You know, sometimes you get a bit keyed up before a big race. I went outside to smoke a cigarette, so as not to disturb Cynthia—"

"But I thought you slept like a spinning top," said the Saint innocently, "and nothing less than the crack of doom would wake Cynthia. On the other hand, if she does sleep so soundly, you might get away to do almost anything without her knowing. But why go to such lengths for a cigarette? When I saw you, you were just getting out of a car, which you'd just driven in and parked." With the basic fiction safely sold, there was no reason not to clinch it with trimmings. "Did you have to drive far enough away so that she wouldn't hear you strike the match? Were you afraid she'd think you were lighting some Venezuelan oil?"

Quillen's mouth opened and shut, without saying anything. His eyes went from side to side, from Simon to Charlie and to Peter. His face seemed uncertain whether to laugh or bluster, but it did neither, and that damning indecision was as good as a confession that was irrevocably underlined by each lengthening second of silence.

The silence was only relative, against the background of a thousand nondescript voices and noises, above which came the rising drone of more machinery approaching. Looking over Quillen's shoulder, Simon saw a dark green car come around the Esso bend into what they call Sassoon's Straight, which runs a furlong or so behind the box stand and very slightly off parallel to it. Teresa had stolen the lead somewhere in the back reaches. But the white Bristol was still in the running: it came out of the turn next, a couple of lengths behind and swinging a little wide and wild, but gathering itself and pouring on the coal for a screaming pursuit that began eating up the lost ground at an electrifying rate. The Saint's stroboscopic flash of relief at seeing both cars still rolling winked out as the new picture became as clear and steady to his mind as if he had been sitting beside Cynthia in the cockpit. He could see with clairvoyant vividness her mouth drawn into a gash, her teeth clenched, her eyes blazing, her knuckles white, her right foot flat on the floor. Furious at having been passed, perhaps goaded even more by some professional trick that Teresa might have used to accomplish it, Cynthia Quillen had simply seen red and was determined to even the score regardless of anything she might have been taught about race driving. One basic tenet of which is that there may be more dangerous places in which to lose one's temper than at the helm of a hot pan in a road race, but not much is known about them, because the experimenters who discover them seldom survive to describe them.

Cynthia was recklessly feeding her horses all the gas they needed to overtake the Maserati, and they were doing it at a rate which drew a vague kind of communal shout from the crowd. But to anyone who could make an educated estimate of the ballistic and dynamic factors involved, it was a performance to bring a cold sweat to the palms. For all straights come to an end, and this one ended at the extreme northeast tip of the course with two approximately right-angled turns which reversed it like a broad hairpin to run back into the starting and finishing stretch. At Cynthia's rate of acceleration she could pass Teresa, all right, but in doing it she would build up a velocity that no braking system might be able to cut down again fast enough to navigate the next corner against the immutable drag of centrifugal force . . . even without any mechanical failure.

"He needn't've gone to all that trouble," Peter said, as if half hypnotized. "They'll kill each other anyhow."

"We'd better stop the race," Charlie said, with quiet tenseness.

"You talk to the stewards," Simon snapped.

It may have been a somewhat superfluous directive, for Charlie was already turning towards the press box. But the Saint had a chill fear that even that procedure might be too slow—might perhaps be already too late. At this stage in his career he had become a trifle diffident about some of the more flamboyant performances which he once found irresistible. But this was one situation in which what could be literally called a grandstand play seemed to be forced on him.

With an almost instantaneous assessment of the physical and formal obstacles between him and the track via the nearest stairway, he swung his long legs over the nearest balcony rail and dropped an easy ten feet to the ground between some only moderately startled camp followers. With hardly a pause in motion he raced through an empty pit stall and across the open tarmac to the assortment of signal flags in their row of sockets beside the starter's box. He grabbed the red one which means "The race has been stopped," and in his other hand the yellow one which says "Caution," and stepped out into the track, waving them both frantically.

Even so, he was only just in time to get an acknowledging lift of one of Teresa Montesino's green-gloved hands as the Maserati streaked by and he saw its brakes begin to smoke.

But the Bristol did not follow, and as he moved farther out into the fairway, ignoring the frenzied injunctions of the public-address system, his heart sank as he saw a car of a different color swooping down towards the bridge, while in the distance a few tiny figures could be seen running like perturbed ants towards some indiscernible center of fascination behind the far turn.

"The biggest joke of it is," Peter commented later, "that if Cynthia'd tried to make that turn, at the speed she was going, she'd've been practically certain to spin out and roll over and probably break her neck. But that loose nut on the steering arm just happened to fall off in the straight, and she already had the brakes on as hard as she could, and when she tried to turn the wheel nothing happened at all, and so she went ploughing right on off the track into a lot of soft sand that stopped her like a feather pillow. Well, almost. Anyway, if Godfrey hadn't been so bloody clever, she'd probably be stone cold dead in de market, instead of just nursing a few bruises."

"That should make him feel a lot better," said the Saint.

"What else will he have to worry about?"

"Oh, the stewards and some other people had quite a talk with him," Charlie said impersonally. "It isn't the sort of thing we want a lot of publicity about. He'll be leaving the island on the next plane—but I don't think Cynthia will be with him."

"Or Mrs Santander either," Brenda put in. "You may think you were awfully discreet, but I bet the story's all over Nassau before midnight."

"You've got to admit he was no piker," Peter mused. "It even shook me a bit when we found the Montesino gal's steering fixed the same way, except that hers was still holding by half a thread. One more rough corner, and she could've been another wreck. The kind of sabotage that even a first-class mechanic mightn't spot—and him pretending he didn't know one end of an engine from the other. If it hadn't been for this suspicious Templar character, he might've got rid of all his problems in one happy afternoon."

"Poor Simon," Betty Bethell said. "Now you'll be hounded to death by grateful women."

The Saint grinned undoubtedly, and waved a languid hand at a white-coated waiter who was conveniently headed in their direction across the Country Club lounge.

"Let's have another round of that Old Curio," he said.

"Yes, Mr Templar," said the man. "Right away, sir. But I was comin' to tell you you're wanted on the phone, sir. Some lady callin', sir."

FLORIDA: THE JOLLY

"Sometimes," Simon Templar pronounced once, "I think that critics make far too much fuss about the use of coincidence in detective stories. In real life, mysteries are solved by coincidence at least half the time—because some chance witness happened to notice and remember something, or the criminal accidentally lost a button at the scene. An alibi goes blooey because an unpredictable fire stops the schemer getting back to his apartment in time for the phone call he's arranged to answer. And how many plays and movies have you seen where the perfect crime was all laid out at the start, and you sat happily on the edge of your seat waiting for the inevitable coincidence to foul it up—the incalculable old lady who comes looking for her wandering Fido, or the power failure that stops the electric clock that should have fired the bomb? The plain truth is that without some sort of fluke there'd usually be no story or no suspense. Coincidences happen to everyone, but they're only branded as far-fetched when somebody does something with one."

One such coincidence which he might have been recalling was not really extravagant at all, reduced to its prime essentials, which consisted of :

A: reading about, and being mildly intrigued by, a minor offense committed against an individual of no obvious importance and certainly unknown to him: and

B: having that victim pointed out to him less than 48 hours later, before he had time to forget the association.

That is, if you exclude the third factor, that such coincidences seemed to happen to the Saint with exceptional frequency. But modern insurance studies have revealed that it is not purely accidental that some people have more accidents than others, and can be properly called "accident-prone." In the same way, Simon Templar seemed to attract interesting coincidences, perhaps because he made better use of them than ordinary people. This, therefore, on the best actuarial authority, should not even be called a coincidence.

The first ingredient, then, was an item in a Palm Beach, Florida, newspaper reporting that a Funeral Home in Lake Worth operated by an undertaker with the rather delightful name of Aloysius Prend had been broken into during the night, but appeared to have rewarded the robbers with no more than $7.18 and some postage stamps, the contents of a petty cash box in an office drawer.

"Now, what would give any burglar the idea of cracking an undertaker's shop?" Simon apostrophized the counter girl in the coffee shop where he was eating breakfast.

"Those guys've got more money than anybody," she said darkly. "Inflation, depression, recession, whatever, people keep dying just the same. There's one business can always be sure of customers."

"And the worse a depression gets, the more it might boom, with more people committing suicide," Simon admitted, following her cheerful trend of thought. "But no matter how fast the bodies roll in, an undertaker doesn't normally ring up cash sales like a supermarket. He presents a nice consolidated bill for his assorted services, which is pretty certain to be big enough to be paid by check. So why would anyone expect to find any more in his desk than small change?"

"Could be they were looking for gold teeth in the stiffs."

Simon found himself liking her more every minute, but he had to point out, "It says here, there was no other damage except the window they broke to get in."

"I bet he's got plenty of it socked away, anyhow," she said, reverting to her original thesis. "You only got to walk around Lake Worth and see 'em tottering about the shuffleboard courts or sitting in those everlasting auction rooms. It should make an undertaker feel like Moses with a claim staked in the Promised Land. Everyone ninety years old, and just waiting to keel over till maybe they're driving a car and can take someone else with them."

"Honestly, I'm disgustingly healthy. And I can still lick all my grandchildren."

"Oh, I can see that. I just wish I saw more fellows around here like you."

She was a comely wench, and she had that look in her eye, but he already had a fairly promising social calendar for that visit, and he decided not to complicate it with this additional prospect, at least for the present.

The established playgrounds of the spoiled sophisticates, socially registered or columnist-created, are forced to struggle with one perennial blight: a dearth of eligible playboys. This may be because the widows and divorcees are too durable; or the influx of their would-be successors too torrential; or because the men who have yet to earn their own wherewithal are still tied to their jobs and projects in less glamorous but more lucrative centers; or those who inherited it have been decimated by a preference for mixed drinks and/or mixed genders. There is a whole rubric of hypotheses which this chronicler may examine at some other time. The fact remains that in such places any unattached male with reasonable manners, charm, alcoholic tolerance, stamina, and affinity for empty chatter, can be assured of enough invitations to guarantee him his choice of gastritis or cirrhosis, or both, and what is so descriptively called the Florida Gold Coast is no exception.

Simon Templar had never made any systematic effort to crash this exclusively dubious society, but there were times when it amused him to be a fringe free-loader, and he had not fled from the northern blizzards to the subtropical sunshine to enjoy himself like a hermit. He shared any intelligent man's disdain for cocktail parties, in principle, but he knew no easier way for a comparative stranger in town to make a lot of assorted acquaintances quickly.

"This is my house guest, Betty Winchester," said his hostess.

"How do you do," murmured the Saint, like anyone else.

"You're going to take her to dinner," his hostess informed him regally, then she saw some more guests arriving. "Oh, excuse me—you tell him about it, Betty."

The girl was actually blushing—an olde-worlde phenomenon which Simon found quite exotic.

"You don't really have to, of course," she assured him. "She's worried because she has to leave me tonight—an emergency meeting of some charity committee she's on—and she thinks it's dreadful to have to abandon me to myself. Please don't think any more about it."

She had black hair and very large hazel eyes in a face that was pert and appealing now, and within the next seven years would decide whether to be stodgy or sensual or sulky, just as her nubile figure might become voluptuous or gross. But at that moment Simon was not shopping for futures. He estimated her age at a barely possible twenty-two.

"But I'd like to think about it," he said. "I didn't have any better ideas. Unless you did?"

"No. I haven't been going out much. I came down here to stay with my uncle, who'd been very sick, and when he died these nice people insisted that I move in with them till after the funeral."

"Had you known them before?" he asked. The usual small talk.

"I went to high school with their daughter, and we still see each other sometimes."

"Where do you live, then?"

"In New York. And she's married and living in Philadelphia. Do you live here?"

"No. I'm just another tourist, too . . . When was this funeral?"

"Yesterday."

"I'm sorry. But I take it you're not in total mourning."

"Oh, no. Although my cousin and I were his only last relatives. But we weren't really so close to him, all the same. And I don't think it would do him any good now if I went around being tragic for months, would it?"

"With all due respect to Uncle, I agree," Simon said. "So about this dinner—is there anything special you feel an appetite for?"

She thought.

"Only one thing I haven't been able to get, at least not the way I remember them: stone crabs! We used to go to a place, Joe's, right at the south end of Miami Beach—"

"That's a lot longer haul than it used to be, since this coast got practically built up all the way. But I discovered another place last season, a bit closer, on the Seventy-ninth Street Causeway, where the claws are just as luscious and sometimes even bigger." He consulted his watch. "I could get you there in not much more than an hour on the Parkway, and if you had one more good drink before we took off you'd hardly know you'd missed anything. That is, unless there's something about this brawl that we mustn't miss?"

The answer was that they dined sumptuously at Nick & Arthur's, stifling for temporary logistic reasons the nostalgic loyalty to Joe's, and sentimentally comparing the size and succulence of the specimens served by both establishments.

"Anyway," Simon concluded, "they are Florida's unique and wonderful contribution to the hungry tummy. And what more could Lucullus ask?"

She didn't try to answer that, most probably having never heard of Lucullus, but she happily finished everything that could be put on her plate, and had some coconut cream pie after it while he finished the bottle of Dienhard Steinwein '59 with which they had launched those supreme crustaceans. After which it ultimately and inevitably came to a question of what they should do next.

Since the Saint's adventures nearly always seem to get dated by something or other, it may as well be stated right away that this happened during the epoch when a so-called dance called the Twist had spread like an epidemic from a place called the Peppermint Lounge in New York where it first broke out, across the United States and even beyond the seas, and on countless nightclub floors devotees who had hitherto seemed at least superficially rational were disjointing vertebrae and spraining knees in frenzied attempts to imitate the writhings of an inexpert Fijian fire-walker trying to help himself across the coals by holding on to a live wire.

As they came out of the restaurant, Simon noticed that they were next door to a new manifestation which had moved in since the last time he had been there: an establishment which proclaimed itself, in splendid neon, to be "New York's Peppermint Lounge." Discounting any fantastic possibility that the original New York incubator of the current mania had physically uprooted itself and followed its vacationing habitués to Miami Beach, it seemed as if this must at least be an authorized and authentic branch of the mother lodge, and he was reminded of a shocking deficiency in his spectrum of experience.

"Do you know, Betty," he said, "that you are out tonight with not just a square, but a four-dimensional cube? I still haven't seen a Twist session in full swing. Would you chaperone me in there for just long enough to see what it's all about?"

"That's the last thing I'd have expected you to suggest," she said respectfully. "Let's try it."

It was still early enough for the place to be packed only half-way to suffocation, but they were able to find one stool to share at the bar while they waited for a table which Simon felt cynically prepared to decline if and when it was finally offered. Meanwhile he absorbed the scene which he had come in to see, endeavoring in what he felt must have been a rectangular way to fathom the motivations of the customers who wriggled and twitched to a simple monotonous beat like a horde of frenetic dervishes freshly sprinkled with itching powder.

"Well?" she teased at last. "Don't you want to try it?"

"Thank you," sighed the Saint. "But I'm old-fashioned. Dancing went out for me when it stopped being an excuse to snuggle a girl up close and whisper wicked suggestions in her ear with a helpful background of seductive music. These arm's-length athletics—the Jitterbug, the Rumba, and now this—seem like an awful waste of energy and opportunity."

"You sound as if you had a one-track mind," she said, but she smiled.

"Doesn't everyone, any more? In my young days, they did . . . "

Suddenly she was no longer listening. She was staring into the quivering mob with a fixity that seemed scarcely justified by any of their individual contortions. Her hand fell on his arm.

"Look—over there! The elderly man in the Madras jacket, with the platinum babe in the red sweater."

Simon found it easier to track the assigned target through the babe, who stood out not only because of the color of her sweater but by reason of what filled it. Even at his most chivalrous, he could not take issue with the "Babe" description, which fitted not only the artificial whiteness of the hair but the blend of hardness and looseness in the face. If she was not the kind of company available to any lonesome visitor for a phone call and a fee, she had certainly made a democratic effort to look like it.

Her partner, who was identifiable mainly because she looked and shook in his direction more than in any other, was a man of entirely average size with rimless glasses and insufficient strands of gray hair meticulously plastered over the top of his head in a laborious but absurdly vain attempt to disguise the fact that there was no supporting growth underneath them. His other features somewhat resembled those of a puritanical rabbit, with a reservation that at that moment it was apparently playing truant. Simon guessed him to be no older than fifty, and reflected sadly that the adjective "elderly" was as descriptive of the person who used it as of the person it was applied to.

"Anybody you know?" he asked.

"It's Mr Prend—the undertaker who handled my uncle's funeral!"

"Not Aloysius?"

"Yes. Did you ever hear of such a name?"

He decided that it was hardly worth giving her a discourse on St Aloysius Gonzaga of Catiglione, who died of the plague in Rome in 1591 at the tender age of twenty-three, and was designated the patron saint of young people, but Mr Aloysius Prend was certainly doing credit to his name in the youthful if untrained exuberance with which he quivered and cavorted in uninhibited emulation of his tarty companion.

"After all," Simon reasoned at length, "I suppose even undertakers have to relax sometimes. He wouldn't dare be seen looking anything but solemn and mournful around Lake Worth, so he has to go out of town to let off steam. And it's a million to one that none of his prospective customers would catch him in a place like this."

"And that babe he's with!"

"I expect he has to take what he can get. It wouldn't be too easy for him to date a nice home-town gal who knew what business he was in. Be charitable, and try not to let him see you. It'd only ruin his evening."

"It seems almost indecent," she persisted. "You'd think he was celebrating something. And his place was burgled only the other night. Who on earth would do a thing like that?"

"Most likely some juvenile delinquents on a dare," said the Saint. "And he's celebrating because they didn't drink up his expensive embalming fluid. Now could you stand it if we moved on to some joint with a floor show more suitable for my hardening arteries?"

He was able to get her out before Mr Prend seemed to have noticed her, but his flippant dismissal of the subject of Mr Prend's incongruous relaxation was activated only by a reluctance to argue about it with an interlocutor who was not likely to contribute any more to his peculiar sensitivities.

But the truth was that he had become intensely interested in Mr Aloysius Prend.

The Saint had an apperception of oddities of behavior and circumstance like the reaction of a musician to a false note. It was nothing that could be taught or acquired, or explained to anyone whose inner hearing was not so finely tuned. Nor was he governed by the sterile assumption that anything unusual or unconventional must have some reprehensible connection; far from it. But he conceded that all crime is a deviation from the current norm, and it was his instinct for the kind of abnormality most likely to be linked with skulduggery in the process of cooking-up or concealment that had led him into more strange situations perhaps than any other single factor in the complex equation of his life.

During the next few hours, he tried to fill in a picture of the uncle whose mortal disposition had accidentally enabled Betty Winchester to discover the incongruous other side of Mr Prend.

Ernest Cardman, he learned by assembling and coordinating a great variety of disorganized and personalized information which he coaxed from her as innocuously as possible, as the elder brother of two sisters who had selfishly flipped off and got married before he felt qualified for such a plunge, had been left holding the bag (if we may be excused the expression in this context) and had been forced to become the comforter, counsellor, and companion of their widowed mother, who had lingered through manifold ailments until she was well over eighty. By that time, Uncle Ernest had either become habituated to his way of life or had decided that he liked it, for he took no advantage of his belated liberation. He went on living in the same modest beach house on South Ocean Boulevard down towards Lake Worth, although the land it stood on could by then have been sold to a hotel or motel for five times the value of the building, with no friends and no apparent ambition to make any, poring endlessly over the charts and analyses supplied by a dozen or more stock market advisory services to which he subscribed, which were his only recreation and his only reading except for the world news which had to be studied for its potential reflection in the markets.

He punctiliously invited Betty and her cousin, the son of his other sister, to visit him for a week each year during the season, but made no effort to give them entertainment, and seemed to derive nothing from their company except the relief they volunteered him from his household chores. He still did his own shopping, cooking, and housekeeping, as he had done it for his mother, who in her later years became so temperamental and exacting that no paid servant would stay with her. That was, until a couple of years ago, when his own health betrayed him and he had been obliged to hire a former hospital nurse who was willing to double as housekeeper to take care of him.

"She's quite a jewel—not that she doesn't know it," was the description of Mrs Velma Yanstead. "The motherly sort, even though she's a good deal younger than Uncle Ernest. But I suppose that was just what he wanted."

At any rate, Mrs Yanstead had stayed on, even after he made a partial recovery from the "intestinal flu" which had brought her in, and cared for him solicitously through the increasingly frequent gastric upsets which he became prone to, until the final acute attack to which he succumbed.

"I guess you could qualify for the Freud Trophy," Simon concurred, gravely, and then hastily explained, "that's a sort of head-shrinkers' Oscar. He should have been grateful to find another apron-string."

"He was," Betty said, so bitterly that he now understood the tinge of spite that had faintly discoloured her previous praise. "He left her practically everything!"

"He did?"

"Well, he left me and my cousin two thousand dollars each, like showing he hadn't forgotten us. But she got the house and all the rest."

"And there was a lot more?"

"His attorney said he had stocks worth about a quarter of a million."

Ernest Cardman's single-minded study of the oscillations of Wall Street had not been unprofitable. Yet with perhaps typical parsimony, he had saved himself a legal fee by disposing of that considerable estate in a simple one-page will written in his own crabbed and shaky hand. As a holograph will, it required no witnesses, and had been sent by ordinary mail to his attorney, who had been out of town at the time and who had not even seen it until he returned the day after his client died.

"Was it a shock to you?"

"Was it! We had no idea he was so well off, but still he'd always let us understand that whatever there was would come to us. In fact, I can remember him saying he wouldn't even waste his time making a will at all, because as his next-of-kin we'd automatically inherit anyhow. And all he'd done before that was leave a letter with his attorney willing his body to the University of Miami Medical School. Henry—my cousin—was fit to be tied, He was staying with Uncle Ernest before I came down, and he never got any kind of idea what was cooking. He says we ought to contest the will."

The phantom electric needles of unfocused intuition tried to stitch their way up the Saint's spine.

"I believe there is something called 'undue influence,' " he hazarded.

"So Henry says. But I must admit, I never saw her get out of line when I was there. She was always sweet."

"Doesn't Henry think it was forged, then?"

"He's talked about that too. But Velma said she wished it could be checked by a handwriting expert. I couldn't help feeling sorry for her, in a way."

Most of this was not actually a connected conversation, as it appears—which would have been difficult in some of the places and situations they were in—but it is so presented to spare the reader all the irrelevant interruptions. And the Saint had his own way of teasing out information over a period of time, without seeming to cross-examine as it might sound from nothing but the relevant exchanges.

They were driving unhurriedly back to Palm Beach on the coast road before he brought the topic casually back to the background of her cousin.

"Was Henry at the party tonight? I don't remember meeting him."

"No. He isn't staying there. He moved out to a motel after the will was read, though Velma did say he was welcome to stay. I expect he had some other date—he'd like to be a playboy, but he can't often afford it."

"And now at least he's got two thousand to play with. What does he do for money between legacies?"

"He has a job in an advertising agency."

"And thinks he should be an account executive—with a fat expense account?"

"He'd like to be."

Simon looked at her again from another angle.

"And what about you, Betty? What do you do in New York?"

"I'm a cosmetician," she said, and added defensively, "That doesn't mean I work in a beauty parlor. I advise people what to buy, what would do the most for them, and I probably help more men than women—about choosing those kind of gifts, I mean."

She named the Fifth Avenue department store where she performed this invaluable service, but it did not awe him out of kidding her most irreverently about the qualifications for her profession and its importance to the economy.

Nevertheless, when they got back to the mansion where she was staying, she was the one who said, "Shall I be seeing you again?"

"When are you going back to the magic mud-packs?" he asked.

"On Sunday. I can't take another week off, the way it's turned out."

"How about dinner tomorrow?" He glanced pointedly at his watch. "I mean really tomorrow, not a little later today."

"Go."

(We already warned that this incident would be bound to get dated, like all the others.)

At the door, she kissed him spontaneously on the lips, but with a swiftness that was there and gone before anything but surmise could be made of it, and he drove away with one more question raised instead of answered in his mind.

In the morning, however, he was out at a very reasonably early hour, heading for the address of the late Ernest Cardman, which he located with no trouble in the phone book—he had interrogated Betty Winchester quite enough not to want to have overloaded his inquisition with that last detail.

As he had been told, it was a comparatively modest house for its prime location, and when his ring on the bell was answered he found Mrs Velma Yanstead no less modest, in a neck-high housecoat of some starchy material which was so studiously respectable that it proclaimed almost aggressively that her virtue mattered more to her than her comfort. And yet, somewhat paradoxically, that did not make her forbidding. She was fat and forty and heartily uncomplicated.

"I'm from *The Miami Guardian*," he said, with conscienceless aplomb. "As you know, we have a Palm Beach section in our Sunday edition, and of course we'll have to print something about Mr Cardman and his will. Is there anything you'd like to say about it for publication?"

"Well, really!" She was neither coy nor antagonistic, but just diffident enough to be likeable. "I'd no idea that would be news."

"A quarter of a million dollars is still news, Mrs Yanstead, even in these inflated times. May I come in for a few minutes?"

The living-room was like a million middle-class Florida living-rooms, undistinguished by planned interior decoration or obtrusive eccentricity. It was furnished with what can best be described as furniture—more or less functional things with legs, arms, seats, or flat surfaces. The general tone, especially of the bric-a-brac, perhaps had a grandmotherly or old-maidish tinge which Mr Cardman had clearly had no solitary urge to change, but it was not strenuously slanted towards the antique, and it certainly did not suggest wealth or extravagance.

"You sound rather like him," Mrs Yanstead said amiably. "Always talking about inflation, he was, and twenty-five cent dollars and recessions and I don't know what else. I never argued with him—that was his hobby, and it was none of my business."

"You had no idea how wealthy he was?"

"I never thought about it. I knew he must've been fairly comfortably off, but he didn't spend as if he had it to throw away."

"You weren't in his confidence at all personally?"

The question could hardly have been phrased more perfectly, without the slightest hint at which she could have taken offense, but open to her to answer as fully as she might be inclined.

"He was just like any other patient, but I've always got on well with my patients." She stated it as a matter of professional pride warmed by human satisfaction. "You can't do them much good if you don't get on with them. I wasn't like a servant, of course—we played cribbage and watched television together, and everything like that. But there was nothing romantic about it."

"Then the will was as much a surprise to you as to anyone?"

"You could've knocked me down with a feather."

Simon scribbled solemnly on the back of an envelope, like a stage reporter, recording the brilliant cliché for quotation, in case he forgot it.

He changed the subject for a moment: "What exactly did Mr Cardman die of?"

"Acute gastro-enteritis. He'd suffered a lot with it, off and on, ever since he got that intestinal virus that had me brought in."

"There wasn't anything the doctor could do?"

"He had prescriptions. But I suppose his insides were damaged more than they could repair, at his age. And he was always trying out diets on his own, or dosing himself with medicines and health syrups that he saw advertised. I think they did him more harm than good. I used to get quite cross with Mr Utterly for encouraging him."

The Saint was briefly puzzled.

"Mr Utterly?"

"His nephew."

"Oh, yes. There's a niece, too, isn't there?"

"Miss Winchester. A pretty girl, and I think she was Mr Cardman's favorite. But Mr Utterly was naughty, always encouraging him by sending him things from New York—seaweed pills and grass powder and I don't know what else. Just trying to make up to his uncle, I know, but it was no help."

"You were always on good terms with both of them—I mean, the nephew and niece?"

"I thought so."

"So you thought they'd be understanding about being sort of disinherited in your favor?"

This time perhaps he was not quite subtle enough, for he struck a spark from her deep-set black eyes before the plump wrinkles creased around them again.

"I did feel badly at first," she said. "Until Mr Utterly turned rather nasty—have you seen him?"

"No."

"Well, he said some very nasty things, about me taking advantage of his uncle. So then I stopped feeling sorry for him. I thought, if he's going to be a bad sport, because he didn't manage to cut out his cousin with those pills and things that he kept working on Mr Cardman with, then why should I get in a family battle? I thought, Mr Cardman made up his own mind, and if this is what he wanted I've got a right to take it, and bless him."

"Do you have a picture of him?"

Mrs Yanstead looked around vaguely. There were a few framed photographs on walls and ledges, but the Saint's surreptitious wandering glances had identified most of them as plates from a sentimental biography of a woman who could only have been Mr Cardman's mother, a recurrent face from an old misty-edged sepia vignette of a demure young girl to a modern skilfully-retouched portrait of a prim old matriarch. Mr Cardman's inclusion in a group with his sisters, gathered around her in their self-consciously angelic adolescence, was not what Simon had in mind, but Mrs Yanstead's obliging exploration discovered a very contemporary snapshot tucked into one corner of phonus-period velvet frame.

"He never was one to have his picture taken," she said, "but this is one that Miss Winchester took right after she came down this season."

It was the typical box-camera enlargement, obviously taken against one side of the house, with Mrs Yanstead and Mr Cardman standing awkwardly side by side (but at a discreet distance) and both, looking straight into the lens and grinning in the pointless mechanical way beloved of the amateur artists who are the bread and butter of the photographic-supply industry, but partly on that account it had the virtue of presenting a facial facsimile that was recognizable in the same brutal way that a passport photo or a prison mug shot may be recognizable. It showed Mr Cardman with a predatory nose but a weak chin, a cocky but frail figure beside the foster-mother of his senility, who seemed to make an earthily honest effort to hold back and avoid eclipsing him with her superior bulk and vitality.

"May I borrow this?" Simon asked. "It won't be damaged, and I'll send it back in a day or two."

"I suppose so."

"One other thing," he said as he was leaving: "where can I find Mr Utterly?"

"He went to the Tradewind—that's the first motel you come to down the road. I expect he'll have plenty to say about me." She pursed her lips, then shrugged and smiled again. "Well, I don't live in a glass house, so I shouldn't worry about who throws stones."

Simon drove on to the motel, and after inquiring at the office he was directed to the Terrace Snack Bar, which was beside the swimming pool, which had considerately been provided for the indulgence of guests who either found a hundred-yard walk to the beach too fatiguing or were appalled by the potential perils of the rippling ocean. There he found Cousin Henry eating an improbably early lunch, or more likely a very belated breakfast, consisting of corned beef hash and black coffee.

Henry Utterly was a broad-shouldered young man with a premature paunch bulging over the top of his Hawaiian-print shorts. His black hair was slicked down in graceful sweeps over his head and his ears, but below that it sprouted in thin curls all over him except in the conventionally scraped facial areas, which had the dark sheen of gun-metal. He had the still red and unfinished tan of the typical tourist, and another rosy tinge in his eyeballs which some Yankee visitors acquire under the palm-trees and others bring with them from a lunch diet of dry martinis. This season he still had a certain fast and superficial charm, and in a very few years, unless he found the end of his rainbow, he could be just another slob.

He received the Saint with practised Madison-Avenue affability—a blend of pressurized brightness and defensive flexibility.

"*The Guardian*? Of course, the best newspaper in the South, I tell everybody—except people from the other papers. But are you selling space or trying to fill some?"

"Would you like to make any statement about your late uncle's will?" Simon asked.

"I'd like to make several, but not to you. I don't want to have something printed that I could be sued for."

"I suppose we could safely say that you were surprised."

"I think so. Also astounded, staggered, flabbergasted—and perhaps even incredulous."

"And if you did make a statement it might be uncomplimentary to someone?"

"It might be," Mr Utterly said. He tugged at his lower lip with mock judiciousness. "Yes, I think you can safely say that. Very uncomplimentary. Would you like some mocha Java, or just any coffee?"

"I'm a bit farther ahead in the day," Simon said negatively. "But a Dry Sack on the rocks would go down nicely."

"Good idea." Utterly repeated the order to a waitress, adding: "And I'll have a Bloody Mary."

Simon resumed, "I can understand that you'd want to be careful, Mr Utterly, but it's true that you're thinking of contesting the will, isn't it?"

"I've discussed it with my attorneys, yes. We're having another meeting on it this afternoon. It's in what I would call the survey stage. We turn the pros and cons loose in the pond and see what they spawn."

"Are you hoping to prove the will was forged?"

"That might be difficult. I'm not giving much away, but everyone concerned knows that my uncle had a fairly bad stroke a few years ago, and his right hand and arm never recovered completely. So it might be a bit marginal to rely on handwriting experts. On the other hand, anyone with enough motive to forge a will would be even more capable of getting the old man to write it himself."

"You mean what they call 'undue influence'?"

"That's something like the beat of the legal jazz."

Simon circulated his drink in the glass which had been delivered to him, and sipped it appreciatively.

"Did that stroke affect Mr Cardman anywhere besides the arm?" he inquired, without flippancy.

"Like in the head? Now you approach the cosmic. You invoke the definition that makes politics, religion, philosophy, and low comedy. Who is nuts and who isn't? Well, I'd hate to claim that my own uncle was insane, but he'd reached an age when his mind was certainly not as sharp as it was when he was younger. There's plenty of evidence that he was eccentric, to say the least. Even Mrs Yanstead, unless she perjures herself, will have to admit that he had to be coaxed or bullied to take his doctor's medicine, but he'd try anything he heard of from some quack advertisement."

"And she says you encouraged him, sending him all kinds of health foods and herb remedies and what not."

Utterly shot him a hard stare, without a flicker of embarrassment.

"Oh, you've already talked to her." It was a statement, not a question. "I don't deny it. Harmless placebos—I made sure of that. Things that I knew couldn't hurt him, and may even have given him a few extra vitamins. I went along with the gag, and if it made him happy, what was wrong with that?"

"And since you're a relative, that couldn't be called 'undue influence' in your case," Simon said.

His tone was so impeccably neutral that for the first time Henry Utterly seemed uncertain—but whether of himself or of the Saint's intention would have been a very ticklish nuance to bet on.

"My dear sir, you're not aiming a muckraker at the American Family image? Making subversive suggestions that the affection they lavish on Rich Uncle is magnetized by his credit rating? Don't apologize. Even if that's what you were thinking, it's obvious that I didn't try too hard—even if I did commit the crime of trying to be more sympathetic than my cousin Betty. The proof is that neither of us got in the real money. We were left out in the pasture by a nag with no form at all—pardon my choice of metaphor. And we hadn't even thought she was in the running. Therefore one may legitimately wonder if the race was fixed. But in such a case one suspects the winner, not the losers. Do you excavate, gate?"

"I dig," said the Saint, but regretfully decided that it would not be in keeping with his role to complete the rhyme. "Although it's still hard for me to see how a man can be influenced into actually making a will like that, cutting off his own family in favor of a comparative stranger. I mean, without thumbscrews, or that sort of persuasion."

Utterly waved his hands with a commanding eloquence that was somehow reminiscent of an orchestra conductor in full flourish.

"Psychology, my friend." He was genial again, as his confidence recovered and re-inflated. "That's something I understand. It's my business. Why do you smoke what you smoke, shave with whatever you use, brush your teeth with that toothpaste? Because they were sold to you. Now don't be offended; you think you chose them. But I have news for you. You only chose what you chose because somebody knew how to get through your resistance and make you want it. My uncle was conditioned for twenty years and more to a Mother fixation. He was a pushover for the next person who came along who could fit into that Mother-image."

"And all your psychology couldn't compete with her?"

"Does my cousin Betty look like a Mother? Only if you include the kind that you find in homes for wayward girls. Do I look like a Mother? Be careful how you answer that." Utterly grinned, and emptied his Bloody Mary. By now he was hugely pleased with himself. "You know we didn't stand a chance against a real Mother-type, if she went out to exploit it. Whether a Court will agree is another matter. So I don't think I can say any more without the risk of damaging my own case. You understand?"

"Yes, but—"

"Then good-bye." Utterly stood up, holding out his hand, pleasantly, but offensively secure in his privilege and his savoir faire. "Call me after the verdict, and I might have some more Pulitzer material for you."

He turned away and plunged into the pool, ungracefully but finally enough, and Simon let it go at that. The Saint was not yet prepared, for purely private satisfaction, to explode the innocuous anonymity with which he seemed to have saddled himself. But only a much more rarified objective could have controlled the temptation.

And now he had one, beyond any doubt, for he was sure that Mr Ernest Cardman's death, though it could hardly be called untimely, had nevertheless been artificially expedited.

But cerebral certainty is not proof, and even the Saint in his most lawless days, with all his impatience with the finicky rules of legal evidence and his delight in clearing his own short cuts to justice, had always required some positive verification, satisfactory at least to him if not to all technical criteria. And nobody knew better than he that any law-abiding police agency would be still more hesitant to turn on the sirens and rush hither and yon merely because he, Simon Templar, walked in and said he felt sure he had discovered a murder.

Luckily (and if this sounds like one more coincidence, let the statisticians make the most of it) he had a fairly direct access to the next facility he needed which for a while at least allowed him to be himself again. The Saint had friends, acquaintances, and contacts everywhere: they were a sort of human stock-in-trade, a fringe of his life which made much of the core possible. He had acquired many of them in highly improbable ways, haphazard as often as adventurous, but when it was necessary he had no compunction about calling on any of them.

He had met Julian D Corrington, Professor Emeritus and at that time head of the Zoology Department of the University of Miami, by correspondence over a magazine article that Dr Corrington had written about Sherlock Holmes; for Dr Corrington, in a small part of his spare time, happened also to be one of the many distinguished intellectuals who have made a whimsical cult of studying the detective writings of Conan Doyle as minutely as a theologian analyzes the scriptures, and often with resultant discoveries which must exert as much graveyard torque on that Master as similar diversions may apply to this chronicler in due time.

A person-to-person phone call established at no cost that Dr Corrington was still tied up with his bi-weekly histology class, but would be in his office in the afternoon, and Simon shamelessly cheated the telephone company to the enrichment of the petroleum industry by driving down to Coral Gables and presenting himself in person after lunch, which he ate rather late but unhurriedly before heading down Le Jeune Road to the University.

Directed to a room on the third floor of the Anastasia Building, on the North Campus, he found an alert good-natured man with plentiful gray hair and gray mustache, whose trim and erect figure belied the seventy years he laid claim to.

"Are you really the man I've read so much about?" he said. "I never thought I'd actually meet you in person."

They chatted for a while in generalities, until Simon felt he could broach the purpose of his call without sounding too cavalier about it.

The Professor listened to him thoughtfully, and said, "I think I should take you to see the head of the Department of Anatomy—it would be under his jurisdiction, and he knows all the law about these things. I expect you'll find you have to get a court order, or at least a formal request from the police."

"Knowing who I am, can you see the police doing me any favors?" Simon objected. "And I haven't enough to go on to get a court order, at this moment. I doubt if I could even impress the head of your Anatomy Department. And yet this is urgent. If anything happens to that body, it'll be almost impossible to make it a murder case."

"It may be hard to locate the body even now," Corrington said. "As I understand the procedure, they try to make a cadaver anonymous as soon as possible."

"But somebody must sign a receipt for it when it's delivered," Simon argued. "Somebody must unpack it and put it wherever they keep the supplies for the dissecting rooms. This was so recent that it might still be possible to trace it—if only too much time isn't wasted."

"I suppose we can make inquiries. I can take you over there, at any rate, unofficially of course, like any personal friend I'm showing around, and you can see what answers you get."

"That'd be a step forward, anyhow. If it isn't asking too much."

"It would be amusing to be the Saint's Dr. Watson, even in such a minor way." Corrington's eyes twinkled. "And I can't be held responsible for what questions you ask the janitor, or what he chooses to tell you."

He steered the Saint briskly out to his car in the parking lot behind the building, and chauffeured him a half-dozen blocks along Riviera Drive to a building which to Simon looked reminiscent of the pre-war

Coral Gables Biltmore Hotel, a sister caravanserai of Miami Beach's Roney Plaza which somehow got separately orphaned when the Coral Gables development failed to match the Beach as another southern Samarkand.

"That's what it is," Corrington told him. "And this first building we're coming to was the old servants' quarters. Now it's part of our Medical School, temporarily, until they finish the new buildings."

"How are the mighty fallen," Simon murmured, thinking also of Mr Cardman, who despite his thriftiness, when the hotel and himself were equally in flower, would probably never have dreamed of using any entrance but the front.

The semi-basement storage room to which they were admitted by recognition of Dr Corrington had even fewer prospects as a tourist attraction, having been converted into something like a giant filing or safe-deposit vault smelling of formaldehyde and the clammy by-products of refrigeration. The individual in charge, however, was contrastingly warm and cheerful—perhaps because, as he immediately explained, he was only temporarily replacing the regular incumbent, hospitalized for a minor ailment, and did not think he wanted to make a career of it.

"Yeah, I remember that one, because I'm still lookin' to see where they come from," he said, without hesitation. "Like kids collect stamps or car tags. This was the only one I had from Lake Worth since I been on the job. Come in only yesterday. I know exactly where I put him."

Simon said to Corrington, "Would there be any chance of getting some friendly pathologist on the faculty to take a look at it? I don't mean a regular autopsy, but enough to see if there might be *prima facie* grounds to ask for one."

"Good heavens, that would be completely out of order! I couldn't ask anyone to risk losing his job like that."

"Well, then, at least see if you can't get this body put on one side for a few days, just long enough for me to—"

"Here," said the temporary custodian of cadavers.

He had pulled out one of the oversize drawers banked along one wall, in which the pathetic but essential materials for scientific study were impersonally stored.

Simon looked in, at the naked corpse of a short flabby male in his fifties, with a round face and a snub Irish nose, and felt for a second as if the terrazzo floor was falling from under him.

He finally recovered his voice.

"That isn't Cardman," he stated.

"Are you sure?" Corrington asked dubiously. "Death sometimes seems to change people."

Simon took out the snapshot that he had borrowed from Mrs Yanstead, and showed it.

"As much as that?"

"This is the one from Lake Worth, anyhow," said the custodian.

"Couldn't you possibly be mistaken?" insisted the Saint. "May I look in the other drawers?"

"If you think I'm an idiot," was the aggrieved retort, "help yourself. And I'll get my book and look up the record."

Simon accepted the invitation literally, and pulled open every other drawer. There was no face in any of them that could ever have been the face in the snapshot, even allowing for the maximum transfigurations of death. But the custodian returned more stubbornly affirmative than ever.

"That's the one," he said. "Come from Prend's Funeral Home in Lake Worth."

"Could it by any chance have been taken out for dissection and another body put in the same drawer since?"

"Not by any chance. There's been no cadavers taken out for two days."

Simon caught the Professor's eye and indicated with a slight motion of his head that they should leave.

Outside, he said, "I think we've got to believe him. On the other hand, I'm not mistaken either. Which leaves only one possible explanation. Cardman's body was switched for another one before the coffin was delivered here."

"In order to hide something?"

"Exactly. Because somebody was afraid that when it was taken apart in the lab, some professor or precocious student might notice that there was something wrong with it—something that didn't gibe with the assigned diagnosis. I suppose that in spite of the anonymity angle, a body would have to go to the lab with some presumed cause of death attached to it, so that the students could be warned about what was normal and what was abnormal?"

"I don't really know how they handle that here. But—"

"Anyhow, all that matters now is to prevent the trail getting any more confused. The guy in charge in there positively identifies the body he showed us as the one he received from Lake Worth. I have a picture that contradicts him. It shouldn't be any problem to decide who's right, with witnesses who knew Cardman, dental charts, maybe even fingerprints—just so long as nothing is messed up. Now, surely you can arrange somehow to get this body put on ice, so to speak, for at least twenty-four hours, till I fill in the holes that the police would pick on."

"Why don't you let me take you to the head of the Department—"

"Because it would take too long, and I'd start getting entangled in red tape, which makes me break out in a rash. And if the police clomp into this too soon, with their big boots, they could still louse it up or be too late. Just give me this much leeway, Dr Corrington.

Make sure, somehow, that nothing happens to that body. Even if I'm as wrong as anyone can be, it'll be just as useful a cadaver tomorrow. And what on earth could you be accused of if you merely helped to keep it untouched for one day?"

The Professor Emeritus cogitated this carefully and profoundly, and finally came up with a grin that was as young as the season.

"They're going to retire me as it is," he said. "Now they'll have to accuse me of being a juvenile delinquent."

When Simon Templar got back to Palm Beach, it was late enough for the telephone to report no reply from Mr Prend's Funeral Home (as he found it was actually listed) or from Ernest Cardman's recent number, now maintained by Mrs Yanstead. He was less surprised to learn from the Tradewind Motel that Mr Utterly's room also did not answer, and did not even bother to try the minor palazzo where Betty Winchester was guesting.

He called Corrington's home and learned that the body which was not Cardman's had been set aside pending further developments, and with that reassurance he was able to enjoy a quiet dinner at the Petite Marmite, and go to bed early with a book for company, and sleep for eight hours without a troublesome thought about death, murder, or deceit. Some of which stemmed from a hunch hardening into certainty that he now had all the threads of this incident gathered up and ready to be tied.

At ten o'clock in the morning, which seemed to him a safe and uncomplicating time, he arrived at Prend's Funeral Home. This was an edifice of modest but calculated dignity, rather suggestive of a miniature White House, located far enough from any cemetery to offer a choice of processional routes to suit all budgets, A touch on the bell button elicited a deep tolling from within, of a cathedral solemnity which could only irreverently have been called a chime, and after a suitable pause the door oozed ponderously open, disclosing the over-extended hair and rabbit features of Mr Prend himself.

Except for the physical shell, however, it was an effort to connect this apparition with the celebrant whom Simon had seen Twisting at the Peppermint Lounge. In vocational costume, instead of a snazzy Madras jacket and light tight pants, Mr Prend wore a suit of dull definitive black and sufficiently antique cut to underline its impregnable propriety. His face was composed into pliable blobs and blanks of potential compassion attention, tolerance, efficiency, sympathy, and a ruthless ability to distinguish the cheapskates from the sincere mourners who would blow the works for a properly expensive casket. Only the red-rimmed eyes behind his semi-invisible bifocals might have caused an initiated cynic to wonder if he had spent another night at the Peppermint Lounge or elsewhere, but to less mundane observers they could still have passed for nothing worse than the penalties of excessive condolence.

"Good morning, sir," intoned Mr Prend, with infinite discretion. "Can I help you?"

His voice was as consciously deep as the door-bell, and the Saint was hard put to sustain his own gravity.

He used his *Miami Guardian* masquerade again to get as far as the reception room, which was furnished in ebony wood and black leather, with a very deep purple carpet and matching velvet drapes, and gray walls on one of which hung a large chromolithograph of the Resurrection.

"There are not many questions I can answer," Mr Prend warned him. "As far as most details are concerned, I am bound by professional secrecy, just like a doctor or a lawyer."

"As a matter of general principle," Simon said, "how do you handle a body that's been willed to a hospital?"

"No differently from any other, for most of the proceedings. We embalm it and dress it and lay it in a casket for those who may wish to look their last on the remains—"

"Why embalm it, if it's going to be dissected anyway?"

"That makes the preservation even more important. And the institutions prefer us to do it. It is an art which we are highly trained for and experienced in."

"Is the body complete? I mean, with all its innards?"

Mr Prend winced.

"Of course. Without the internal organs, it would be of much less value for research."

"So then do they have a regular funeral?"

"That is entirely at the option of the relatives. There can be a procession to a church, if they wish, or a ceremony can be performed in the chapel which is attached to most of the better Funeral Homes. If the purpose of your article is to enlighten readers who may be thinking of bequeathing their remains to a research institution, you can assure them that everything can be handled with dignity and as reverently as any other disposal."

"Up to the point where the coffin isn't buried or cremated."

"That is the only difference. The mourners leave, having paid all their respects to the loved one, and as far as they are concerned it is all over. The Funeral Director then takes charge of the remains and delivers them as soon as possible to the designated institution, from whom he obtains a receipt. And that is the end of it."

It was coming to one of those situations where the Saint mentally craved the gesture of lighting a cigarette, but he knew that a genuine reporter from *The Miami Guardian* would have been too respectful of his surroundings and the pompous side of Mr Prend to succumb to it.

"In the case of Mr Cardman, whom you processed recently," he said, "how did that work out?"

"There was a simple service in our chapel, attended only by his immediate kin. And the remains were delivered to the University of Miami, as he wished, the next day."

"So they were here overnight, after any of the relatives saw them."

"Yes."

"The night during which your place was burgled, wasn't it?"

Mr Prend seemed to make an effort of recollection.

"Yes, it would have been that night."

"Then is it possible," said the Saint, "that the real object of whoever broke in was to switch Cardman's body for another one that you had here?"

"Preposterous!" Prend ejaculated. "What makes you think—"

"The body that you delivered to the University of Miami has already been un-identified: whoever it is, it isn't Cardman."

Mr Prend stared at him stiffly.

"But why would anyone do that?" he protested mechanically.

"To destroy the evidence of a murder. Someone who knew the ropes realized that if Cardman's body went to the University—which was something they hadn't counted on till that part of the will showed up—somebody in the lab might spot the signs of poisoning in those internal organs. The easy answer was a switch to another coffin that was booked for something final like a crematorium."

Mr Prend's roseate optics kindled at last like the tail lights of a car whose driver has belatedly trampled the brakes.

"That could explain it!" he gasped. "I never thought of it before . . . But who? Mr Cardman's niece was so charming. His nephew was a little difficult. But—"

"Neither of them made the funeral arrangements, did they? Being comparative strangers in town, they'd have had to ask someone who lived here to recommend an undertaker. Someone with previous experience."

"Yes, I suppose so. We rely a great deal on recommendations."

"In Cardman's case, it was probably Mrs Yanstead."

"Yes—yes, I suppose it was."

"Aloysius," said the Saint, chummily, "how much of the take did she cut you in on for shuffling the bodies?"

Mr Prend remained rigid for so long that Simon wondered briefly whether he had inadvertently become a candidate for his own services. But at last his catalepsy resolved itself into the wrathful indignation which after all was the only plausible form it could have taken.

"How dare you—"

"Aloysius," said the Saint, still more mildly, "according to your own explanation, Cardman's body would have to be switched for another one which wasn't going to be inspected by tender-hearted relatives who might actually look at it and start screaming about the new face you put on Uncle George. Nobody who busted in here out of the blue would know which of the corpses you had in stock would be good for the switch. Only the boss could have handled everything—but also been smart enough to set up some evidence of a bogus burglary to make it look like an outside job, just in case something went sour and he had to answer embarrassing questions. Should I take it that you're all organized and set up and ready to take a murder rap?"

"What gives you the right to talk about a murder?"

"I believe that's called an educated guess. First, you look for a motive. Anyone who expected to inherit his money could have that. And might have had an awful shock when a will turned up that left it all to somebody else. Then we ask, if he was poisoned—and he certainly wasn't shot or stabbed—who had the best chance to do it? At least two people. But who would have been most aware of the risks of poisoning, which had tripped up so many amateurs? Who would have been best placed to mislead the doctor about symptoms? Who would have realized first that Cardman's surprise bequest of his body to the

University could upset the whole beautiful applecart, who would know enough about the routines to see how it could still be propped up, who would know the local undertakers and which one would be most likely to go along with a little persuasion—"

"That's all," said a voice behind him.

Simon turned.

It was Velma Yanstead, as his ears had already told him, but his ears could not have told him that she would be holding an automatic in her pudgy hand, levelled at him from a distance at which it would be difficult to miss.

"I thought you were too smooth and good-looking to be a real reporter," she said, libellously. "But you don't talk like a policeman, either. What's your real name and what's your business?"

"Madam," Simon replied, courteously, "I'm best known as The Saint. I'm a meddler."

The name registered visibly on both of them, in different ways. Mr Prend seemed to wilt and deflate as if struck by a dreadful blight, but Mrs Yanstead seemed to swell and harden in the same proportion. There must have been something after all, Simon reflected with incurable philosophy, in that old adage about the female of the species.

"Well, you meddled once too often this time," she said. "I've read enough about you to know how you work. You're on your own, and you keep everything to yourself till you think it's all wrapped up. So you can just disappear, and it'll be months before anyone even wonders where you went."

"Such is fame," sighed the Saint.

Mrs Yanstead was no more amused than Queen Victoria. She had come in from the hallway, as had the Saint, but now she indicated a door on the other side of Mr Prend.

"We got to get rid of him now," she said sternly. "And you'll be no worse off than you are already."

She was now addressing Mr Prend, who gulped and swallowed his tonsils, his larynx, and possibly other things.

"But—"

"Go along with it, Al," Simon advised him, kindly. "Surely you can find room for me in there, in one of your king-sized caskets, alongside some scrawny stiff who's paid for a cremation. And no one will ever know . . . Except you might have to marry her, and give up that bleached blonde you've been dating in Miami Beach—"

"That's quite enough," Mrs Yanstead said, and prodded the Saint with her gun.

This was one of the most foolish things she ever did. Not because Simon was unduly stuffy or ticklish about being prodded, but because the touch of the gun enabled him to locate its position exactly without telegraphing any hint of his intention by glancing at it. His hands moved together like striking snakes, his left hand catching her wrist, his right hand striking the gun and bending her hand backwards with it. The one shot she fired shook the room like a thunderclap, but the muzzle of the automatic was already deflected before she could react and pull the trigger.

Simon Templar sat down in Mr Aloysius Prend's place at the desk, using the same gun to cover the two of them, and picked up the telephone.

"We can deny all of this," Mrs Yanstead said to her accomplice, who was now visibly trembling with a subtle but definite vibration that might have started a new wave at the Peppermint Lounge if it could only have been demonstrated there. "It's only his word against ours, and there are two of us—"

"I wouldn't bet too much on that," said the Saint dishearteningly. "I didn't wear a jacket on a warm day like this just to look like the correct respectable costume for visiting Funeral Homes. I wanted a place to hang a microphone and carry a miniature tape recorder, because

I know how skeptical some authorities are about my unsupported testimony." He opened his coat and showed them. "Wonderful things, these transistors. I wonder what Sherlock Holmes would have done with them—I must ask a friend of mine. Now would you like to give me the police number or have I got to ask the operator?"

LUCERNE: THE
RUSSIAN PRISONER

"Excuse me. You are the Saint. You must help me."

By that time Simon Templar thought he must have heard all the approaches, all the elegant variations. Some were amusing, some were insulting, some were unusual, most were routine, a few tried self-consciously to be original and attention-getting. He had, regrettably, become as accustomed to them as any Arthurian knight-errant must eventually have become. After all, how many breeds of dragons were there? And how many different shapes and colorations of damsels in distress?

This one would have about chalked up her first quarter-century, and would have weighed in at about five pounds per annum—not the high-fashion model's ratio, but more carnally interesting. She had prominent cheek-bones to build shadow frames around blindingly light blue eyes, and flax-white hair that really looked as if it had been born with her and not processed later. She was beautiful like some kind of mythological ice-maiden.

And she had the distinction of having condensed a sequence of inescapable clichés to a quintessence which could only have been surpassed by a chemical formula.

"Do sit down," Simon said calmly. "I'm sure your problem is desperate, or you wouldn't be bringing it to a perfect stranger—but have you heard of an old English duck called Drake? When they told him the Spanish Armada was coming, he insisted on finishing his game of bowls before he'd go out to cope with it. I've got a rather nice bowl here myself, and it would be a shame to leave it."

He carefully fixed a cube of coarse farmhouse bread on the small tines of his long-shafted fork, and dipped it in the luscious goo that barely bubbled in the chafing dish before him. When it was soaked and coated to its maximum burthen, he transferred it neatly to his mouth. Far from being an ostentatious vulgarity, this was a display of epicurean technique and respect, for he was eating fondue—perhaps the most truly national of Swiss delectables, that ambrosial blend of melted cheese perfumed with kirsch and other things, which is made nowhere better, than at the Old Swiss House in Lucerne, where he was lunching.

"I like that," she said.

He pushed the bread plate towards her and offered a fork, hospitably.

"Have some."

"No, thank you. I meant that I like the story about Drake. And I like it that you are the same—a man who is so sure of himself that he does not have to get excited. I have already had lunch. I was inside, and I could see you through the window. Some people at the next table recognized you and were talking about you. I heard the name, and it was like winning a big prize which I had not even hoped for."

She spoke excellent English, quickly, but in a rather stilted way that seemed to have been learned from books or vocal drill rather than light conversation, with an accent which he could not place immediately.

"A glass of wine, then? Or a liqueur?"

"A Benedictine, if you like. And some coffee, may I?"

He beckoned a waitress who happened to come out, and gave the order.

"You seem to know something about me," he said, spearing another piece of bread. "Is one supposed to know something about you, or are you a Mystery Woman?"

"I am Irina Jorovitch."

"Good for you. It doesn't have to be your real name, but at least it gives me something to call you." He speared another chunk of bread. "Now, you tell me your trouble. It's tedious, but we have to go through this in most of my stories, because I'm only a second-rate mind reader."

"I am Russian, originally," she said. "My family are from the part of Finland where the two countries meet, but since 1940 it has been all

Soviet. My father is Karel Jorovitch, and he was named for the district we came from. He is a scientist."

"Any particular science, or just a genius?"

"I don't know. He is a professor at the University of Leningrad. Of physics, I think. I do not remember seeing him except in pictures. During the war, my mother was separated from him, and she escaped with me to Sweden."

"You don't have a Swedish accent."

"Perhaps because I learnt English first from her, and I suppose she had a Finnish or a Russian accent. Then there were all sorts of teachers in Swedish schools. I speak everything like a mixture. But I learnt enough languages to get a job in a travel agency in Stockholm. My father could not get permission to leave Russia after the war, and my mother had learned to prefer the capitalist life and would not go back to join him. I don't think she was too much in love with him. At last there was a divorce, and she married a man with a small hotel in Göteborg, who adopted me so that I could have a passport and travel myself. But soon after, they were both killed in a car accident."

"I see . . . or do I? Your problem is that you don't know how to run a hotel?"

"No, that is for his own sons. But I thought that my father should be told that she was dead. I wrote to him, and somehow he received the letter—he was still at the University. He wrote back, wanting to know all about me. We began to write often. Now I didn't even have a mother, I had nobody, it was exciting to discover a real father and try to find out all about him. But then, one day, I got another letter from him which had been smuggled out, which was different from all the others."

The Saint sipped his wine. It was a native Johannisberg Rhonegold, light and bone-dry, the perfect punctuation for the glutinous goodness into which he was dunking.

"How different?"

"He said he could not stand it any more, the way he was living and what he was doing, and he wished he could escape to the West. He asked if I would be ready to help him. Of course I said Yes. But how? We exchanged several letters, discussing possibilities, quite apart from the other letters which he went on writing for the censors to read."

"How did you work that?"

"Through the travel agency, it was not so hard to find ways. And at last the opportunity came. He was to be sent to Geneva, to a meeting of the disarmament conference—not to take part himself, but to be on hand to advise the Soviet delegate about scientific questions. It seemed as if everything was solved. He only had to get out of the Soviet embassy, here in Switzerland, and he would be free."

The Saint's ease was no longer gently quizzical. His blue eyes, many southern shades darker than hers, had hardened as if sapphires were crystallizing in them. He was listening now with both ears and all his mind, but he went on eating with undiminished deference to the cuisine.

"So what's the score now?"

"I came here to meet him with some money, and to help him. When he escaped, of course, he would have nothing. And he speaks only Russian and Finnish . . . But something went wrong."

"What, exactly?"

"I don't know."

Until then, she had been contained, precise, reciting a synopsis that she must have vowed to deliver without emotion, to acquit herself in advance of the charge of being just another hysterical female with helpful hallucinations. But now she was leaning across the table towards him, twisting her fingers together, and letting her cold lovely face be twisted into unbecoming lines of tortured anxiety.

"Someone betrayed us. We had to trust many people who carried our letters. Who knows which one? I only know that yesterday, when he was to do it, I waited all day up the street where I could watch the entrance, in a car which I had hired, and in the evening he came out. But not by himself, as we had planned. He was driven out in an embassy car, sitting between two men who looked like gangsters—the secret police! I could only just recognize him, from a recent photograph he had sent me, looking around desperately as if he hoped to see me, as if I could have rescued him."

Her coffee and Benedictine arrived, and Simon said to the waitress, "You can bring me the same, in about five minutes."

He harpooned a prize corner crust, and set about mopping the dish clean of the last traces of fondue. He said, "You should have got here sooner. There's an old Swiss tradition which says that when fondue is being eaten, anyone who loses the bread off their fork has to kiss everyone else at the table. It must make for nice sociable eating . . . So what happened?"

"I followed them. It was all I could think of. If I lost him then, I knew I would lose him for ever. I thought at first they were taking him to the airport, to send him back to Russia, and I could make a fuss there. But no. They went to Lausanne, then on to here, and then still farther, to a house on the lake, with high walls and guards, and they took him in . . . Then I went to the police."

"And?"

"They told me they could do nothing. It was part of the Soviet embassy, officially rented for diplomatic purposes, and it could not be touched. The Russians can do whatever they like there, as if they were in Russia. And I know what they are doing. They are keeping my father there until they can send him back to Moscow—and then to Siberia. Unless they kill him first."

"Wouldn't that have been easier from Geneva?"

"There is another airport at Zürich, almost as close from this house, and without the newspaper men who will be at Geneva for the conference."

Letting his eyes wander around the quiet little square, Simon thought that you really had to have a paperback mind to believe tales like that in such a setting. The table where they sat outside the restaurant was under the shade of the awning, but he could have stretched a hand out into the sunshine which made it the kind of summer's day that travel brochures are always photographed on. And gratefully enjoying their full advertised money's worth, tourists of all shapes and sizes, the importance of that event, or trudging up the hill to gawk at the Lion Memorial carved in the rock to commemorate the Swiss mercenaries who died in Paris with unprofitable heroism defending the Tuileries against the French Revolution, or to the Glacier Garden above that which preserves the strange natural sculpture of much more ancient turnings—all with their minds happily emptied of everything but the perennial vacation problem of paying for their extra extravagances and souvenirs. Not one of them, probably, would have believed in this plot unless they saw it at home on television. But the Saint knew perhaps better than any man living how thinly the crust of peace and normalcy covered volcanic lavas everywhere in the modern world.

He turned back to Irina Jorovitch, and his voice was just as tolerantly good-humored as it had been ever since she had intruded herself with her grisly reminder of what to him were only the facts of life. He said, "And you think it should be a picnic for me to rescue him."

She said, "Not a picnic. No. But if any man on earth can do it, you can."

"You know, you could be right. But I was trying to take a holiday from all that."

"If you would want money," she said, "I have nothing worth your time to offer. But I could try to get it. I would do anything—anything!"

It was altogether disgraceful, he admitted, but he could do nothing to inhibit an inward reflex of response except try not to think about it.

"Gentleman adventurers aren't supposed to take advantage of offers like that," he said, with unfeigned regret.

"You must help me," she said again. "Please."

He sighed.

"All right," he said. "I suppose I must."

Her face lit up with a gladness that did the same things for it that the Aurora Borealis does to the Arctic snows. It was a reaction that he had seen many times, as if his mere consent to have a bash had vaporized all barriers. It would have been fatally intoxicating if he ever forgot how precariously, time after time, he had succeeded in justifying so much faith.

"It isn't done yet, darling," he reminded her. "Tell me more about this house."

It was on the southern shore of the Vierwaldstättersee, he learned, the more rugged and less accessible side which rises to the mingled tripper-traps and tax-dodger chalets of Bürgenstock, and by land it was reachable only by a second-to-secondary road which served nothing but a few other similarly isolated hermitages. Although it was dark when she passed it, she was sure there was no other residence nearby, so that anyone approaching in daylight would certainly be under observation long before he got close. The walls around the grounds were about seven feet high, topped with barbed wire, but with slits that the inmates could peep through—to say nothing of what electronic devices might augment their vigilance. Added to which, she had heard dogs barking as she drove past.

"Nothing to it," said the Saint, "if I hadn't forgotten to bring my invisible and radar-proof helicopter."

"You will think of something," she said, with rapturous confidence.

He lighted a cigarette and meditated for almost a minute. "You say this house is right on the lake?"

"Yes. Because at the next turning after I passed, my headlights showed the water."

"Do you think you could recognize it again, from the lake side?"

"I think so."

"Good. Then let's take a little boat ride."

He paid his bill, and finished his coffee while he waited for the change. Then they walked down the Löwenstrasse and across the tree-shaded promenades of the Nationalquai to the lake front. Just a few yards to the left there was a small marina offering a variety of water craft for hire, which he had already casually scouted without dreaming that he would ever use it in this way. With the same kind of companionship, perhaps, but not for this kind of mission . . . The Saint chose a small but comfortably upholstered runabout, the type of boat that would automatically catch the eye of a man who was out to impress a pretty girl—and that was precisely how he wanted them to be categorized by anyone who had a motive for studying them closely. Taking advantage of the weather and the informal customs of the country, he was wearing only a pair of light slacks and a tartan sport shirt, and Irina was dressed in a simple white blouse and gaily patterned dirndl, so that there was nothing except their own uncommon faces to differentiate them from any other holiday-making twosome.

And as he aimed the speedboat diagonally south-eastwards across the lake, with the breeze of their own transit tousling her short white-blond hair and moulding the filmy blouse like a tantalizing second skin against the thrusting mounds of her breasts, he had leisure to wish that they had been brought together by nothing more pre-emptive than one of those random holiday magnetisms which provide inexhaustible grist for the world's marriage and divorce mills in self-compensating proportions.

She had put on a pair of sunglasses when they left the restaurant, and out on the water the light was strong enough for Simon to take out a pair of his own which had been tucked in his shirt pocket. But they would be useful for more than protection against the glare.

"Get the most out of these cheaters when we start looking for the house," he told her as he put them on. "Don't turn your head and look at anything directly, just turn your eyes and keep facing somewhere else. Behind the glasses, anybody watching us won't be able to tell what we're really looking at.

"You think of everything. I will try to remember."

"About how far did you drive out of Lucerne to this house?"

"I cannot be sure. It seemed quite far, but the road was winding."

This was so femininely vague that he resigned himself to covering the entire southern shore if necessary. On such an afternoon, and with such a comely companion, it was a martyrdom which he could endure with beatific stoicism. Having reached the nearest probable starting point which he had mentally selected, he cut the engine down to a smooth idling gait and steered parallel to the meandering coast line, keeping a distance of about a hundred yards from the shore.

"Relax, Irina," he said. "Any house that's on this stretch of lake, we'll see. Meanwhile, we should look as if we're just out for the ride."

To improve this visual effect, he lowered himself from his hot-water-rodder's perch on the gunwale to the cushion behind the wheel, and she snuggled up to him. "Like this?" she asked seriously.

"More or less," he approved, with fragile gravity, and slipped an arm around her shoulders.

It was only when they had passed Kehrsiten, the landing where the funicular takes off up the sheer palisade to the hotels of Bürgenstock on its crest, that he began to wonder if she had overestimated her ability to identify the house to which Karel Jorovitch had been taken from an aspect which she had never seen. But he felt no change of tension in her as the boat purred along for some kilometers after that, until suddenly she stiffened and clutched him—but with the magnificent presence of mind to turn towards him instead of to the shore.

"There, I have seen it!" she gasped. "The white house with the three tall chimneys! I remember them!"

He looked to his right, over her flaxen head which had a disconcertingly pure smell which reminded him somehow of new-mown hay, and saw the only edifice she could have been referring to.

The tingle that went through him was an involuntary psychosomatic acknowledgement that the adventure had now become real, and he was well and truly hooked.

In order to study the place thoroughly and unhurriedly, he turned towards Irina, folded her tenderly in his arms, and applied his lips to hers. In that position, he could continue to keep his eyes on the house whilst giving the appearance of being totally preoccupied with radically unconnected pursuits.

It was surprisingly unpretentious, for a diplomatic enclave. He would have taken it for a large old-fashioned family house—or a house for a large old-fashioned family, according to the semantic preference of the phrase-maker. At any rate, it was not a refurbished mansion or a small re-converted hotel. Its most unusual feature was what she had already mentioned: the extraordinarily high wire-topped garden walls which came down at a respectable distance on both sides of it—not merely to the lake edge, but extending about twelve feet out into the water. And for the further discouragement of anyone who might still have contemplated going around them, those two barriers were joined by a rope linking a semicircle of small bright red buoys such as might have marked the limits of a safe bathing area, but which also served to bar an approach to the shore by boat—even if they were not anchored to some underwater obstruction which would have made access altogether impossible.

And on the back porch of the house, facing the lake, a square-shouldered man in a deck chair raised a pair of binoculars and examined them lengthily.

Simon was able to make all these observations in spite of the fact that Irina Jorovitch was cooperating in his camouflage with an ungrudging enthusiasm which was no aid at all to concentration.

Finally they came to a small headland beyond which there was a cove into which he could steer the boat out of sight of the watcher on the porch. Only then did the Saint release her, not without reluctance, and switched off the engine to become crisply businesslike again.

"Excuse the familiarity," he said. "But you know why I had to do it."

"I liked it, too," she said, demurely.

As the boat drifted to a stop, Simon unstrapped his wrist watch and laid it on the deck over the dashboard. He held his pen upright beside it to cast a shadow from the sun, and turned the watch to align the hour hand with the shadow, while Irina watched fascinated.

"Now, according to my boy scout training, halfway between the hour hand and twelve o'clock on the dial is due south," he explained. "I need a bearing on this place, to be able to come straight to it next time—and at night."

From there, he could no longer see anything useful of Lucerne. But across the lake, on the north side, he spotted the high peaked roof of the Park Hotel at Viznau, and settled on that as a landmark with multiple advantages. He sighted on it several times, until he was satisfied that he had established an angle accurately enough for any need he would have.

"This is all we can do right now," he said. "In broad daylight, we wouldn't have a prayer of getting him out. I don't even know what the odds will be after dark, but I'll try to think of some way to improve them."

The beautiful cold face—which he had discovered could be anything but cold at contact range—was strained and entreating.

"But what if they take him away before tonight?"

"Then we'll have lost a bet," he said grimly. "We could hustle back to Lucerne, get a car, come back here by road—I could find the place now, all right—and mount guard until they try to drive away with him. Then we could try an interception and rescue—supposing he isn't already gone, or they don't take him away even before we get back. On the other hand, they might keep him here for a week, and how could we watch all that time? Instead of waiting, we could be breaking in tonight . . . It's the kind of choice that generals are paid and pilloried for making."

She held her head in her hands.

"What can I say?"

Simon Templar prodded the starter button, and turned the wheel to point the little speedboat back towards Lucerne.

"You'll have to make up your own mind, Irina," he said relentlessly. "It's your father. You tell me, and we'll play it in your key."

There was little conversation on the return drive. The decision could only be left to her. He did not want to influence it, and he was glad it was not up to him, for either alternative seemed to have the same potentiality of being as catastrophically wrong as the other.

When he had brought the boat alongside the dock and helped her out, he said simply: "Well?"

"Tonight," she replied resolutely. "That is the way it must be."

"How did you decide?"

"As you would have, I think. If the nearest man on the dock when we landed wore a dark shirt, I would say tonight. It was a way of tossing up, without a coin. How else could I choose?"

Simon turned to the man in the blue jersey who was nearest, who was securing the boat to its mooring rings.

"Could we reserve it again tonight?" he inquired in German. "The Fräulein would like to take a run in the moonlight."

"At what time?" asked the attendant, unmoved by romantic visions. "Usually I close up at eight."

"At about nine," said the Saint, ostentatiously unfolding a hundred-franc note from his wad. "I will give you two more of these when I take the boat, and you need not wait for us. I will tie it up safely when we come back."

"*Jawohl, mein Herr!*" agreed the man, with alacrity. "Whenever you come, at nine or later, I shall be here."

Simon and Irina walked back over the planking to the paved promenade where natives and visitors were now crisscrossing, at indicatively different speeds, on their homeward routes. The sun had already dropped below the high horizons to the west, and the long summer twilight would soon begin.

"Suppose we succeed in this crazy project," he said. "Have you thought about what we do next?"

"My father will be free. I will book passage on a plane and take him back to Sweden with me."

"Your father will be free, but will you? And will I? Or for how long? Has it occurred to you, sweetheart, that the Swiss government takes a notoriously dim view of piratical operations on their nice neutral soil, even with the best of motives? And the Russkis won't hesitate to howl their heads off at this violation of their extra-territorial rights."

Her step faltered, and she caught his arm.

"I am so stupid," she said humbly. "I should have thought of that. Instead, I was asking you to become a criminal, to the Swiss Government, instead of a hero. Forgive me." Then she looked up at him in near terror. "Will you give it up because of that?"

He shook his head, with a shrug and a wry smile.

"I've been in trouble before. I'm always trying to keep out of it, but Fate seems to be against me."

"Through the travel agency, perhaps I can arrange something to help us to get away. Let me go back to my hotel and make some telephoning."

"Where are you staying?"

"A small hotel, down that way." She pointed vaguely in the general direction of the Schwanenplatz and the older town which lies along the river under the ancient walls which protected it five centuries ago. "It is all I can afford," she said defensively. "I suppose you are staying here? Or at the Palace?"

They were at the corner of the Grand National Hotel and the Haldenstrasse.

"Here. It's the sort of place where travel bureaux like yours send people like me," he murmured. "So you go home and see what you can organize, and I'll see what I can work out myself. Meet me back here at seven. I'm in room 129." He flagged a taxi which came cruising by. "Dress up prettily for dinner, but nothing fussy—and bring a sweater, because it'll be chilly later on that thar lake."

This time he didn't have to take advantage of a situation. She put her lips with a readiness which left no doubt as to how far she would have been willing to develop the contact in a less public place.

"See you soon," he said, and closed the taxi door after her, thoughtfully.

He had a lot to think about.

Without unchivalrously depreciating the value of any ideas she might have or phone calls she could make, he would not have been the Saint if he could have relied on them without some independent backing of his own. He had softened in many ways, over the years, but not to the extent of leaving himself entirely in the hands of any female, no matter how entrancing.

By seven o'clock, when she arrived, he had some of the answers, but his plan only went to a certain point and he could not project beyond that.

"I think I've figured a way to get into that house," he told her. "And if the garrison isn't too large and lively we may get out again with your father. But what happens after that depends on how hot the hue and cry may be."

She put down her sweater and purse on one of the beds—she had found her way to his room unannounced, and knocked on the door, and when he opened it she had been there.

"I have been telephoning about that, as I promised," she said. "I have arranged for a hired car and a driver to be waiting for us at Brunnen—that is at the other end of the lake, closer to the house than this, and just about as close to Zürich. He will drive us to the airport. Then, I have ordered through the travel agency to have a small private plane waiting to fly us all out."

"A private charter plane—how nice and simple," he murmured. "But can you afford it?"

"Of course not. I told them it was for a very rich invalid, with his private nurse and doctor. That will be you and I. When we are in Sweden and they give us the bill I shall have to explain everything, and I shall lose my job, but my father will be safe and they cannot bring us back."

He laughed with honest admiration.

"You're quite amazing."

"Did I do wrong?" She was crestfallen like a child that has been suddenly turned on, in fear of a slap.

"No, I mean it. You worked all that out while you were changing your clothes and fixing your hair, and you make it sound so easy and obvious. Which it is—now you've told me. But I recognize genius when I see it. And what a lot of footling obstacles disappear when it isn't hampered by scruples!"

"How can I have them when I must save my father's life? But what you have to do is still harder. What is your plan?"

"I'll tell you at dinner."

In an instant she was all femininity again.

"Do I look all right?"

She invited inspection with a ballerina's pirouette. She had put on a simple dress that matched her eyes and moulded her figure exactly where it should, without vulgar ostentation but clearly enough to be difficult to stop looking at. The Saint did not risk rupturing himself from such an effort.

"You're only sensational," he assured her. "If you weren't, I wouldn't be hooked on this caper."

"Please?"

"I wouldn't be chancing a bullet or a jail sentence to help you."

"I know. How can I thank you?" She reached out and took his right hand in both of hers. "Only to tell you my heart will never forget."

With an impulsively dramatic gesture, she drew his hand to her and placed it directly over her heart. The fact that a somewhat less symbolic organ intervened did not seem to occur to her, but it imposed on him some of the same restraint that a seismograph would require to remain unmoved at the epicenter of an earthquake.

"Don't I still have to earn that?" said the Saint, with remarkable mildness.

When they got to the Mignon Grill at the Palace Hotel on the other side of the Kursaal ("*I promised Dino last night I'd come in for his special Lobster Thermidor, before I had any idea what else I'd be doing tonight,*" Simon explained, "*but anyhow we should have one more good meal before they put us on bread and water.*"), he told her how he was hoping to carry out the abduction, and once again she was completely impersonal and businesslike, listening with intense attention.

"I think it could work," she said at the end, nodding with preternatural gravity. "Unless . . . There is one thing you may not have thought of."

"There could be a dozen," he admitted. "Which one have you spotted?"

"Suppose they have already begun to brain-wash him—so that he does not trust us."

Simon frowned.

"Do you think they could?"

"You know how everyone in a Soviet trial always pleads guilty and begs to be punished? They have some horrible secret method . . . If they have done it to him, he might not even want to be rescued."

"That would make it a bit sticky," he said, reflectively. "I wonder how you un-brain-wash somebody?"

"Only a psychologist would know. But first we must get him to one. If it is like that, you must not hesitate because of me. If you must knock him out, I promise not to become silly and hysterical."

"That'll help, anyway," said the Saint grimly.

The baby lobster were delicious, and he was blessed with the nerveless appetite to enjoy every bite. In fact, the prospect that lay ahead was a celestial seasoning that no chef could have concocted from all the herbs and spices in his pharmacopeia.

But the time came when anticipation could not be prolonged any more, and had to attain reality. They walked back to the Grand National, and he picked up a bag which he had left at the hall porter's desk when they went out. It was one of those handy zippered plastic bags with a shoulder strap which airlines emblazon with their insignia and distribute to overseas passengers to be stuffed with all those odds and ends which travellers never seem able to get into their ordinary luggage, and Simon had packed it with certain requisites for their expedition which would have been fatal to the elegant drape of his coat if he had tried to crowd all of them into various pockets. The boat was waiting at the marina, and in a transition that seemed to flow with the smoothness of a cinematic effect they were aboard and on their way into the dark expanse of the lake.

Simon followed the shore line to Viznau before he turned away to the right. From his bag he had produced a hiker's luminous compass, with the aid of which he was able to set a sufficiently accurate course to retrace the makeshift bearing be had taken that afternoon between his wrist watch and the sun. He opened the throttle, and the boat lifted gently and skimmed. Irina Jorovitch put on her cardigan and buttoned it, keeping down in the shelter of the windshield. They no longer talked, for it would only have been idle chatter.

The water was liquid glass, dimpling lazily to catch the reflection of a light or a star, except where the wake stretched behind like a trail of swift-melting snow. Above the blackness ahead, the twinkling façades of Bürgenstock high against the star-powdered sky were a landmark this time to be kept well towards the starboard beam. Halfway across, as best he could judge it, he broke the first law by switching off the running lights, but there were no other boats out there to threaten a collision. Then when the scattered lights on the shore ahead drew closer he slacked speed again to let the engine noise sink to a soothing purr that would have been scarcely audible from the shore, or at least vague enough to seem distant and unalarming.

He thought he should have earned full marks for navigation. The three tall chimneys that he had to find rose black against the Milky Way as he came within perception range of curtained windows glowing dimly over the starboard bow, and he cruised softly on beyond them into the cove where he had paused on the afternoon reconnaissance.

This time, however, he let the boat drift all the way in to the shore where his cat's eyes could pick out a tiny promontory that was almost as good as a private pier. He jumped off as the bow touched, carrying the anchor, which he wedged down into a crevice to hold the boat snugly against the land.

Back in the boat, he stripped quickly down to the swimming trunks which he had worn under his clothes. From the airline bag he took a pair of wire-cutting pliers, and one of those bulky "pocket" knives equipped with a small tool-shop of gadgets besides the conventional blades, which he stuffed securely under the waistband of his trunks. Then came a flashlight, which he gave to Irina, and a small automatic pistol.

"Do you know how to use this, if you have to?" he asked.

"Yes. And I shall not be afraid to. I have done a lot of shooting—for sport."

"The safety catch is here."

He gave her the gun and guided her thumb to feel it.

She put it in her bag, and then he helped her ashore.

"The road has to be over there," he said, "and it has to take you to the gates which you saw from your car. You can't possibly go wrong. And you remember what we worked out. Your car has broken down, and you want to use their phone to call a garage."

"How could I forget? And when they don't want to let me in, I shall go on talking and begging as long as I can."

"I'm sure you can keep them listening for a while, at any rate. Is your watch still the same as mine?" They put their wrists together and she turned on the flashlight for an instant. "Good. Just give me until exactly half-past before you go into action . . . Good luck!"

"Good luck," she said, and her arms went around him and her lips searched for his once more before he turned away.

The water that he waded into was cold enough to quench any wistful ardour that might have distracted his concentration from the task ahead. He swam very hard, to stimulate his circulation, until his system had struck a balance with the chill, out and around the western arm of the little bay, and then as he curved his course towards the house with the three chimneys he slackened his pace to reduce the churning sounds of motion, until by the time he was within earshot of anyone in the walled garden he was sliding through the water as silently as an otter.

By that time his eyes had accommodated to the darkness so thoroughly that he could see one of the dogs sniffing at a bush at one corner of the back porch, but he did not see any human sentinel. And presently the dog trotted off around the side of the house without becoming aware of his presence.

Simon touched the rope connecting two of the marker buoys enclosing the private beach, feeling around it with a touch like a feather, but he could detect no wire intertwined with it. If there were any alarm device connected with it, therefore, it was probably something mechanically attached to the ends which would be activated by any tug on the rope. The Saint took great care not to do this as he cut through it with the blade of his boy-scout knife. But hardly a hand's breadth below the surface of the water, making the passage too shallow to swim through, his delicately exploring fingers traced a barrier of stout wire netting supported by the buoys and stretched between their moorings, which would have rudely halted any small boat that tried to shoot in to the shore. He could feel that the wire was bare, apparently not electrified, but just in case it might also be attached to some warning trigger he touched it no less gingerly as he used his wire-cutters to snip out a section large enough to let him float through.

The luminous dial of his watch showed that he still had almost five minutes to spare from the time he had allowed himself. He waited patiently, close to the projecting side wall, until the first dog barked on the other side of the house.

A moment later, the other one chimed in.

A man came out of the back door and descended the verandah steps, peering to left and right in the direction of the lake. But coming from the lighted house, it would have to take several minutes for his pupils to dilate sufficiently for his retinas to detect a half-submerged dark head drifting soundlessly shorewards in the star-shadow of the wall. Secure in that physiological certainty, the Saint paddled silently on into the lake bank, using only his hands like fins and making no more disturbance than a roving fish.

Apparently satisfied that there was no threat from that side, the man turned and started back up the porch steps.

Simon slithered out of the water as noiselessly as a snake, and darted after him. The man had no more than set one foot on the verandah when the Saint's arm whipped around his throat from behind, and tightened with a subtle but expert pressure . . .

As the man went limp, Simon lowered him quietly to the boards. Then he swiftly peeled off his victim's jacket and trousers and put them on himself. They were a scarecrow fit, but for that nonce the Saint was not thinking of appearances: his main object was to confuse the watchdogs' sense of smell.

The back door was still slightly ajar, and if there were any alarms wired to it the guard must have switched them off before he opened it. The Saint went through without hesitation, and found himself in a large old-fashioned kitchen. Another door on the opposite side logically led to the main entrance hall. Past the staircase was the front door of the house, which was also ajar, meaning that another guard had gone out to investigate the disturbance at the entrance gate. The Saint crossed the hall like a hasty ghost and went on out after him.

The dogs were still barking vociferously in spite of having already aroused the attention they were supposed to, as is the immoderate habit of dogs, and their redundant clamor was ear-splitting enough to have drowned much louder noises than the Saint's barefoot approach. One of them did look over its shoulder at him as he came down the drive, but was deceived as he had hoped it would be by the familiar scent of his borrowed clothing and by the innocuous direction from which he came; it turned and resumed its blustering baying at Irina, who was pleading with the burly man who stood inside the gate.

The whole scene was almost too plainly illuminated under the glare of an overhead floodlight, but the man was completely preoccupied with what was in front of him, doubtfully twirling a large iron key around a stubby forefinger, as Simon came up behind him and slashed one hand down on the back of his neck with a sharp smacking sound. The man started to turn, from pure reflex, and could have seen the Saint's hand raised again for a lethal follow-up before his eyes rolled up and he crumpled where he stood. The dogs stopped yapping at last and licked him happily, enjoying the game, as Simon took the key from him and put it in the massive lock. Antique as it looked, its tumblers turned with the smoothness of fresh oil, and Simon pulled the gate open.

"How wonderful!" she breathed. "I was afraid to believe you could really do it."

"I wasn't certain myself, but I had to find out."

"But why—" She fingered the sleeve that reached only halfway between his elbow and his wrist.

"I'll explain another time," he said. "Come on—but be quiet, in case there are any more of them."

She tiptoed with him back to the house. The hallway was deathly still, the silent emptiness of the ground floor emphasized by the metronome ticking of a clock. Simon touched her and pointed upwards, and she climbed the stairs behind him.

The upper landing was dark, so that a thin strip of light underlining one door helpfully indicated the only occupied room. The Saint took out his knife again and opened the longest blade, holding it ready for lightning use as a silent weapon if the door proved to be unlocked— which it did. He felt no resistance to a tentative fractional pressure after he had stealthily turned the door-knob. He balanced himself, flung it open, and went in.

The only occupant, a pale shock-headed man in trousers and shirtsleeves, shrank back in the chair where he sat, staring.

"Professor Jorovitch, I presume?" said the Saint unoriginally.

Irina brushed past him.

"Papa!" she cried.

Jorovitch's eyes dilated, fixed on the automatic which Simon had lent her, which waved in her hand as if she had forgotten she had it. Bewilderment and terror were the only expressions on his face.

Irina turned frantically to the Saint.

"You see, they have done it!" she wailed. "Just as I was afraid. We must get him away. Quick—do what you have to!"

Simon Templar shook his head slowly.

"No," he said. "I can't do that."

She stared at him.

"Why? You promised—"

"No, I didn't, exactly. But you did your best to plant the idea in my head. Unfortunately, that was after I'd decided there was something wrong with your story. I was bothered by the language you used, like 'the capitalist life,' and always carefully saying 'Soviet' where most people say 'Russian,' and saying that hearing my name was 'like winning a big prize' instead of calling it a miracle or an answer to prayer, as most people brought up on this side of the Curtain would do. And being so defensive about your hotel. And then when we came over this afternoon I noticed there was no Russian flag flying here, as there would be on diplomatic property."

"You're mad," she whispered.

"I was, rather," he admitted, "when I suspected you might be trying to con me into doing your dirty work for you. So I called an old acquaintance of mine in the local police, to check on some of the facts."

The gun in her hand levelled and cracked.

The Saint blinked, but did not stagger. He reached out and grabbed her hand as she squeezed the trigger again, and twisted the automatic out of her fingers.

"It's only loaded with blanks," he explained apologetically. "I thought it was safer to plant that on you, rather than risk having you produce a gun of your own, with real bullets in it."

"A very sensible precaution," said a gentle new voice. It belonged to a short rotund man in a pork-pie hat, with a round face and round-rimmed glasses, who emerged with as much dignity as possible from the partly-open door of the wardrobe.

Simon said, "May I introduce Inspector Oscar Kleinhaus? He was able to tell me the true story—that Karel Jorovitch had already defected, weeks ago, and had been given asylum without any publicity, and that he was living here with a guard of Swiss security officers until he completed all the information he could give about the Russian espionage apparatus in Switzerland. Oscar allowed me to go along with your gag for a while—partly to help you convict yourself beyond any hope of a legal quibble, and partly as an exercise to check the protection arrangements."

"Which apparently leave something to be desired," Kleinhaus observed, mildly.

"But who would have thought it'd be me they had to keep out?" Simon consoled him magnanimously.

The two guards from the bank and the front of the house came in from the landing, looking physically none the worse for wear but somewhat sheepish—especially the one who was clad only in his underthings.

"They weren't told anything about my plan, only that they were going to be tested," Simon explained, as he considerately shucked off and returned the borrowed garments. "But they were told that if I snuck close enough to grab them or slap them they were to assume they could just as well have been killed, and to fall down and play dead. We even thought of playing out the abduction all the way to Zürich."

"That would have been going too far," Kleinhaus said. "But I would like to know what was to happen if you got away from here."

"She said she'd arrange for a car to pick us up at Brunnen, and there would be a light plane waiting for a supposed invalid at the Zürich airport—which would have taken him at least as far as East Germany."

"They will be easy to pick up," Kleinhaus sighed. "Take her away."

She spat at the Saint as the guards went to her, and would have clawed out his eyes if they had not held her efficiently.

"I'm sorry, darling," the Saint said to her. "I'm sorry it had to turn out like this. I liked your story much better."

The irony was that he meant it. And that she would never believe him.

PROVENCE: THE

HOPELESS HEIRESS

Simon Templar saw her again as he was sampling the *Chausson du Roi* at La Petite Auberge at Noyes.

A *chausson* means, literally, a bedroom slipper, hence, in the vocabulary of French cuisine, it is also the word for a sort of apple turnover, which bears a superficial resemblance to a folded slipper with the heel tucked into the toe. The *Chausson du Roi,* however, as befits its royal distinction, is not a dessert, and contains nothing so commonplace as apples. It envelops sweetbreads liberally blended with the regal richness of truffles, and it is one of the specially famous entrées of La Petite Auberge, whose name so modestly means only "the little inn," but which is one of the mere dozen restaurants in all of France decorated by the canonical *Guide Michelin* with the three stars which are its highest accolade. Noyes is in the south, not far from Avignon of the celebrated bridge, and is a very small village of absolutely no importance except to its nearest neighbors, which hardly anyone else would ever have heard of but for the procession of gourmets beating a path to a superior munch-trap. And she personified one rather prevalent concept of the type to be expected in such company.

She had truly brown hair, the rare and wonderful natural color of the finest leather, styled with careless simplicity, with large brown eyes to match, a small nose, a generous mouth, and exquisitely even teeth, all assembled with a symmetry that might have been breath-taking—if it had been seen in a slightly concave mirror.

Because she was fat.

Simon estimated that she probably scaled about 180 pounds bone dry, the same as himself. Except that his pounds were all muscle stretched over more than two yards of frame, whereas she had to carry too many of them horizontally, with a head less height, in billows of rotundity that might have delighted Rubens but would have appalled Vargas. It was a great pity, he thought, for without that excess weight even her figure might have been beautiful: her ankles were still trim and her calves not too enlarged, and her hands were small and shapely. But from the way she was tucking into the provender on her plate there seemed to be little prospect of her central sections being restored to proportion with her extremities.

She wore no ring on the third finger of her left hand, and the man with her was certainly old enough to be her father, but there was no physical similarity between them. He was gray-haired and gray-eyed, with a thin, meticulously sculptured, gray mustache, and the rest of him was also as thin as she was obese. But nothing else about him confirmed the ascetic promise of his slenderness. To mitigate the warmth of the summer evening, his dark gray suit had been custom tailored of some special fabric, perhaps even custom woven, which combined the conventionally imperative drab-ness of correct male attire with the obvious lightness of a tissue of feathers; his snowy shirt was just solid enough to be opaque without pretending to be as substantial as the least useful handkerchief; his cuff-links were cabochon emeralds no bigger than peanuts, and his wrist watch was merely one different link in a broad loose bracelet which anyone without Simon Templar's assayer's eye would have dismissed as Mexican silver instead of the solid platinum that it was. In every detail, examined closely enough, there was revealed a man who carved nothing but the best of everything—but with a discrimination refined to the ultimate snobbery of modesty.

Simon seized a chance to satisfy his curiosity when the dining-room hostess (he had noted an increasing number of personable and competent young women in such posts of recent years, and wondered if it would be correct to call them *maîtresses d'hôtel*) came by to inquire whether everything was to his pleasure.

"At the corner table?" she said, answering his return question. "That is Mr Saville Wakerose. I should have thought you would know him. Isn't he one of your greatest gourmets?"

The Saint had never set eyes on Mr Wakerose before that summer, but the name was instantly familiar, and at once it became hardly a coincidence at all that they should have been eating in the same restaurants on three consecutive days—the Côte d'Or at Saulieu, the Pyramide at Vienne, and now the Petite Auberge at Noyes. For each one was a three-starred shrine of culinary art, and they were spaced along the route from Paris to the Mediterranean at distances which could only suggest an irresistible schedule to any gastrophilic pilgrim with the time to spare. In which category Simon Templar was an enthusiastic amateur when other obligations and temptations permitted, but Saville Wakerose was a dean of professionals. In twenty years of magazine articles, newspaper columns, lecture tours, and general publicity, he had established his authority as a connoisseur of food and wine and an arbiter of general elegance at such an altitude that even princes and presidents were reported to cringe from his critiques of their hospitality. And he had not merely parlayed his avocation into a comfortable living in which the best things in life were free or deductible, but he had climaxed it some four years ago by marrying the former Adeline Inglis, the last scion of one of those pre-welfare-state fortunes, who in her débutante days had inspired ribald parodists to warble:

> *Sweet Adeline,*
> *For you I pine;*
> *Your dough divine*
> *Should mate with mine . . .*

Since then she had had five or six husbands, in spite of whom she still had plenty of dough left when Saville Wakerose added himself to the highly variegated roster. He was to be the last of the list, for a couple of years later, before the habitual rift could develop in their marital bliss, a simple case of influenza followed by common pneumonia suddenly retired her for all time from the matrimonial market, leaving him presumably well consoled in his bereavement.

"He has a very young wife," Simon observed, with intentional discretion.

The hostess smiled.

"That is not his wife. She is his *belle-fille*, Miss Flane."

Belle-fille does not mean what it might suggest to anyone with a mere smattering of French. The fat girl was Wakerose's step-daughter. And with that information another card spun out of the Saint's mental index of trivial recollections from his catholic acquaintance with all forms of journalism. One of Adeline Inglis's earliest husbands, and the father of her only experiment in maternity, had been Orlando Flane, a film star who had shone in the last fabulous days before Hollywood became only a suburb instead of the capital of the moving picture world.

That, then, would have to be the one-time photographers' darling Rowena Flane, whose father had never had much talent and was rated nothing but an alcoholic problem after the divorce, and who blew out what was left of his brains soon afterwards, but who had left her those still discernible traits of the sheer impossible beauty which had made him the idol of millions of sex-starved females before their fickle frustrations transferred themselves to the school of scratching, mumbling, or jittering goons who had succeeded him.

Adeline Inglis, Simon seemed to recall, searching his memory for the imprint of some inconsequential news photo, had taken advantage of the best coiffeurs, couturiers, and cosmeticians that money could buy to succeed in looking like a nice well-groomed middle-class matron dolled up for a community bridge party. Her daughter, fortuitously endowed with a far better basic structure, had not given it a fraction of that break. But he wondered why somebody close to her hadn't pointed out that even if she suffered from some glandular misfortune, there were better treatments for it than to indulge her appetite as she seemed inclined to do. Most especially somebody like Saville Wakerose, who through all his professional gourmandizing had taken obvious pride in preserving the figure of an aesthete.

And from that not so casual speculation began an incident which brought the Saint to the brink of a fate worse than . . . But let us not be jumping the gun.

Although he had never been so crude as to even glance towards Rowena Flane and her step-father while making his inquiries, Simon knew that the recognition had been mutual, and when the hostess's peregrinations took her to the corner table he had no doubt that some equally sophisticated inquiry was made about himself. But he would not have predicted that it would have the result it did.

It was one of those mild and ideal evenings in May, when summer often begins in Provence, and after succumbing to an exquisite miniature *Soufflé au Grand Marnier* he was happy to accede to the suggestion of having his coffee served outside under the trees. Wakerose and Rowena had started and finished before him and were already at a table on the front terrace which Simon had to pass in search of one for himself, and Mr Wakerose stood up and said: "Excuse me, Mr Templar. We seem destined to keep crossing paths on this trip. Why not give in to it and join us?"

"Why not?" Simon said agreeably, but looked at the fat girl for his cue.

She smiled her endorsement with a readiness which suggested that the invitation could actually have been her idea.

"Thank you," Simon said, and sat down beside her.

Liqueurs came with the coffee—a Benedictine for her, a Châtelaine Armagnac for Mr Wakerose. Simon decided to join him in the latter.

"It makes an interesting change," said Mr Wakerose. "And I like to enjoy the libations of the territory, whenever they are reasonably potable. And after all, we are nowhere near Cognac, but much nearer the latitude of Bordeaux,"

"And those black-oak Gascon casks make all the difference from ageing in the *limousins*," Simon concurred, tasting appreciatively. "I think it takes a harder and drier brandy to follow the more rugged wines of the Rhône—like this."

As an exercise in one-upmanship it was perhaps a trifle flashy, but he had the satisfaction of seeing Saville Wakerose blink.

"Are you just on the trail of food and drink?" Rowena asked. "Or is it something more exciting?"

"Just eating my way around," said the Saint carelessly, having accustomed himself to these gambits as a formality that had to be suffered with good humor. "That can be exciting enough, in places like this."

"You sound as if you'd evolved a formula for handling silly questions. But I suppose you've had to."

It was Simon's turn to blink—though he was sufficiently on guard, from instinct and habit, to permit himself no more than a smile. But it was a smile warmed by the surprised recognition of a perceptivity which he had been guilty of failing to expect from a poor little fat rich girl.

"You've probably had to do the same, haven't you?" he said, and it was almost an apology.

"It appears that we all know each other," Mr Wakerose observed drily. "Although I did forget the ceremonial introductions. But I'm sure Mr Templar made the same subtle inquiries about us that we made about him."

Simon realized that Wakerose was also a gamesman, and nodded his sporting acknowledgement of the ploy.

"Doesn't everybody?" he returned blandly. "However, I was telling the truth. The only clues I'm following are in menus. I stopped looking for trouble years ago—because quite enough of it started looking for me."

Saville Wakerose trimmed his cigar.

"We haven't only been eating our way around, as you put it, in all those places where you've been seeing us," he said. "We've also been seeing all the historic sights. Are you familiar with the history of these parts, Mr Templar?"

Simon joyously spotted the trap from afar.

"Only what I've read in the guide books, like everyone else," he said, skirting it neatly and leaving the other to follow.

Wakerose just as gracefully sidestepped his own pitfall.

"Rowena loves history, or at least historical novels," he explained, "and I prefer to read cook books. But I let her drag me around the ancient monuments, and she lets me show her the temples of the table, and it makes an interesting symbiosis."

It was a stand-off, like two duellists stopped by a mutual discovery of respect for the other's skill, and accepting a tacit truce while deciding how—or whether—to continue.

Simon was perfectly content to leave it that way. He turned to Rowena again with a new friendliness, and said, "Historical novels cover a lot of ground, between deluges—from the Flood to Prohibition. Do you like all of 'em, or are you hooked on any particular period?"

"It's not the period so much as the atmosphere," she said. "When I want to relax and be entertained, I want romance and glamor and a happy ending. I can't stand this modern obsession with everything sordid and complicated and depressing."

"But you don't think life only started to be sordid and depressing less than a hundred years ago?"

"Of course not. I know that in many ways it was much worse. But for some reason, when writers look at the world around them they only seem to see the worst of it, or that's all they want to talk about. But when they look back, they bring out the best and the happiest things."

"And that's all you want to see?"

"Yes, if I'm paying for it. Why spend money to be depressed?"

"I could see your point," Simon said deliberately, "if you were a poor struggling working girl with indigent parents and a thriftless husband, dreaming of an escape she'll never have. But if we put the cards on the table, and pretend we know who you are—why do you need that escape?"

Wakerose had suddenly begun to beam like an emaciated Buddha.

"This is prodigious," he said. "Mr Templar is putting you on, Rowena."

"I didn't mean to," Simon said quickly, but without taking his eyes off her. "It was meant as an honest question."

"Then you tell me honestly," she said, "why a rich girl with no worries shouldn't prefer to dream about knights in shining armor or dashing cavaliers, instead of the kind of men she sees all the time."

"Because she should be sophisticated enough to know that they're the only kind she could live with—or who could live with her. The day after this historical hero swept her off her feet, she'd start trying to housebreak him. She'd decide that she couldn't stand the battered old tin suit he rescued her in, and take him down to the smithy for a new one, which she would pick for him. The cavalier who spread his coat over a puddle for her to walk on with her dainty feet would find that she expected to repeat the performance at home while he was wearing it."

"Is that really what you think about women—or just about me, Mr Templar?"

"It couldn't possibly be personal, Miss Flane, because I never had any reason to think about you before," said the Saint calmly and pleasantly. "It's what I think about most modern women, and especially American women. They want a lion as far as the altar, and a lap-dog from there on. They think that chivalry is a great wheeze for getting cigarettes lighted and doors opened and lots of alimony, but they insist that they're just as good as a man in every field where there's no advantage in pleading femininity. So being accustomed to having the best of it both ways, they'd go running back to Mother or their lawyers if the fine swaggering male who swept them off their feet had the nerve to think he could go on being the boss after he'd carried them over the bridal threshold. The difference is that some motherless poor girls might figure it was better to put up with that horrible brute of a Prince than go back to being Cinderella, but the rich girl has no such problem."

Her big brown eyes darkened, but it was not with anger. And he was finding it a little less easy to meet her gaze.

"How do you know what other problems she has?" she retorted. "Or does being called the Robin Hood of Modern Crime make you feel you have to hate all rich people on principle?"

"Not for a moment," he said. "Some of my best friends are millionaires. I've even become fairly rich myself—not by your standards, of course, but enough so that nobody could write a check that'd make me do anything I didn't want to. Which is all I ever wanted."

"Well spoken, sir," murmured Wakerose with delighted irony. "Rowena will be glad to know that at last she's met one man who isn't a fortune hunter."

"Thank you," said the Saint. "At this stage of my chameleon career, it's cheering to find one crime I still haven't been accused of."

"I didn't mean to be rude with that Robin Hood crack," Rowena said. "It was meant as an honest question, like yours."

"And an understandable one," Simon said cheerfully. "So if you're worried about all the jewels you've got with you, I give you my word of honor I won't steal them while you're here. Where is your next stop?"

Wakerose chuckled again.

"I'm afraid we're staying here for at least a week, while Rowena explores all the ruins within reasonable driving range, before and after the luncheon stops which I shall select. I have convinced her that this is a much more civilized procedure than trying to combine transit with tourism, unpacking in a different hotel every night and having to pack up again every morning to set forth like gypsies without even a bathroom to call our own. Here we are assured of modern rooms and comfortable beds and clean clothes hung up in our closets, and returning in the evening is a relaxation instead of a scramble. So you will have left long before us."

"I knew there'd be a catch somewhere. So what are you planning to see tomorrow?"

"Nothing but a very unhistoric local garage, unfortunately. The fuel pump on my car elected to break down this afternoon—luckily, we were only just outside Châteaurenard. I expect to spend tomorrow spurring on the mechanic to get the repair finished by the end of the day and pretending I know exactly what he should be doing, while hoping that he will not detect my ignorance and take advantage of it to manufacture lengthy and expensive complications."

Simon could not have told anyone what made him do it, except that in a vague but superbly Saintly way it might have seemed too rare an opportunity to pass up, to take the wind out of Saville Wakerose's too meticulously trimmed sails, but he said at once, "That sounds rather dull for Rowena, I'd be happy to take her sightseeing in my car, while you keep a stern eye on the mechanical shenanigans."

Rowena Flane stared at him from behind a mask that seemed to have been hastily and incompletely improvised to cover her total startlement.

"Why should you do that?" she asked.

He shrugged, with twinkling sapphires in his gaze.

"I hadn't any definite plans for tomorrow. And I told you I didn't have to do anything I didn't want to."

"We couldn't impose on you like that," Wakerose said. "Rowena has plenty of books to read—"

"It's no imposition. But if she'd feel very stuffy about being obligated to a stranger, and it would make her feel better, she can buy the gas."

"And the lunch," she said.

"Oh, no. You couldn't afford that. The lunch will be mine."

Suddenly she laughed.

She had an extra chin and ballooning bosoms to make a billowy travesty of her merriment, yet it had something that lighted up her face, which was in absolute contrast to her stepfather's polite and faultless smile.

And from that moment the Saint knew that his strange instinct had once again proved wiser than reason, and that he was not wasting his time . . .

She was half an hour late in the morning, but went far beyond perfunctory apologies when she finally came downstairs.

"I'm sure you'll think I'm always like this, and I don't blame you. But Saville promised to call me, and he overslept; I was furious. I think there's nothing more insulting to people than to make them wait for you. Who was it who said that 'Punctuality is the politeness of princes'?"

"I like the thought," Simon said. "Who was it?"

"I don't know. I wish I did."

"That makes me feel better already. Now I won't be quite so much in awe of your historical knowledge."

"Honestly, it's not as frightening as Saville tries to make out." She held up the Michelin volume on Provence, "I just read the guide books, like you."

"All right," he said amiably, as he settled beside her at the wheel of his car, and opened a road map. "You name it, and I'll find it."

It was a busy morning. In spite of their belated start, they were able to walk the full circuit of the Promenade du Rocher around the Palace of the Popes in Avignon, enjoying its panoramas of the town and countryside and the immortal bridge which still goes only halfway across the Rhône, before taking the hour-long guided tour of the Palace itself, which the Saint found anticlimactically dull, having no temperament for that sort of historical study. He endured the education with good grace, but was glad of the release when he could drive her over the modern highway across the river, a few kilometers out to the less pretentious cousin-town of Villeneuve-les-Avignon, for lunch at the *Prieuré*.

It was not that she had made the sightseeing any more painful for him than it had to be—in fact, she had displayed an irreverence towards the more pompous exhibits which had encouraged his own iconoclastic sense of humor—but the bones of the past would never be able to compete for his interest with the flesh of the present, even when it was as excessive as Rowena Flane's.

The shaded garden restaurant was quiet and peaceful, and a Pernod and water with plenty of ice tinkling in the glass was simultaneously refreshing to the eye, the hand, the palate, and the soul.

"Of all civilized blessings," he remarked, "I think ice would be one of the hardest to give up. And you must admit that it improves even historical epics when you can watch them in an air-conditioned theater, and enjoy the poor extras sweating up the Pyramids while you sit and wish you'd worn a sweater."

"The Roman emperors had ice," she said. "They had it brought down from the Alps."

"So I've heard. A slave runner set out with a two-hundred-pound chunk, and arrived at the palace with an ice cube. I guess it was just as good as a Frigidaire if you were in the right set. But who daydreams about being a slave?"

"Unless she catches the eye of the handsome hero."

"I know," said the Saint. "The kind of part your father used to play so well."

He saw her stiffen, and the careless gaiety drained down from her eyes.

"Was anything wrong with that?" she challenged coldly.

"Nothing," he said disarmingly. "It was a job, and he did it damned well."

The head waiter came then, and they ordered the *crêpes du Prieuré*, the delicately stuffed rolled pancakes which he remembered from a past visit, and to follow them a *gigot à la broche aux herbes de Provence* which he knew could not fail them, with a bottle of Ste Roseline rosé to counter the warmth of the day.

But after that interruption, she stubbornly refused its opportunity to change the subject.

"I suppose," she said deliberately, "you were like everyone else. When he stopped playing those parts so well, you joined in calling him a drunken bum."

Simon made no attempt to evade the showdown.

"Eventually, that's what he was. It was a shame, when you remember what he did and what he looked like, before the juice wore him down. Unfortunately that was the only period when I knew him."

Her brown eyes darkened and tightened.

"You knew him?"

"So very slightly—and at the wrong time. Just before he committed suicide. I wish I'd known him before. He must have been quite a guy."

She studied him suspiciously for several seconds, but he faced the probe just as frankly and unwaveringly as the preceding challenge.

"I'm glad you said that," she told him finally. "That's how I try to think of him. And I think you meant it."

"I'm glad you believe that," he answered. "Now I won't have spoiled your appetite. That would have been a crime, with what we're looking forward to. That's another department where I'd prefer to keep my history in the surroundings: food. When these walls around us were new, the *spécialité de la maison* was probably something like boiled hair shirts. I'd love to see the face of a *Michelin* inspector being served the product of an ancient French kitchen. Did you know that it was about a century and a half after the Popes took their dyspepsia back from Avignon to Rome before the French learned the elements of the fancy cooking they're now so proud of?"

"Yes, I know. And it was another Italian who brought it—Catherine de' Medici, when she married Henri the Second and became queen of France. Saville taught me that—"

The conversation slanted off into diverting but safely impersonal byways which brought them smoothly through their two main courses and surprised the Saint with more discoveries of her range of knowledge and breadth of interests.

Of course, he remembered, she had had the advantage of the best tutors, conventional schools, and finishing schools that money could buy. But she was a living advertisement for the system. Sometimes she was so fluent and original that he found himself fascinated, listening as he might have listened to some prefabricated sex-pot with a press-agent's contrived and memorized line of dialectic, completely forgetting how different she looked from anything like that.

On the other hand, having convinced herself of his sincerity, his attention seemed to draw her out to an extent that he would hardly have expected even when he had promised himself the attempt the night before. And as her defensiveness disappeared, it seemed to make room for a personal warmth towards him to grow in the same ratio, as if in gratitude for his help in letting down her guard.

A discreet interval after they had disposed of the last of the pink and succulent lamb, the head waiter was at the table again with his final temptations. Rowena unhesitatingly and ecstatically went for the *Charlotte Prieuré*, while the Saint was happy to settle for a fresh peach.

"I'm sure you think I'm awful," she said, "finishing all my potatoes and then topping them with this rich sweet goo. You're like Saville— you can enjoy all the tastiest things, and hold back on the fattening ones, and keep a figure like a saint. The hungry kind, I mean."

By this time they were on the verge of being old friends.

"I guess we're the worrying types," he said. "Or the vain ones. A longish while ago, I took a good look at some of the characters who had the same tastes that I have, and decided that I could beat the game. I wanted to live like them without looking like them. I figured that the solution might be to have your cake and not eat all of it. Anyway, it seemed like an idea."

"So you could always be young and beautiful, like Orlando in his prime."

"I should be so lucky. But there are worse things to try for."

"Such as being a fat slob like me."

"Not a slob," he said carefully. "But why don't you do something about being fat?"

"Because I can't," she said. "I know you think it's just because I eat too much. That's how it started, of course. When I was a child I felt unwanted, so I took to desserts and candy in the same way that people become alcoholics or drug addicts. The psychologists have a word for it . . . Then, in my teens, because I was so fat, I didn't get any dates, and the other girls always made fun of me. They were jealous of all the other things I had, and were just looking for something to torment me with.

So I just stuffed myself with more desserts and candy, to show I didn't care. And so I ended up with adipochria."

"With who?"

"It means a need for fat. Just before my mother died, I'd finally started trying to go on a diet, and I'd lost some weight, but I began to feel awful. Tired all the time, and feeling sick after meals, and getting headaches constantly. So Saville took me to a specialist, and that's what he said it was. I'd conditioned my metabolism to so much rich food and sweets, all my life, that something glandular had atrophied and now I can't get along without them."

The Saint stared at her.

"And the remedy is to keep eating more of the same?"

"It isn't a remedy—it's a necessity. If I cut them out, it's like a normal person being starved. In a month or two I'd die of anaemia and malnutrition."

"And that's all he could tell you? To stay fat and get fatter?"

"Just about. Well, he gave me a lot of pills, which he hopes will change my condition eventually. But he absolutely forbade me to try any more dieting until I feel a positive loathing for any sweet taste. He said that would be the first symptom that my system was starting to become normal." Simon shook his head incredulously. "That's the damnedest disease I ever heard of."

"Isn't it?" she said, resignedly. "That's another reason why I escape into those historical romances. They're what I'll have to be satisfied with until some hero comes along who likes fat girls."

But there was a soft moistness in her eyes that he did not want to look at, and he concentrated on peeling a second peach.

"Why not?" he said. "The *Vogue* model type would never have got a tumble from any of those old-time swashbucklers, to go by the contemporary prints and paintings. They didn't need skinny little waifs to make them feel robust. And yet the interesting thing is that when it came to architecture they put up buildings that were big but graceful, and full of ornament, too much of it sometimes, but always delicate. No huge lumpish monstrosities like some of the modern jobs I've seen. Talking of which, what ancient memorials are we heading for this afternoon?"

"I wanted to see the Pont du Gard at Uzès, and . . . "

And once again the conversation was steered back into a safe impersonal channel.

He drove to Uzès and parked down beside the river, and they walked to survey the magnificent Roman aqueduct from both levels and across the span. Then it was only another fifteen miles to Nîmes, where they parked in front of the extraordinarily preserved Arenas, which could still have served as a movie set if they had backgrounded chariots instead of Citroëns, and walked on up the Boulevard Victor Hugo to visit the somewhat disappointing Maison Carrée, and then on to the Jardin de la Fontaine for the view from the Tour Magne, which—But this is not the script of a travelog. Let us leave it that they walked a lot and saw a lot which has no direct bearing on this story, and that the Saint was not truly sorry when they came to Tarascon on the way home and found it was too late to visit the Château, though it was picturesque enough from the outside.

"I'll have to make it another day," Rowena said. "I couldn't go away without seeing it. *Tartarni de Tarascon* was the first French classic I had to read in school, and I can still remember that it made me cry, I was so sorry for the poor silly man."

"Don Quijote was another poor silly man," Simon said. "And so am I, maybe. Lord, have mercy on such as we—as the song says. But thank the Lord, a few people do . . . Why did you feel an unwanted child?" he asked abruptly.

She took about a mile to answer, so that he began to think she was resenting the question, but she was only brooding around it.

"I suppose because I never seemed to have any parents like the other girls. I had a series of stepfathers who sometimes pretended to be interested in me, but that was only to impress Mother. They weren't really fatherly types, and they soon stopped when they found that she couldn't have cared less. Motherhood was something she had to try once, like everything else, so she tried it, but after a few years it was just another bore. So I was pushed on to governesses and tutors and all kinds of boarding schools—anything to keep me out of her hair. And yet she must have loved me, in a funny way, or else she still had a strong sense of duty."

"Why—how did she show it?"

"Well, she did leave me everything in her will. I don't get control of it until I get married or until I'm thirty—until then, Saville's my guardian and trustee—but in the end it all comes to me."

It went through the Saint's head like the breaking of a string on some supernal harp, the reverberation which is vulgarly rendered as "*boinng*," but amplified to the volume of a cathedral bell as it would sound in the belfry.

He didn't look at her. He couldn't.

But she had spoken in perfect innocence. His ears told him that.

His hands were light on the wheel, and the car had not swerved. The moment of understanding had only been vertiginous in his mind, exactly as its subsonic boom had sounded in no other ears.

"You get on better with Saville than the other stepfathers, I take it."

"Well, I was a lot older when he came along, so he didn't have to pretend to like children. As a matter of fact, he loathes them. But he's been very good to me."

"I'm sure there's a moral," Simon said trivially. "We're always reading about misunderstood children, but you don't hear much about misunderstood parents. And yet all parents were children themselves once. I wonder why they forget how to communicate when they change places."

"I must try to remember, if I'm ever a mother."

It was only another half-hour's drive back to the Petite Auberge, and he was glad it was no longer.

He had a little thinking to do alone, and there would not be much time for it.

As they turned in at the entrance and headed up the long driveway through the orchards, she said, "It's been a wonderful day. For me. And you must have been terribly bored."

"On the contrary, I wouldn't have missed it for anything," he said, truthfully.

"I might have believed you if you'd let me pay for lunch.

But that crack of yours, that I couldn't afford it—it still sticks in my mind. You meant something snide, didn't you?"

He brought the car to a gentle stop in front of the inn.

"I meant that if I let you buy my lunch you might have thought you could buy more than that, and then I'd've had to prove how expensive I can be to people I don't like. And I'd begun to like you."

"Then do you still like me enough to join us for dinner, if Saville pays?"

He smiled.

"Consider me seduced."

She leaned over and kissed him on the cheek, and got out before he could open the door.

The Saint shaved and showered and changed unhurriedly, and sauntered out on to the terrace to find Saville Wakerose sipping a dry martini.

"Hi there," he said breezily. "How's the ailing automobile?"

"Immobile," Wakerose said lugubriously. "May I offer you one of these? They really make them quite potably here."

"Thank you." Simon sat down. "What's the trouble—did the mechanic outsmart you?"

"The mountebank took the fuel pump apart and found something broken which he couldn't repair. We went all over the province looking for something to replace it with, but being an American car nobody had anything that would fit. Finally I had to telephone the dealers in Paris and have them put a pump on the train, which won't get to Avignon till tomorrow morning. And after he picks it up, the charlatan at the garage will probably take at least half the day to install it."

"Aren't you being a bit hard on him?" Simon argued. "You'd be liable to run into the same thing if you took a French car into a small-town American garage. Just like they say you should drink the wine of the country, I believe in driving the car of the country you're in, or at least of the continent."

"When they make air-conditioned cars in Europe," Wakerose said, earnestly, "I shall have to consider one."

Simon had forgotten during the course of the day that Wakerose was a lifeman who never stopped playing, but he accepted the loss of a round with great good nature and without any undignified scramble to retrieve it. He could afford to bide his time.

Rowena gave him the first opening, as he knew she must, when she came down and joined them.

"I suppose you've heard the news," she said. "Isn't it aggravating?"

"Not to me," Simon said cheerily.

"I know, you can take your sightseeing or leave it alone. But tomorrow is market day in Arles, and I've read that it's one of the biggest and best in all the South, and it's heartbreaking to miss it—"

"Can't you hire a car?"

"I've been trying to make inquiries," Wakerose said. "But this isn't exactly Hertz territory. And I can't send Rowena off with some local taxi-driver who doesn't speak English, in an unsanitary rattletrap—"

"Which might break down anywhere, like the best American limousine," Simon said sympathetically. "I see your problem. But if Rowena could stand another day in my non-air-conditioned Common-Market jalopy, I'd be glad to offer an encore."

It was extraordinary how beautiful her face was, when you looked at it centrally and the dim light made the outer margins indefinite, especially when that luminous warmth rose in her eyes.

"It's too much!" she said. "I know how you hate that sort of thing, and yet you know I'll just have to take you up on it. How can you be such an angel?"

"It comes naturally to a saint," he drawled. "And I get my kick out of seeing the kick you get out of everything. As I told you last night, I'm not on any timetable, and another day makes no difference to me."

"A rare and remarkable attitude in these days," Wakerose said, "when anyone who claims to be respectable is supposed to have a Purpose In Life, no matter how idiotic. I envy you your freedom from that bourgeois problem. But not your marketing excursion tomorrow. Rowena will quite certainly transmute you from a cavalier into a beast of burden, laden with every gewgaw and encumbrance that attracts her fancy. You need not try to look chivalrously skeptical, Mr Templar. I have been with her to the Flea Market in Paris."

"I promise," Rowena said. "Anything I buy I'll carry myself."

"And don't think I won't hold you to that," Simon grinned at her.

"You've got a witness," she smiled back.

Wakerose heaved a sigh of tastefully controlled depth.

"You must both rest your feet at the Jules César," he said. "It is right in the middle of the main street, and as I recall it they serve a most edible lunch. And Rowena should appreciate a hotel named after such a genuine historical hero instead of some parvenu tycoon as they usually are in America. Come to think of it, I believe there are six or seven different towns called Rome in the United States, and I'll wager that not one of them has even a motel called the Julius Caesar."

The conversation continued with light and random variety through dinner.

Characteristically, Wakerose suggested Parma ham and melon for a start, followed by flamed quail and a green salad, to which Simon was quite contented to agree, but for Rowena it was *foie gras* to begin with, and then chicken in a cream sauce with tarragon, and *pommes Dauphine*.

"I would propose a glass of Chante Alouette '59 for all of us to start with," Wakerose said, studying the wine list, "and Rowena can finish the bottle with her chicken. You and I, Mr Templar, can wash down our *cailles* with a red Rhône. Do you have any preference? They have a most impressive selection here. Or are you one of those people to whom all Châteauneuf du Pape is the same?"

"The Montredon is very good, I think," Simon said, without glancing at the list. "Especially the '55."

The meal ended with the score about even and all the amenities observed, though by the end of it the Saint thought there was an infinitesimal fraying at the edges of Wakerose's cultivated smoothness, and thought that he could surmise the reason. It was not that Wakerose would be seriously exasperated to have encountered an adversary who could meet him on level terms in his own specialty of going one better. Something more important seemed to preoccupy him, and the strain was cramping his style.

For dessert, Wakerose chose an almost calorie-free sorbet, but clairvoyantly anticipated Rowena's yearning for the *crêpes flambées* which the Petite Auberge, proud of its own recipe, disdains to call *Suzette*. But this time the Saint decided that he had been dietetically discreet enough all day, and could afford the indulgence of leaving Wakerose alone in his austerity.

"I'm so glad you can at least pretend to dissipate with me," Rowena said, glowingly. "It makes me feel just a little less of a freak, even if you're only doing it to be polite. I love you for it."

Wakerose looked at her oddly.

"Mr Templar has that wonderful knack of making everybody feel like somebody special," he commented. "It must have required superhuman will-power for him to remain a bachelor."

"Maybe I just haven't been lucky yet," Simon said, easily. "I'm corny enough to be stuck with the old romantic notion that for every person there's an ideal mate wandering somewhere in the world, and when they meet, the bells ring and things light up and there's no argument. The *coup de foudre*, as the French call it. Some people settle for less, or too soon, and some people never find it, but that doesn't prove that it can't happen."

His gaze shifted once from Wakerose to Rowena and back again, as it might in any normal generality of discussion, but he knew that her eyes never left his face.

"One might call it the 'Some Enchanted Evening' syndrome," Wakerose said sardonically. "Well, each of us to our superstitions. I cling to the one which maintains that brandy or a liqueur at the end of a meal is a digestive, although I know that medical authority contradicts me. Rowena enjoys a Benedictine. What would appeal to you?"

"I shall be completely neutral," said the Saint, "and have a B-and-B."

They took their coffee and liqueurs outside on the terrace. Rowena ordered her coffee in a large cup, *liégeois*, with a dollop of ice cream in it, and used it to swallow a pill from a little jewelled box, but the caffeine was not sufficient to stop her contributions to the conversational rally becoming more and more infrequent and desultory, and Wakerose had still not finished his long cigar when she stifled a yawn and excused herself.

"I'm folding," she said. "And I want to be bright tomorrow. Will you forgive me?" She stood up and gave her hand to the Saint, and he kissed it with an impudent flourish. "Thank you again for today—and what time does the private tour leave in the morning?"

"Shall we say ten o'clock again?"

"You're the boss. And tonight I'll leave my own call at the desk, so you won't be kept waiting. Goodnight, Saville."

Wakerose tracked her departure with elegantly lofted eyebrows, and made a fastidious business of savoring another puff of smoke.

"My felicitations," he said at last. "You appear to have her marvellously intimidated, which is no mean feat. But I would advise you, if I may, not to presume too much on this docility. I've seen it before, and I feel I have a duty to warn you. Behind that submissiveness there lurks a tiger which even professional hunters have mistaken for a fat cat."

There was an inherent laziness in the balmy Provencal evening which allowed the Saint to take a long leisurely pause before any answer was essential, which helped to cushion the abruptness of the transition he had to make.

"There was something I wanted to talk to you about," he said, "but not quite as publicly as this." He turned his head from side to side to indicate the other guests at adjacent tables, within potentially embarrassing earshot. "I wonder if you'd like to see my room? I don't know what yours is like, but I think mine is exceptionally nice, and you might find it worth remembering if you ever come here again."

Wakerose's brows repeated their eloquent elevation, but after a pointedly puzzled pause he said, "Certainly, that sounds interesting."

They went in through the foyer and past the stairs. Simon's room was on the ground floor, in a wing beyond the inner lounge. He unlocked the door, ushered Wakerose in, and shut the door again behind them.

Wakerose looked methodically around, put his head in the bathroom, and said, "Very nice indeed. But you had something more than comparative accommodations to talk about, didn't you?"

The Saint opened his suitcase, rummaged in it and took out a pack of cigarettes, and dropped the lid again. He opened the package and then put it down nervously without taking a cigarette.

"I haven't seen you smoking before," Wakerose said.

"I'm trying to quit," Simon explained, and went on suddenly: "I won't waste your time beating about the bush. I want to marry your step-daughter."

Wakerose rocked back on his heels, and anything he had previously done with his eyebrows became a mere quiver compared with the way they now arched up into his hair line.

"Indeed? And what does Rowena think about it?"

"I haven't asked her yet. It may be an old-fashioned formality, but I felt I should tell you first. I thought that a gentleman of the old school like yourself would appreciate that."

"I do. Oh, I do, most emphatically. But you can't seriously imagine that I would be so overwhelmed that I should give my permission, let alone my blessing, to a suitor such as yourself?"

"If Rowena isn't twenty-one yet, she can't be far from it. So she'd be able to make up her own mind soon enough. I just wanted to be honest about my intentions, and I hoped you'd respect them, and that we could be friends."

Wakerose widened his eyes again elaborately.

"Honest? Respect?" he echoed. "After you gave your word of honor—"

"Not to steal her jewels," Simon said. "Her heart isn't a diamond—I hope. We've only spent one day together, but I think she feels a little the same about me as I do about her."

"I could scarcely help noticing the feeling," Wakerose said. "But I beg to doubt if its nature is the same. Rowena is a sweet girl, but you can't seriously expect me to believe that she is attractive in that way to such a man as yourself,"

"When I take her to a good specialist, and she loses about fifty pounds," Simon said steadily, "I think she'll be one of the most beautiful young women that anyone ever saw."

Wakerose laughed hollowly.

"My poor fellow. Now I begin to comprehend your delusion. Obviously she hasn't told you what's the matter with her."

"About that 'adipochria'?" Simon said steadily. "Yes, she has. And I'm prepared to bet my matrimonial future that there's no such disease known to medical science, and that the doctor who diagnosed it is nothing but an unscrupulous quack."

The other's eyes narrowed.

"That is an extremely dangerous statement, Mr Templar."

"It'll be easily proved or disproved when she gets an independent opinion from a first-class reputable clinic," said the Saint calmly. "And if I'm right, I shall then go on to theorize that it was you who snuck something into her food or her vitamin pills when she tried going on a diet, to produce the symptoms which gave you an excuse to lug her off to the first bogus specialist, whom you'd already suborned to prescribe still more carbohydrates and some pills which are probably tranquillizers or something to slow down her metabolism even more. That you deliberately plotted to make her as unattractive as possible, so as to keep her unmarried and leave her mother's fortune in your hands until you could siphon off all that you wanted."

He had confirmation enough to satisfy himself in the long silence that followed, before there was any verbal answer.

Saville Wakerose took one more light pull at his cigar, grimaced slightly, and carefully extinguished it in an ashtray.

"One should never try to smoke the last two-and-a-half inches. Very well," he said briskly, "how much do you want?"

"For conniving to destroy a human being even more cruelly than if you poisoned her?"

"Come now, my dear fellow, let us not overdo the knightly act. There is no admiring audience. And blackmail is not such a pretty crime, either—that is the technical name for your purpose, isn't it?"

"Then you admit to something you'd rather I kept quiet about?"

"I admit nothing. I am merely looking for a civilized alternative to a great deal of crude unpleasantness and publicity. Shall we say a quarter of a million Swiss francs?"

"Don't you think it's degrading to start the bidding as low as that?"

"Half a million, then. Paid into any account you care to name, and quite untraceable."

The Saint shook his head.

"For such a brilliant man, you can be very dense, Saville. All I want is to give Rowena a fair chance for a happy normal life, in spite of her money."

"Don't bid your hand too high," Wakerose said with brittle restraint. "You are assuming that Rowena will immediately believe these fantastic accusations, regardless of who is making them and what obvious motives can be imputed to him. If it should come to what they call on television a showdown between us, although I would go to great lengths to avoid anything so unsavory, I hope she would prefer to believe my version of this *tête-à-tête*."

Simon Templar smiled benignly.

He turned back to his suitcase, opened it again, pushed a soiled shirt aside, and extracted a plastic box no bigger than a book. A small metal object dangled from it at the end of a flexible wire, which now seemed to have been hanging outside the suitcase when the lid was closed.

217

"Have you seen these portable tape recorders?" he asked chattily. "Completely transistorized, battery operated, and frightfully efficient. Of course, their capacity is limited, so I had to use that cigarette routine for an excuse to switch it on when we came in. And the sound quality isn't hi-fi by musicians' standards, but voices are unmistakably recognizable. I wonder what version you can give Rowena that'll cancel out this one?"

"How delightfully droll!" All of Wakerose's face seemed to have gradually turned as gray as his hair, but it can be stated that he did not flinch. "I should not have been so caustic at the expense of television, but I thought that was the only place where these things actually happened. So what is your price now?"

Simon was neatly coiling the flexible link to the microphone, preparatory to tucking it away in the interior of his gadget, but still leaving it operational for the last syllables that it could absorb.

"This will be hard for you to digest, Saville," he said, "but since anything you paid me would probably be money that you ought to be giving back to Rowena, my conscience would bother me, even if she has got plenty to spare. On the other hand, I'd like to get her out of your clutches without any messy headlines. So I'll give you a break. If you back me up tomorrow evening when I suggest that she ought to see another doctor—whom I'll suggest—and if you can think up a good excuse to resign voluntarily as her guardian and trustee, I won't have to play this tape to her."

Wakerose compressed his lips and stared grimly about the room. With his hands locked tensely behind his back, he paced across it to the open window and stood looking out into the night. The hunch of his shoulders gave the impression that if it had been on a higher floor he might have thrown himself out.

After a full minute, he turned.

"I shall think about it," he said, and walked towards the door.

"Think very hard," said the Saint. "Because I'm not quite sure that it mightn't be better for Rowena to know the whole horrible truth about you and your slimy scheme. And whatever brilliant inspirations you have about how to double-cross me and retrieve the situation, I'll always have this little recording."

Wakerose sneered silently at him, and went out without another word.

He came back soon after three o'clock in the morning, through the open window, and crossed in slow-motion tiptoe to the bed where the covers humped over a peacefully insensible occupant. There was enough starlight to define clearly the dark head-shape buried in the pillow but half uncovered by the sheet, and he swung mightily at it with the heavy candlestick which he carried in one gloved hand . . .

The massive base bit solidly and accurately into its target, but with no solid crunch of bone, only a soggy resistance—which was natural, since the "head" consisted of a crumpled towel balled up inside a dark pullover and artistically moulded and arranged to give the right appearance. At the same time, a blinding luminance dispelled the treacherous dimness for a fraction of a second before the Saint switched on a less painfully dazzling light.

He stood in the bathroom doorway, holding a Polaroid camera with flash attachment in one hand.

"I was beginning to be afraid you were never coming, Saville," he murmured genially. "But I kept telling myself that you were clever enough to realize that you ought to get rid of me and my tape record, no matter what, if you ever wanted to sleep well again. Or I hoped you would, because a picture like this would clinch any ambiguities in the sound track, which you might have been just slippery enough to think you could explain away."

Wakerose stood frozen in a kind of catalepsy, while Simon deftly changed the bulb in his flash and snapped one more after-the-crime souvenir, admittedly not an action shot, but just for luck.

"Of course, this washes out the previous deal," he said. "I don't want to spoil Rowena's day tomorrow, so I'm not going to play the tape to her till we come home. By that time I hope your air-conditioned juggernaut will have been repaired so that you can have taken off, leaving behind a signed confession which I think I can persuade her not to use as long as your accounts are in order and you never bother her again. Otherwise, chum, you may find yourself trying to sell *Gourmet* some novel articles on prison cuisine."

"Yes," said Rowena Flane. "Yes, now I understand—everything except why you've done so much and wouldn't take anything when you could have."

"Because," Simon said, "one day I'll get so much more out of it when I see you as slim and lovely as you should be, and I can think that I made it happen."

"Like in a fairy tale. So the prince kissed the toad, and broke the spell, and it turned into a beautiful princess. Oh, it's hard to believe it's coming true." But she was sad. "Only by then you won't be threatening to marry me anymore."

"Why don't we wait a couple of years," said the Saint, gently, "and see whether you're still single too?"

PUBLICATION
HISTORY

The stories in this book first appeared in *The Saint Detective Magazine* (and *The Saint Mystery Magazine*, as it would later be rechristened) prior to book publication in November 1963 (if you were in America) or 25 May 1964 (if you were in Great Britain).

This book is notable for it being the last one that was written by Leslie Charteris alone; by the early 1960s he was keen to retire yet, prompted largely by the success of the first TV series, he was keen to see the literary Saint kept alive, so after the publication of this book he started collaborating with other writers.

Of the stories in this volume three were adapted for *The Saint* with Roger Moore; "The Russian Prisoner" first aired on Friday, 14 October 1966 whilst "The Better Mousetrap," which included a marvellous performance from comedian Ronnie Barker as a bumbling police detective, popped up a few weeks later on Friday, 25 November 1966. "The Fast Women" which starred Kate O'Mara as one of the eponymous ladies, aired Friday, 13 January 1967.

Uniquely for a Saint book, only one foreign language translation has ever appeared: a French edition entitled *Le Saint au soleil*, which was published in 1966.

ABOUT THE AUTHOR

I'm mad enough to believe in romance. And I'm sick and tired of this age—tired of the miserable little mildewed things that people racked their brains about, and wrote books about, and called life. I wanted something more elementary and honest—battle, murder, sudden death, with plenty of good beer and damsels in distress, and a complete callousness about blipping the ungodly over the beezer. It mayn't be life as we know it, but it ought to be.

—Leslie Charteris in a 1935 BBC radio interview

Leslie Charteris was born Leslie Charles Bowyer-Yin in Singapore on 12 May 1907.

He was the son of a Chinese doctor and his English wife, who'd met in London a few years earlier. Young Leslie found friends hard to come by in colonial Singapore. The English children had been told not to play with Eurasians, and the Chinese children had been told not to play with Europeans. Leslie was caught in between and took refuge in reading.

"I read a great many good books and enjoyed them because nobody had told me that they were classics. I also read a great many bad books which nobody told me not to read . . . I read a great many popular scientific articles and acquired from them an astonishing amount of general knowledge before I discovered that this acquisition was supposed to be a chore."[1]

One of his favourite things to read was a magazine called *Chums*. "The Best and Brightest Paper for Boys" (if you believe the adverts) was a monthly paper full of swashbuckling adventure stories aimed at boys, encouraging them to be honourable and moral and perhaps even "upright citizens with furled umbrellas."[2] Undoubtedly these types of stories would influence his later work.

When his parents split up shortly after the end of World War I, Charteris accompanied his mother and brother back to England, where he was sent to Rossall School in Fleetwood, Lancashire. Rossall was then a very stereotypical English public school, and it struggled to cope with this multilingual mixed-race boy just into his teens who'd already seen more of the world than many of his peers would see in their lifetimes. He was an outsider.

He left Rossall in 1924. Keen to pursue a creative career, he decided to study art in Paris—after all, that was where the great artists went—but soon found that the life of a literally starving artist didn't appeal. He continued writing, firing off speculative stories to magazines, and it was the sale of a short story to *Windsor Magazine* that saved him from penury.

He returned to London in 1925, as his parents—particularly his father—wanted him to become a lawyer, and he was sent to study law at Cambridge University. In the mid-1920s, Cambridge was full of Bright Young Things—aristocrats and bohemians somewhat typified in the Evelyn Waugh novel *Vile Bodies*—and again the mixed-race Bowyer-Yin found that he didn't fit in. He was an outsider who preferred to make his own way in the world and wasn't one of the privileged upper class. It didn't help that he found his studies boring and decided it was more fun contemplating ways to circumvent the law. This inspired him to write a novel, and when publishers Ward Lock & Co. offered him a three-book deal on the strength of it, he abandoned his studies to pursue a writing career.

When his father learnt of this, he was not impressed, as he considered writers to be "rogues and vagabonds." Charteris would later recall that "I wanted to be a writer, he wanted me to become a lawyer. I was stubborn, he said I would end up in the gutter. So I left home. Later on, when I had a little success, we were reconciled by letter, but I never saw him again."[3]

X Esquire, his first novel, appeared in April 1927. The lead character, X Esquire, is a mysterious hero, hunting down and killing the businessmen trying to wipe out Britain by distributing quantities of free poisoned cigarettes. His second novel, *The White Rider*, was published the following spring, and in one memorable scene shows the hero chasing after his damsel in distress, only for him to overtake the villains, leap into their car . . . and promptly faint.

These two plot highlights may go some way to explaining Charteris's comment on *Meet—the Tiger!*, published in September 1928, that "it was only the third book I'd written, and the best, I would say, for it was that the first two were even worse."[4]

Twenty-one-year-old authors are naturally self-critical. Despite reasonably good reviews, the Saint didn't set the world on fire, and Charteris moved on to a new hero for his next book. This was *The Bandit*, an adventure story featuring Ramon Francisco De Castilla y Espronceda Manrique, published in the summer of 1929 after its serialisation in the *Empire News*, a now long-forgotten Sunday newspaper. But sales of *The Bandit* were less than impressive, and Charteris began to question his choice of career. It was all very well writing—but if nobody wants to read what you write, what's the point?

"I had to succeed, because before me loomed the only alternative, the dreadful penalty of failure . . . the routine office hours, the five-day week . . . the lethal assimilation into the ranks of honest, hard-working, conformist, God-fearing pillars of the community."[5]

However his fortunes—and the Saint's—were about to change. In late 1928, Leslie had met Monty Haydon, a London-based editor who was looking for writers to pen stories for his new paper, *The Thriller*— "The Paper with a Thousand Thrills." Charteris later recalled that "he said he was starting a new magazine, had read one of my books and would like some stories from me. I couldn't have been more grateful, both from the point of view of vanity and finance!"[6]

The paper launched in early 1929, and Leslie's first work, "The Story of a Dead Man," featuring Jimmy Traill, appeared in issue 4 (published on 2 March 1929). That was followed just over a month later with "The Secret of Beacon Inn," starring Rameses "Pip" Smith. At the same time, Leslie finished writing another non-Saint novel, *Daredevil*, which would be published in late 1929. Storm Arden was the hero; more notably, the book saw the first introduction of a Scotland Yard inspector by the name of Claud Eustace Teal.

The Saint returned in the thirteenth issue of *The Thriller*. The byline proclaimed that the tale was "A Thrilling Complete Story of the Underworld"; the title was "The Five Kings," and it actually featured Four Kings and a Joker. Simon Templar, of course, was the Joker.

Charteris spent the rest of 1929 telling the adventures of the Five Kings in five subsequent *The Thriller* stories. "It was very hard work, for the pay was lousy, but Monty Haydon was a brilliant and stimulating editor, full of ideas. While he didn't actually help shape the Saint as a character, he did suggest story lines. He would take me out to lunch and say, 'What are you going to write about next?' I'd often say I was damned if I knew. And Monty would say, 'Well, I was reading something the other day . . .' He had a fund of ideas and we would talk them over, and then I would go away and write a story. He was a great creative editor."[7]

Charteris would have one more attempt at writing about a hero other than Simon Templar, in three novelettes published in *The Thriller* in early 1930, but he swiftly returned to the Saint. This was partly due to his self-confessed laziness—he wanted to write more stories for *The Thriller* and other magazines, and creating a new hero for every story was hard work—but mainly due to feedback from Monty Haydon. It seemed people wanted to read more adventures of the Saint . . .

Charteris would contribute over forty stories to *The Thriller* throughout the 1930s. Shortly after their debut, he persuaded publisher Hodder & Stoughton that if he collected some of these stories and rewrote them a little, they could publish them as a Saint book. *Enter the Saint* was first published in August 1930, and the reaction was good enough for the publishers to bring out another collection. And another . . .

Of the twenty Saint books published in the 1930s, almost all have their origins in those magazine stories.

Why was the Saint so popular throughout the decade? Aside from the charm and ability of Charteris's storytelling, the stories, particularly those published in the first half of the '30s, are full of energy and joie de vivre. With economic depression rampant throughout the period, the public at large seemed to want some escapism.

And Simon Templar's appeal was wide-ranging: he wasn't an upper-class hero like so many of the period. With no obvious background and no attachment to the Old School Tie, no friends in high places who could provide a get-out-of-jail-free card, the Saint was uniquely classless. Not unlike his creator.

Throughout Leslie's formative years, his heritage had been an issue. In his early days in Singapore, during his time at school, at Cambridge University or even just in everyday life, he couldn't avoid the fact that for many people his mixed parentage was a problem. He would later tell a story of how he was chased up the road by a stick-waving typical

English gent who took offence to his daughter being escorted around town by a foreigner.

Like the Saint, he was an outsider. And although he had spent a significant portion of his formative years in England, he couldn't settle.

As a young boy he had read of an America "peopled largely by Indians, and characters in fringed buckskin jackets who fought nobly against them. I spent a great deal of time day-dreaming about a visit to this prodigious and exciting country."[8]

It was time to realise this wish. Charteris and his first wife, Pauline, whom he'd met in London when they were both teenagers and married in 1931, set sail for the States in late 1932; the Saint had already made his debut in America courtesy of the publisher Doubleday. Charteris and his wife found a New York still experiencing the tail end of Prohibition, and times were tough at first. Despite sales to *The American Magazine* and others, it wasn't until a chance meeting with writer turned Hollywood executive Bartlett McCormack in their favourite speakeasy that Charteris's career stepped up a gear.

Soon Charteris was in Hollywood, working on what would become the 1933 movie *Midnight Club*. However, Hollywood's treatment of writers wasn't to Charteris's taste, and he began to yearn for home. Within a few months, he returned to the UK and began writing more Saint stories for Monty Haydon and Bill McElroy.

He also rewrote a story he'd sketched out whilst in the States, a version of which had been published in *The American Magazine* in September 1934. This new novel, *The Saint in New York*, published in 1935, was a significant advance for the Saint and Leslie Charteris. Gone were the high jinks and the badinage. The youthful exuberance evident in the Saint's early adventures had evolved into something a little darker, a little more hard-boiled. It was the next stage in development for the author and his creation, and readers loved it. It became a bestseller on both sides of the Atlantic.

Having spent his formative years in places as far apart as Singapore and England, with substantial travel in between, it should be no surprise that Leslie had a serious case of wanderlust. With a bestseller under his belt, he now had the means to see more of the world.

Nineteen thirty-six found him in Tenerife, researching another Saint adventure alongside translating the biography of Juan Belmonte, a well-known Spanish matador. Estranged for several months, Leslie and Pauline divorced in 1937. The following year, Leslie married an American, Barbara Meyer, who'd accompanied him to Tenerife. In early 1938, Charteris and his new bride set off in a trailer of his own design and spent eighteen months travelling round America and Canada.

The Saint in New York had reminded Hollywood of Charteris's talents, and film rights to the novel were sold prior to publication in 1935. Although the proposed 1935 film production was rejected by the Hays Office for its violent content, RKO's eventual 1938 production persuaded Charteris to try his luck once more in Hollywood.

New opportunities had opened up, and throughout the 1940s the Saint appeared not only in books and movies but in a newspaper strip, a comic-book series, and on radio.

Anyone wishing to adapt the character in any medium found a stern taskmaster in Charteris. He was never completely satisfied, nor was he shy of showing his displeasure. He did, however, ensure that copyright in any Saint adventure belonged to him, even if scripted by another writer—a contractual obligation that he was to insist on throughout his career.

Charteris was soon spread thin, overseeing movies, comics, newspapers, and radio versions of his creation, and this, along with his self-proclaimed laziness, meant that Saint books were becoming fewer and further between. However, he still enjoyed his creation: in 1941 he indulged himself in a spot of fun by playing the Saint—complete with monocle and moustache—in a photo story in *Life* magazine.

In July 1944, he started collaborating under a pseudonym on Sherlock Holmes radio scripts, subsequently writing more adventures for Holmes than Conan Doyle. Not all his ventures were successful—a screenplay he was hired to write for Deanna Durbin, "Lady on a Train," took him a year and ultimately bore little resemblance to the finished film. In the mid-1940s, Charteris successfully sued RKO Pictures for unfair competition after they launched a new series of films starring George Sanders as a debonair crime fighter known as the Falcon. But he kept faith with his original character, and the Saint novels continued to adapt to the times. The transatlantic Saint evolved into something of a private operator, working for the mysterious Hamilton and becoming, not unlike his creator, a world traveller, finding that adventure would seek him out.

"I have never been able to see why a fictional character should not grow up, mature, and develop, the same as anyone else. The same, if you like, as his biographer. The only adequate reason is that—so far as I know—no other fictional character in modern times has survived a sufficient number of years for these changes to be clearly observable. I must confess that a lot of my own selfish pleasure in the Saint has been in watching him grow up."[9]

Charteris maintained his love of travel and was soon to be found sailing round the West Indies with his good friend Gregory Peck. His forays abroad gave him even more material, and he began to write true-crime articles, as well as an occasional column in *Gourmet* magazine.

By the early '50s, Charteris himself was feeling strained. He'd divorced his second wife in 1943 and got together with a New York radio and nightclub singer called Betty Bryant Borst, whom he married in late 1943. That relationship had fallen apart acrimoniously towards the end of the decade, and he roamed the globe restlessly, rarely in one place for longer than a couple of months. He continued to maintain a firm grip on the exploitation of the Saint in various media but was writing little himself. The Saint had become an industry, and Charteris couldn't keep up. He began thinking seriously about an early retirement.

Then in 1951 he met a young actress called Audrey Long when they became next-door neighbours in Hollywood. Within a year they had married, a union that was to last the rest of Leslie's life.

He attacked life with a new vitality. They travelled—Nassau was a favoured escape spot—and he wrote. He struck an agreement with *The New York Herald Tribune* for a Saint comic strip, which would appear daily and be written by Charteris himself. The strip ran for thirteen years, with Charteris sending in his handwritten story lines from wherever he happened to be, relying on mail services around the world to continue the Saint's adventures. New Saint books began to appear, and Charteris reached a height of productivity not seen since his days as a struggling author trying to establish himself. As Leslie and Audrey travelled, so did the Saint, visiting locations just after his creator had been there.

By 1953 the Saint had already enjoyed twenty-five years of success, and *The Saint Detective Magazine* was launched. Charteris had become adept at exploiting his creation to the full, mixing new stories with repackaged older stories, sometimes rewritten, sometimes mixed up in "new" anthologies, sometimes adapted from radio scripts previously written by other writers.

Charteris had been approached several times over the years for television rights in the Saint and had expended much time and effort during the 1950s trying to get the Saint on TV, even going so far as to write sample scripts himself, but it wasn't to be. He finally agreed a deal in autumn 1961 with English film producers Robert S. Baker and Monty Berman. The first episode of *The Saint* television series, starring Roger Moore, went into production in June 1962. The series was an immediate success, though Charteris himself had his reservations. It reached second place in the ratings, but he commented that "in that distinction it was topped by wrestling, which only suggested to me that the competition may not have been so hot; but producers are generally cast in a less modest mould." He resented the implication that the TV series had finally made a success of the Saint after twenty-five years of literary obscurity.

As long as the series lasted, Charteris was not shy about voicing his criticisms both in public and in a constant stream of memos to the producers. "Regular followers of the Saint saga . . . must have noticed that I am almost incapable of simply writing a story and shutting up."[10] Nor was he shy about exploiting this new market by agreeing to a series of tie-in novelisations ghosted by other writers, which he would then rewrite before publication.

Charteris mellowed as the series developed and found elements to praise too. He developed a close friendship with producer Robert S. Baker, which would last until Charteris's death.

In the early '60s, on one of their frequent trips to England, Leslie and Audrey bought a house in Surrey, which became their permanent base. He explored the possibility of a Saint musical and began writing some of it himself.

Charteris no longer needed to work. Now in his sixties, he supervised the Saint from a distance whilst continuing to travel and indulge himself. He and Audrey made seasonal excursions to Ireland and the south of France, where they had residences. He began to write poetry and devised a new universal sign language, Paleneo, based on notes and symbols he used in his diaries. Once Paleneo was released, he decided enough was enough and announced, again, his retirement. This time he meant it.

The Saint continued regardless—there was a long-running Swedish comic strip, and new novels with other writers doing the bulk of the work were complemented in the 1970s with Bob Baker's revival of the TV series, *Return of the Saint*.

Ill-health began to take its toll. By the early 1980s, although he continued a healthy correspondence with the outside world, Charteris felt unable to keep up with the collaborative Saint books and pulled the plug on them.

To entertain himself, Leslie took to "trying to beat the bookies in predicting the relative speed of horses," a hobby which resulted in several of his local betting shops refusing to take "predictions" from him, as he was too successful for their liking.

He still received requests to publish his work abroad but had become completely cynical about further attempts to revive the Saint. A new Saint magazine only lasted three issues, and two TV productions—*The Saint in Manhattan*, with Tom Selleck look-alike Andrew Clarke, and *The Saint*, with Simon Dutton—left him bitterly disappointed. "I fully expect this series to lay eggs everywhere . . . the only satisfaction I have is in looking at my bank balance."[11]

In the early 1990s, Hollywood producers Robert Evans and William J. Macdonald approached him and made a deal for the Saint to return to cinema screens. Charteris still took great care of the Saint's reputation and wrote an outline entitled *The Return of the Saint* in which an older Saint would meet the son he didn't know he had.

Much of his time in his last few years was taken up with the movie. Several scripts were submitted to him—each moving further and further away from his original concept—but the screenwriter from 1940s Hollywood was thoroughly disheartened by the Hollywood of the '90s: "There is still no plot, no real story, no characterisations, no personal interaction, nothing but endless frantic violence . . ." Besides, with producer Bill Macdonald hitting the headlines for the most un-Saintly reasons, he was to add, "How can Bill Macdonald concentrate on my Saint movie when he has Sharon Stone in his bed?"

The Crime Writers' Association of Great Britain presented Leslie with a Lifetime Achievement award in 1992 in a special ceremony at the

House of Lords. Never one for associations and awards, and although visibly unwell, Leslie accepted the award with grace and humour ("I am now only waiting to be carbon-dated," he joked). He suffered a slight stroke in his final weeks, which did not prevent him from dining out locally with family and friends, before he finally passed away at the age of eighty-five on 15 April 1993.

His death severed one of the final links with the classic thriller genre of the 1930s and 1940s, but he left behind a legacy of nearly one hundred books, countless short stories, and TV, film, radio, and comic-strip adaptations of his work which will endure for generations to come.

> *I was always sure that there was a solid place in escape literature for a rambunctious adventurer such as I dreamed up in my youth, who really believed in the old-fashioned romantic ideals and was prepared to lay everything on the line to bring them to life. A joyous exuberance that could not find its fulfilment in pinball machines and pot. I had what may now seem a mad desire to spread the belief that there were worse, and wickeder, nut cases than Don Quixote.*
>
> *Even now, half a century later, when I should be old enough to know better, I still cling to that belief. That there will always be a public for the old-style hero, who had a clear idea of justice, and a more than technical approach to love, and the ability to have some fun with his crusades.*[12]

---

1 *A Letter from the Saint,* 30 August 1946
2 "The Last Word," *The First Saint Omnibus,* Doubleday Crime Club, 1939
3 *The Straits Times,* 29 June 1958, page 9

4 Introduction by Charteris to the September 1980 paperback reprint of *Meet—the Tiger!* (Charter), the last ever print edition.

5 *The Saint: A Complete History,* by Burl Barer (McFarland, 1993)

6 PR material from the 1970s series *Return of the Saint*

7 From "Return of the Saint: Comprehensive Information" issued to help publicise the 1970s TV show

8 *A Letter from the Saint,* 26 July 1946

9 Introduction to "The Million Pound Day," in *The First Saint Omnibus*

10 *A Letter from the Saint,* 12 April 1946

11 Letter from LC to sometime Saint collaborator Peter Bloxsom, 2 August 1989

12 Introduction by Charteris to the September 1980 paperback reprint of *Meet—the Tiger!* (Charter).

WATCH FOR THE SIGN

OF THE SAINT!

THE SAINT CLUB

*And so, my friends, dear bookworms, most noble fellow
drinkers, frustrated burglars, affronted policemen, upright
citizens with furled umbrellas and secret buccaneering
dreams that seems to be very nearly all for now. It has been
nice having you with us, and we hope you will come again,
not once, but many times.*

*Only because of our great love for you, we would like
to take this parting opportunity of mentioning one small
matter which we have very much at heart . . .*

—*Leslie Charteris,* The First Saint Omnibus *(1939)*

Leslie Charteris founded The Saint Club in 1936 with the aim of
providing a constructive fanbase for Saint devotees. Before the War, it
donated profits to a London hospital where, for several years, a Saint
ward was maintained. With the nationalisation of hospitals, profits
were, for many years, donated to the Arbour Youth Centre in Stepney,
London.

In the twenty-first century, we've carried on this tradition but have
also donated to the Red Cross and a number of different children's
charities.

The club acts as a focal point for anyone interested in the adventures of Leslie Charteris and the work of Simon Templar, and offers merchandise that includes DVDs of the old TV series and various Saint-related publications, through to its own exclusive range of notepaper, pin badges, and polo shirts. All profits are donated to charity. The club also maintains two popular websites and supports many more Saint-related sites.

After Leslie Charteris's death, the club recruited three new vice-presidents—Roger Moore, Ian Ogilvy, and Simon Dutton have all pledged their support, whilst Audrey and Patricia Charteris have been retained as Saints-in-Chief. But some things do not change, for the back of the membership card still mischievously proclaims that . . .

> *The bearer of this card is probably a person of hideous*
> *antecedents and low moral character, and upon*
> *apprehension for any cause should be immediately released*
> *in order to save other prisoners from contamination.*

To join . . .

Membership costs £3.50 (or US$7) per year, or £30 (US$60) for life. Find us online at www.lesliecharteris.com for full details.

Made in the USA
Charleston, SC
23 June 2014